Interlocking Monsters

HEIDI ARNESON

ISBN-10: 0997477806
ISBN-13: 978-0-9974778-0-1

Published in 2016 by Stick Pony Press, Minneapolis, Minnesota.
Author and illustrator inquiries may be directed to stickponypress@gmail.com

STICK
PONY
PRESS

For the missing.

Part One

MY PUZZLE

THE DARK UNDOABLE

From where I am now I see everything. I see the bone bits in the barn ash and the blood stains on the ceiling and the body in the cistern of the yellow house, and I can crawl into the heads of the missing boys and into the monster who took them and tell you every detail, down to the mustard smear on the pronto pup and the dew drop on the grass blade, but the summer the first boy disappeared I was ten years old and knew nothing.

That summer I dug my own grave down by the lake. I wanted to see what it felt like to be dead. I took Dad's shovel and dug till I couldn't dig anymore, then lay in the hole and watched the blue rectangle above. One white cloud passed over, an ant crawled on my cheek, a purple thunderhead hovered then it started to rain, so I got out of my grave and washed off with a swim in the lake, but I've always been like that, drawn to the dark side. Dracula slept in our basement skirt box, an old man crouched in our bedroom closet and a witch lived in our living room mirror.

That same summer a kid across the street sold his whole plastic monster collection, yellow fangs, reaching claws, dripping blood. I got two for a quarter as a joke, took them home and put them on top of my dresser. *Very funny ha-ha!*

But when I turned off the light they were not funny. In the dark, Frankenstein and Wolfman became every moonbeam, drive-in movie scream and campfire nightmare condensed like blood in a woodtick. I turned on the lamp, kicked off the covers and swept the monsters into my third drawer down. They stayed shut in all summer among erasers, notebooks and Barbie-dolls, tangled like dancers in love or wrestlers grappling. Each time I opened the drawer I felt their malevolence, the brute-rage of Frankenstein, the flesh hunger of Wolfman. Shut up like that their powers festered.

Then came the danger point. One afternoon in August. No one home but Dad and me. All the others off at work or school or Vietnam; I felt something bad about to happen, some dark undoable, told myself *be brave Cat*, gathered my courage and opened the third drawer down. There were my monsters, locked in their death-dance, like some future snapshot of Dad and Uncle Ned. I grabbed them up, ran to the garage, opened the trash can, threw them atop our flattened spaghetti boxes and squished milk cartons and pressed the lid tight.

GOOD RIDDANCE!

Then the first boy disappeared. I didn't know about Billy Bell till seven years later, and by then it was way too late to throw away the real monsters, but from where I am now I see that night clearly, just as if I was atop the Ferris wheel looking down...

...The Ferris wheel lights of the 1969 Iowa State Fair began to glow. Balloons bobbed and sank. Sleepy heads in strollers bobbed and sank. Families headed home, dragging sticky kids clutching stuffed elephants, monkeys and striped wildcats. Big boys clustered off to the side to pose and smoke. Big girls flocked across, spitting popcorn through pink lip gloss. The Tilt-a-Whirl, Rock an' Roller Coaster and Wall of Death spun circular blurs of red-yellow-blue. Barkers' voices rose as the sun sank. "Five throws for a quarter!" "Win a Bunny!" "Everybody wins!" A child yowled. One firecracker popped off, then five in a row. Bang! Bang! Bang! Bang! Bang! The Merry-Go-Round attendant slapped a mosquito on his cheek. His hand came away bloody. A little girl in a blue sundress got sick at his feet. The temperature dropped three degrees. The twilight gave off scents of the day's feast, cotton candy, onions, sizzling oil, and a barefoot boy in overalls stepped up to the Pronto Pup stand. He held a dollar in his fist. He snapped the bill flat.

One whole dollar left!

His sister snatched at the dollar, "No more Billy!"

Billy tugged back, "Mine!"

The bill ripped in two.

"Billy, look what you did! If you eat another Pronto Pup you're gonna bust!" Becky dug her fingers in. "Give!"

Billy tightened his grip, "Fat chance, lard-ass," then he jerked away with his half and dodged behind the Pronto Pup stand...

Whoa.

Behind the Midway everything was different. The string-lights ended, the sweet air soured, garbage overflowed and black electric cables thick as anacondas twined into the darkness. Becky's calls were muffled by the chugging generators.

"Bill-eee!"

Ditched her! Bitch of a sister! I can spend my damn money any damn way I please!

Billy wiped his hands on his overalls and pushed the torn dollar into his pocket. A Chocolate-Dipped Banana-on-a-Stick, All The Milk You Can Drink for a Dime and Froggy's Frosty Lemonade wrestled in his stomach. He unbuttoned his fly and aimed at a black electric cable.

You are blessed by me, Serpent of Infinity. I'm a cowcatcher. I'm a locomotive. I'm the Green Devil who sprouts horns in the darkness-

"Bill-eee!"

Bitchster. You think you rule me. You don't rule me, I rule me. An' someday when you're sleepin' in your prissy room, I'll sneak in an'-

"Hey. You."

A voice. Nearby, from the shadows behind the Pronto Pup stand. Billy stepped back, tripped on a cable and got the itchy tingles, like when you almost wipe out on your bike, and your ghost jumps ahead and itches when it lands back in. A man stepped forward from the orange circle of a cigarette tip. He had a smile on his face. He held the smile as he spoke.

"Hello."

A flash glinted in the man's hand.

Somethin' silver, somethin' shiny.

Billy sized up the man.

He's not tall, not skinny an' not fat, he's just some old guy, but with that smile pasted on, an' the way he stands, he looks like a giant kindergartner tryin' to get someone to play. Okay…I'll play…

Before kids on milk cartons, before Amber Alert, before the disappearance of Jack Jackoway, Billy Bell took a step toward the Smiling Man.

Stupid Billy!

Becky sat down on a sticky bench. At the other end, an upside-down cone had melted into a chocolate-vanilla pool. She opened her fist and smoothed the half dollar. On the torn edge was a nub that made the first president look as if her were about to cry.

This is the worst night of my life! Not only was my best friend s'posed to meet me by the Popcorn-Ball an' didn't! Then I see her flirtin' with Doug Douglas at the Sweet-Swirl! Then I bump into Doug by the Pronto Pups an' boy did I blush! When'm I gonna teach myself not to blush? An' what'll I do if Doug is in one of my junior high classes? I'll blush if he even looks at me. Then Vomit-face ditches me! An' rips my dollar in two! Vomit-face where are you?

Becky stood on the bench and scanned the crowd at Billy-height. There were teenage couples, fingers slung through each other's belt loops, baggy-shorted old-timers and a little girl in a blue dress, but no Billy. Becky cupped her hands and hollered.

"BILL-EEE!"

The man at Froggy's Lemonade blinked, the little girl in blue squinted and the kids atop the Ferris wheel parroted, "BILL-EEE!"

Behind the concessions, Billy heard but didn't answer.

Let her yell till her face turns blue. I'll come when I'm good an' ready.

He could see Smiling Man clearly now, his apple cheeks, ruddy skin and Cheshire cat grin.

An' that shinin' thing! What was that?

Smiling Man held the gleam out to Billy.

"It's a Ruger Redhawk. Double action. Brand new. Take it. Hold it. See how it feels."

Green lights reflected off the Man's glasses, slipping and sliding like electric eels.

"Go ahead. It won't bite."

One step closer...

Billy touched the gun.

Oh yeah.

The metal was warm from Smiling Man's hand. Billy felt the heat, the heft, the silken surface, stainless steel, rosewood grip and curve of the trigger.

Smiling Man puffed his cigarette. "Give it a try."

Two handed, straight-armed, Billy squinted down the barrel.

Sweet little double action, yeah!

Billy pointed up at the first star.

Beam me up Scotty!

He aimed at the cornfield.

Die, crows, die!

He squinted at the black electric cables.

Anacondas, die!

He spun a circle, imagining black-mustachioed banditos sneaking in from all directions as the night swirled lightening-blue with neon-yellow streaming through, then he planted both feet and aimed at Smiling Man.

"Hey! Careful! That gun is loaded!"

Guy sure barks out orders, like Sarge on Gomer Pyle.

Billy handed the weapon back.

"What is your name, son?"

Someone turned the volume up too high on you Mister.

"Cat got your tongue?"

Billy parted his lips to speak, but his voice dove, quicksilver and hid in the shadows of his hips.

Never Talk to Strangers.

"You deef and dumb?"

I'm gonna pull one over on him, call myself Standish Hammersmith.

But when Billy opened his mouth, his own name slid out.

"What's that?"

"Billy."

"Say again?"

"BILLY!"

"They call you William? Or Bill? Or Will?"

"Call me BILL-I-UM!"

They both laughed. Billy put his hands on his knees. Smiling Man threw down his cigarette and extended his hand.

"How do you do, Billium?"

The hand was hard and soft, warm and cool, all at once.

"You hungry?"

"Nah, I'm not hungry."

"That your name? 'Billy Not-Hungry'?"

"No. Billy Bell."

"Ding Dong Dell! You a relation of Joe Bell?"

"You know my Gramps Joe?"

"Joe Bell and I hunted together. A number of times. At the Rise."

Redtail Rise! Gramps took me there! Lotsa times! Old guys shootin' guns, raisin' beers to the sky.

"Want to go shoot? At the Rise?"

Billy listened to the night, the chugging generators, the shrieking rides and the crickets yelling, "Redtail Rise! Redtail Rise!" He could no longer hear Becky's calls.

"I gotta be home by ten."

Smiling Man nodded and turned towards the chain-link fence that surrounded the fairground. Billy followed, jigging over cables, used napkins and broken glass. Smiling Man touched the padlock and the gate fell open.

Cool to the power of three! Smilin' Man has the Magic Touch!

Billy knew all about picking locks, breaking latches and sneaking in. He and Becky had snuck into the fair back by the farm machinery. *More quarters for the Midway!*

Smiling Man stood beside a mud-green Blazer.

"Climb in."

Wait a minute.

Billy could see there was no room in there for him. The passenger seat was covered in fast food wrappers, Guns and Ammo magazines, open boxes of golden cartridges and red shotgun shells.

Never get in the car with a stranger.

He'd heard that a million times, from his mom, his teachers, his sister-

Last time the Bitchster nagged at me to never get in was way before she got bumps on her chest an' pimples on her face, that day we rolled down the windows, an' stuck out our heads, an' Dad yelled, heads in before you get DECAPITATED! Ha! Funny word! DE-CAP-IT-TATE! Then we-

"HEY! In!"

Smiling Man had cleared off the passenger seat. Billy sniffed: coffee, cigarettes, silage-

An' somethin' sweet-spicy, like red-hots meltin' on a windowsill. An' in back a tumpty of empty mouthwash bottles-

"Hey! What're you waiting for? Christmas?"

Billy hauled himself in.

"Buckle up for Life, Billium."

Billy buckled up. *Ready for adventure!*

Smiling Man started the engine and headed towards Highway

119.

Becky pushed through the crowd, bumping shoulders, checking faces, seeing no one familiar.

She asked Pete's Pronto Pup man, "You seen a boy, this tall?"

"Nope."

She asked the Ferris Wheel man. "You seen a boy in overalls?"

"Nah."

She asked at Froggy's Lemonade, "You seen a barefoot boy in overalls this tall?"

The Lemonade Man set down two sweating cups. "Yup. I seen him."

"You have?"

"Yup, I seen hundreds like him today. Lemonade?"

Slagface!

Becky turned a circle.

Was he at the Chocolate Dipped Banana on a Stick? No. The Tilt-A-Whirl? No. The Rock an' Roller Coaster? No! Already looked there twice!

A wide woman with her arms around a bald man passed so close Becky could smell her strawberry lipstick. Two couples embraced against the Hot Stick. A clot of teens galloped past singing Teen Angel. A fat man shouted Shoot it, Dairy! The whole place stank of piss mixed with onion.

Why's everyone havin' so much fun? Shoot the Bull's Eye, Guess Your Weight, Ring the Bell, Tell Your Fortune, Find Your Baby Brother!

The Danger Drop dipped like an oil derrick, up-down, striking mother-lode after mother-lode of screams, the Midway blurred and Becky wiped her tears away before they made tracks in the fairground dust that clung to everything, shoes, hair, skin.

Shut up everyone! Stop laughin'! Where's Billy? Who cares? Not me. I hope he chokes to death on a pronto pup. An' what's the worst could happen? He run off with the Freaks. SEE BILLY BELL! THE EATIN' MONSTER! SEE HIM EAT THIRTY DOGS IN A

ROW!

Or I know. He biked home with Rick Turd or Dicky Dirt. Or he's hidin' in the corn, back where we snuck in, waitin' to jump out an' say 'BOO'...

The Blazer sped east on Highway 119. Twilight deepened to navy blue. Farm after dark farm rolled by. Smiling Man was no longer smiling. He lit another Chesterfield and puffed in silence. Smoke spiraled out the wing vent. Billy pressed his cheek against the glass and peered up.

Big Dipper. Little Dipper. Cass-ee-oh-pee-ah...

He felt in his pocket for the torn bill.

Still there. An' three pennies, a nickel an' a dime. What could you buy with half a dollar? Half a movie? Half a burger? Half a dead frog? Ha.

Smiling Man pulled a stick from his pocket. "Gum?"

Billy accepted the gift, peeled off the wrapper, folded the silver paper again and again, into the smallest triangle he could fold, pocketed the silver wrapper, sat on his hands and chewed.

Ah, Juicy Fruit...

Light spilled through the driver's side window, and Billy saw his own reflection, a wolf-faced boy with dirty-blonde hair and a boat-shaped scar under his left eye. Billy stared at the boy. The boy stared back. Billy scratched his nose. The boy scratched his. Billy stuck out his tongue. The boy stuck out his, then scowled as if to say, *"NEVER GET IN A CAR WITH A STRANGER!"*

Billy frowned back.

Yeah, I know all that crap. Every dumbhead knows that rule. But be cool. This guy's no stranger. He's a friend a' the family...

Becky hurried past the Swine Barn, Poultry Barn and Cattle

Barn. Just before the Four-H, Doug Douglas stepped in front of her.

Doug Douglas! My crush!

Doug stood wavering. He wore a wet grin, stank of Swisher-Sweets, and his usual gang of buddies wasn't circling him.

Hey Doug, Becky wanted to say. She'd practiced at home in the bathroom mirror for a moment like this, watching her mouth for a sign of weakness:

Hey Doug, what you doin' this summer? Hey Doug, you goin' to Peach Pie Picnic? Hey Doug, you going to Blue Winds Campground? Hey Doug, you seen my runty little brother?

But before she could blush or speak, Doug pulled her behind the Four-H, pressed her up against the corrugated metal and sank his tongue in her mouth. Becky felt a flow between her legs, pushed Doug away and ran without looking back, spitting Doug out as she ran.

French kissed! Before we even held hands!

At Machinery Street she slipped between the tractors and headed back to where she and Billy had snuck in.

Where my favorite shirt got ripped...

As she crawled under, the jutting fence-wire scraped her shoulder again.

"Ow!"

Shh. Gotta keep quiet. Gotta scare Billy...

On the other side she waited for her eyes to adjust, parted the corn and poked her head through. Billy's sneakers were just where he'd left them.

So stupid, that dare, to go barefoot at the Fair! I warned him, didn't I? What if you cut yourself on a pull-tab? Then what? Or a broken bottle? Then what? Or a rusty nail? Then what? Stitches? Tetanus? Lockjaw?

Becky looked down the next row. No Billy.

Keep quiet. Go further.

She parted the next. There was Billy's yellow banana bike beside her blue Schwinn.

Prob'ly he's further in...

"It's past ten, Billy. Mom'll murder us both."

Snap.

"I'M LEAVIN' WITHOUT YOU!"

Snap.

"Billy?"

Becky imagined the snap was Doug Douglas. She imagined Doug followed her, tackled her and kissed her again. She tasted Doug's salty tang and landed an imaginary punch to his chin.

WHAM!

Doug vanished and her mom's hand flew in.

SMACK! You come home late! SMACK! Without your brother?

Becky ducked her imaginary mom, pushed back to her bike and pedaled home, concocting excuses.

Mom, Billy ditched me! An' I looked all over! An' couldn't find him!.. Or how 'bout a lie? To save my hide? How 'bout, we was on our way home, but Billy lost his shoes, an' we couldn't find 'em, so we gave up an' biked home, an' last I looked, he was right behind...

"Not far now, Billium."

Smiling Man turned onto a dirt road. The road rose past three farms, curved, and dead-ended by a row of straw bales tacked with peppered targets.

Redtail Rise!

Billy looked around for his gramp's friends.

Not here yet.

Smiling Man parked the high beams on the targets, grabbed two fresh rolled-up targets from the back and strode toward the bales. "Come on."

Billy felt a pressure in his gut.

Fair food catchin' up.

He gestured toward an old maple.

"Gotta go."

Smiling Man nodded. Billy tiptoed over the weedy ground.

Shit for brains!

What had seemed like the coolest idea, to go barefoot at the fair, now seemed like *one dickhead deal.* He stumbled over a tree root, dropped his overalls, squatted under the spreading maple and looked up.

How many stars up there? An' how far away? An' does it go on forever? Or does it fold in on itself like a stick a' chewin' gum?

An' what'm I gonna wipe my butt with?

Billy felt for a handful of leaves, wiped clean, hiked up his overalls and picked his way back to the straw bales.

Smiling Man nodded, threw down his Chesterfield and straight-armed the target.

BAM! BAM! BAM! BAM! BAM! BAM!

Whoa! So fast!

They both walked back to study the holes.

Not bad. Maybe he'll teach me to shoot like that.

Smiling Man reloaded and handed the Ruger to Billy.

"Your round."

Billy climbed up on the bale. Smiling Man positioned himself behind. He stood close and moved closer. Billy tried not to squirm.

Whoa! Ruger sure feels good, but shit! Does Smilin' Man hafta stand so close? An' breathe his red-hot breath on me? An' I can feel his wiener through his pants. Is he gettin' a boner on me? Yeah, he's gettin' a boner! Why get a boner on me?

The target blurred as the man swelled.

Go ahead, Smilin' Man! Pop your boner! I'm the one with the gun! An' I got a plan! Shoot off five, an' then run hide till Gramps' friends come take me home in their pickup!

Billy focused on the bullseye.

This is for my bitch sister!

He squinted, aimed, squeezed.

BAM!

The kickback shuddered his shoulders, clacked his teeth. Smiling Man repositioned.

Billy refocused.

An' this is for Dicky Dirt stealin' my frog!

BAM!

An' this is for Miss Priss givin' me a F!

BAM!

An' this is for Rick Turd smearin' my face in the dirt!

BAM!

An' this is for Mom smackin' me!
BAM!
An' this is for Smilin' Man!
Billy twisted, jabbed his elbows and bolted.

Becky pedaled home practicing her lie.
Billy was right behind. We was almost home, an' he was right behind.
She turned down Fourth, crossed Bluebird, pedaled past the neighboring stucco box-houses, braked at their little stucco, leaned her bike against the garage and opened the back door braced for trouble.

In the hallway she put her ear to the wall. Her parents laughed with Ed McMahon at a Johnny Carson joke. Their laughter turned to coughing, the Excedrin Headache Number Two Hundred and Three commercial came on, her dad walked to the kitchen for more beers, Doc Severinson's horn swooned, then came the low murmurs of guest-heartthrob Burt Reynolds.

He was right behind...
Becky tiptoed to the bathroom, locked the door and unpeeled her underwear. The fabric stuck to her scant pubic hair. In the center was a reddish-brown smear.

My first period! On the worst night of my life!
She washed the stain out with cold water, reached behind the towels for the flowered box, attached the pad as instructed, and lay across her bed without taking off her clothes, pulling back the covers or turning off the light.

Now I'm a woman. Am I a woman? I don't feel like a woman! I feel like crap! An' I'll never speak to Doug Douglas again! What was he tryin' to do? Push his tongue through to China? An' what'm I gonna do next time I see him? Stick a garter snake down his throat! See how he likes it! An' where's Billy? Off with some pot-smokin' hippie?
Becky imagined her brother in a cramped trailer filled with pierced, tattooed bodies, with plates in their lips, the Fat Lady astride the Living Skeleton, all laughing in a marijuana haze. She

felt in her pocket for the torn bill.

Still there.

She stared up at the ceiling. A crack up there crept out from the light, meandered out in a crooked loop, then turned back towards the light, but didn't quite make it back. Becky completed the crack with her mind, drawing it back to the light, back to the light, nearly back but never quite...

Billy was right behind, right behind. I looked back an' there he was, right behind...

THE BLANK-FACE STRANGER

After Billy Bell more boys went missing, about one a year. Meanwhile I was growing up in the suburb of White Rock Minnesota *oblivious*. One summer passed another down by the lake with my grave gaping and Mom saying "fill that in, Cat," till finally I sodded it over, but the grass never did grow in right.

Seven summers after Billy Bell disappeared, on the morning after my seventeenth birthday, I woke up down by the lake on my sodded-over grave in the gray before sunrise. All dead silent. No birds sang, no fish leapt, mist rose like ghosts over the water and there was a black plastic trash bag beside me filled with something soft and squishy.

I had no idea how I got down there, no idea what was in that bag, and no idea I was about to sneak off in Dad's Dodge Dart Swinger, drive down to Iowa and end up face-to-face with Becky Bell in a mess of spilled pies and shattered glass.

I wasn't supposed to be driving to Iowa. I was SUPPOSED to be having a Bicentennial blast, going to parties, getting blasted, meeting cute boys, waving red, white and blue streamers and GETTING KISSED. But I wasn't getting kissed.

Because I had a black mark on my soul. And a crappy middle name I know. Catherine Mildred McCloud. Pretend you never heard that. My friends called me Cat. If I had friends. But the boys in White Rock barked at me and called me Dog. Because of that black mark.

You couldn't see it. I didn't look like a monster. I looked like a regular teenage girl, average weight and height, with a strawberry shag, green eyes, ten fingers and toes, two arms and legs. There was no huge mole growing on my chin, and no third head growing from my shoulder, my skin wasn't seeping pus, my nose wasn't falling off and my limbs weren't twisted by polio or shrunken by Thalidomide.

But I was repellant.

And all I could do was nothing. Lie down by the lake and do nothing. Lie in my bed and do nothing. Lie in front of the TV and do nothing but smoke a little pot when I could get it, steal booze from Dad's liquor cabinet, masturbate till my hand cramped and wish someone would remove that black mark.

How do you remove a black mark? Wash it off? With what? Comet? Clorox? Scrubbing Bubbles? How do you wash off something you can't see?

This thing was deep inside me. You'd have to be a surgeon, cut me open and slide your scalpel through. Even then you might not find it. Some poisons you can't see.

I did try killing myself. I took Mom's tomato knife and raked it back and forth across my wrist, but I couldn't get under the first layer of skin. Then I tried staying underwater till my lungs burst, but some life-force thrust me up from the water. Then I took a handful of Dad's Fruit-flavored Tums, but they wadded into a chalky ball at the back of my throat and I gagged them up. Then I rubber-banded a Roman Meal bread bag over my head but I was too claustrophobic to stay inside long enough to pass out. Then I was going to go downtown and jump into the Mississippi River from the Hennepin Avenue Bridge, but I didn't have my Driver's License yet, and couldn't find the Number Twenty-nine bus schedule.

I did kill a stranger though.

You may or may not have heard of the boy named Billy with the mustard smear on his face, or the boy named Jimmy who crawled out of his tent in the middle of the night, or Rob who went fishing and left his pole behind. Those boys didn't pack a bag, didn't say goodbye, didn't leave a note. They just vanished.

But you've heard of Jack Jackoway, the cute kid with the crooked grin who got taken by a masked man that warm Halloween. Everybody knows about Jack. Jack was all over, in newspapers, on TV. Jack, Jack, Jack. But famous or not, none of those kids ever came back.

People want to think those boys are still alive. Prayers and all that, hand-written signs. *JACK COME BACK. JIMMY MOMMY MISSES YOU.* Yellow ribbons, teddy bears, flowered wreaths. But when an eleven year old goes missing and he's gone for years, he isn't some grown-up secret agent driving a convertible down a coastal highway surrounded by Playboy Bunnies and holding up a whiskey glass. He's turning into soil somewhere.

Where? That was the question.

I saw those boys when I closed my eyes, when I walked to the Mini-Mart, when I opened my eyes underwater, their noses, their dimples, their cute little chins. I couldn't stop thinking about them, about their last day alive, what they saw, what they smelled, what they tasted. I imagined their last moments in Technicolor, down to the dewdrops on each grass blade and the upside-down reflection in each dewdrop. What were they thinking when they died? Did they scream? Did they cry? Did they know they were going to die? Did they scrape their fingernails against wooden boards or expire from lack of air or loss of blood? No one knew. No one living. *No one but me.*

And I had to keep my mouth shut. Because this is the one story about my family that I'm not supposed to tell. I can tell about us kids laughing down at the lake, or splashing at the yellow house pond with watermelon juice running down our chins, or Uncle Bob's dumb elephant jokes, and Uncle Ned flying so high he could see the shining gold dome of the Iowa

State Capital, and Dad throwing Mark down the stairs. I could even tell Rosy Sue's darkest secret, if I had to.

But not this. Whenever I tried, my tongue went numb, my lips sealed and I couldn't speak. Because to tell would curse my family. Reporters would stick microphones in their faces, people would hiss at us in the street; we'd have to disguise ourselves and move to Canada. And our good family name would be ruined. And we were a good family.

And this wasn't a nice straight line of *once upon a time this happened, and then that.* This is scattered through time, yellow house, car accident, underwear, blah-blah-blah. Whenever I tried to pick up one piece, it turned into a sticky red thread, that tangled up with a sticky blue thread, that tangled up with a sticky yellow, then all the threaded turn into tail-eating snakes, and I was trapped again in a nest of mixed metaphors.

THE QUEEN OF SECRETS

Rosy Sue would know what to do. Rosy Sue was the Queen of Puzzles. When I was little, and she was older, she'd smooth her red hair, push up her kitty-cat glasses, and say, "Let's put together a puzzle, Cat! First get the Royal Crown Cola! Then get the Old Dutch Potato Chips! Now get the Yellow House puzzle! Turn the box upside down! Go ahead! Don't be afraid!"

I was afraid that someone would yell at me for making such a mess but I dumped the box anyway, and out came all the brown-backed bits. "Look at all those pieces, Cat!" Rosy Sue said, "Do you know all those pieces fit together? They do! And do you know what it will look like when we're done? Just like this picture on the box, yellow house, garden and cornfields."

Then she'd pick up a piece in her perfectly manicured fingers and say, "First we have to turn them all right side up, then sort them, like with like. Red with red, blue with blue, flowers with flowers, sky with sky. Now find the edges. Those are the outsides. Make the outsides and work your way in. That is how you put together a puzzle!"

Rosy Sue was so good, one Christmas Mark snuck home with a present for all us girls, THREE POLAR BEARS IN A SNOWSTORM. One thousand interlocking pieces, ALL WHITE. No one could put that puzzle together, but Rosy Sue did in one night. In the morning we all blinked at the white circle on the dining room table.

But by the time I had the missing boy puzzle, Rosy Sue was dead. And this was a 3-D gazillion-piece living puzzle with thrashing arms, kicking legs, eyes that saw and teeth that bit and secrets on secrets, one inside the other. How to sort this? Like with like? Boys with boys? Secrets with secrets? And where were the edges? At our house in White Rock? Or at the yellow house in Pearl Pond? Or further back than I could see? Back with my hairy-ape relatives?

And what did I know? Nothing. Because I was the baby. When you're the baby you never get the whole picture, just bits and pieces. Like the time Dad threw our brother Mark down the stairs. Why did Dad throw Mark down? I didn't know. I was the baby. Babies miss out on a lot. I didn't see Dad throw Mark down, and didn't know what happened before or after. I just heard from my sisters, "Dad threw Mark down the stairs. Dad threw Mark so hard he wet his pajamas."

I saw pictures in my head. Mark a teenager. Dad dragging Mark up by his hair, bump-bump. Dad holding Mark aloft at the top of the stairs, punching his face over and over, and throwing him back down, then Mark crumpled at the bottom of the stairs.

Those were the pieces. But how did it start? And what

happened after? And what was my part? I didn't feel anything, just knocked my head against the wall trying to get in.

Same with this story. I wasn't sure where it ended or where it began, and most of the pieces didn't belong to me, they belonged to other people, some family, some strangers. And all I could do was imagine and gather. Maybe I'd never see the whole picture. Maybe I'd never get all the pieces. Maybe I'd never be able to put it together.

But no one else in White Rock is going to tell. The people there keep their lawns mowed and their houses clean and their mouths shut. We were about the poorest, and we always had food on the table and clothes to wear and chairs to sit, so we fit with all the other stucco houses, shiny cars and mowed lawns that sloped down to the lake. And nobody ever talked about anything but *nice* things at the cookouts and supper-tables and the church across the lake. Like Mom said, "if you can't say anything nice, don't say anything at all." And if we kids did ever talk about anything *not nice*, it was down at the lake, or under a picnic table fort, or in spidery basement corners, *whisper, whisper…*

And people said don't go with a stranger, but they didn't say what happened after. In fairy tales kids got eaten alive, or ground into bread, or pushed into ovens, but no one said what happened in real life. And you couldn't ask.

When I asked my sister Holly what the F-word was, she grabbed my wrist, dragged me to the bathroom, picked up the soap and shoved it in my mouth. I spit out the soap, but couldn't spit out the burn, and I still didn't know what the F-word was. I had no idea it had anything to do with private parts or men or women or secret urges.

I had secret urges. So did my friend Jill the Catholic girl across the street. On summer days when all the other kids played down at the lake, Jill and I took our secret urges down to the basement rec room. One spring day, the first day warm enough for shorts, Jill and I sat out on my front steps, squinting in the sun, studying our winter knees and waiting for something to happen.

Jill had this nice fat scab on her knee, and I asked her if she knew what the F-word was, thinking, *she'll never know.*

She said, "I do know. My brother told me. But he made me promise never tell, cross my heart, hope to die, stick a needle in my eye."

I ran inside, pulled a needle from Mom's pin cushion, ran back out and handed the needle to Jill, saying, "Jill, tell me, and if I tell, you can stick this in!"

Jill held the needle to my eye and said the F-word was what dogs do.

What dogs do? What do dogs do? We didn't have a dog. *What do dogs do? Chase their tails? Scratch for fleas? Lick their butts? Oh, I know! Dogs pooped! They hunched up outside where everyone could see and squeezed out a hard dark poop!*

But Jill said, "The F-word is what two dogs do TOGETHER. And when they do it, they get STUCK."

"Stuck where?"

"Stuck together."

"Stuck together where? At the mouths!?"

I knew about French-kissing teenagers with braces needing a fire-truck to get unstuck.

"No! Stuck at their butts! And my brother, he tried to un-stick them, but they yipped at him, then they nipped at him, and so he had to leave those two poor dogs stuck!"

Then Jill used the needle to pry up the edges of her scab as I imagined two yellow dogs stuck end-to-end, trying to eat, trying to run, trying to sleep. I vowed that if I ever did see those two dogs stuck on our street, even if they yipped at me and nipped at me, I'd use all my strength to pry them apart and set them free. But I never did see any dogs stuck on our street. Jill placed the scab on her tongue like a communion wafer and sucked.

"Now you know what the F-word is."

But I still didn't know.

And I didn't know what parts stuck to what. I knew men had

danglers but never saw any. My brothers were too old and Dad kept his covered. But one day walking home from school, I found a page torn from a magazine. Not any magazine you'll ever see. Not Time or Life or National Geographic. This magazine had pictures of men and women in cowboy hats and cowboy scarves and cowboy belts and cowboy guns and cowboy boots but nothing else. Their private parts were right out in the open. And they weren't cringing or covering up. They were face-front smiling. The women had the familiar hair-triangles of my big sisters, and the men had dangling pink hoses. So I knew about danglers.

And I knew about holes because of rumors.

In private, I looked for my own, but couldn't bend over far enough, so I took a pinwheel stick into my closet and tried to push it up into me. On try number one the stick blind-ended. On try number two the stick blind-ended. On try number three the stick blind-ended. *So I was the only girl in the world without a hole!* Then the stick slid up so far I feared I'd puncture some vital sac, and all my life-juices would seep out unseen, and when Holly called me to help with supper and I didn't come, she'd find me slumped in our closet, *dead by pinwheel stick!*

So I knew about holes and danglers, but didn't know men and women used their private parts to act out secret urges. I just thought they rolled around together fully-clothed, like Jill and I did on summer days when all the other kids played down at the lake, and she and I went down to the rec room, turned off the lights, lit candles, dripped hot wax on our hands, made body-shapes of the wax, breasts and hips imprinted with our life-lines, then lay on the mildewy rollaway cot and pretended to kiss with Kleenex between our lips. And when Jill and I played make-believe in the rec room, one of us was always the MAN and one of us was always the WOMAN. We might be a prince and a maiden, or a spy and a spy, or a doctor and patient, but we were always a man and a woman. We were never a man and a boy. *A man and a boy?* That did not happen, not even in fairy tales. That's why I didn't believe my sister Rosy Sue when she ran up years later and said, "I know who took that missing kid Jack."

I also didn't believe Rosy Sue because she was the QUEEN OF SECRETS. You could be kneeling on the living room floor building a house of cards, or making a Barbie doll staircase out of World Book Encyclopedias, or carving a chalk canoe, and Rosy Sue would come from nowhere, put her face to yours and say, "I have a secret." Then you'd jump a bit and your card-house would fall, or the encyclopedia stairs would topple, or your chalk canoe would snap in two and you'd have to start all over with a new stick, but you wouldn't say, leave me alone Rosy Sue! Or, get out of here Rosy Sue! Or, look what you did, Rosy Sue! Because she was ten years older and charming. Rosy Sue could charm a snake out of its venom. So you had to stop what you were doing and promise not to tell OR ELSE.

And you knew what OR ELSE meant. OR ELSE meant if you ever told, Rosy Sue would know instantly. She'd feel it in the bones of her ear, and come from wherever she was to wherever you were, *zip* she'd be with you. And you couldn't run and you couldn't hide, because no matter how far you ran, she'd find you. She said, "If you run to a straw hut in Africa, or to an igloo on the North Pole, or if you die and hide in another time, in the belly of a Tyrannosaurus Rex or the heart of an Egyptian Mummy or deep in the blue-tube future, I'll smell you out, put my hands round your throat and squeeze the life from you, forever amen, *if you ever tell.*"

When I was a toddler, my face got bashed up somehow, playing with my Fischer-Price Lawnmower, and afterwards Rosy Sue took care of me. She carried me down to her and Anne's room, wiped my tears and put a mirror to my face shiny-side away, so all I saw were the pressed flowers on the back, then said, "Never look in this mirror, Cat. An old woman lives in here, with yellow eyes and bloody teeth, and if you look in, she'll reach through and eat your face, starting with your nose, then your eyes, then your tongue. She'll swallow you down and burp you up, and she'll never be done chewing, and after the eternity of getting chewed and swallowed, she'll poop you out and you'll sink to the bottom of the lake and slowly dissolve in the muck with the bullheads, crayfish and snapping turtles. So never look in this mirror. Or the hall mirror. Or the living room. Or the bathroom. Or any mirror. Not till I tell you it's safe."

When we were visiting the yellow house in Iowa, Rosy Sue took my warty little hand and led me down the back steps, past the hammock and Gram's flowerbed, under the tall trees, out to the gravel road and told me to lie down.

I lay down in the road. Rosy Sue lay beside me. The gravel pressed into my back. Her arm grew cool against mine. The sky went from turquoise to navy to black. The crickets cricked. The stars came out, more stars than at home, and Rosy Sue went on about this boy in the sky.

"Lay still," she said, "be quiet, or he won't come."

"Who won't come?"

"The boy in the sky."

On and on she went about this boy who could fly anywhere, to California, Italy or the moon, or dip his fingers with the dolphins. "But he doesn't fly ANYWHERE," she said, "not to the moon or Italy or with dolphins. All he does is fly these roads and these fields and these farms. And why is that you ask?" I didn't ask, but Rosy Sue went on and on, and a June bug flew in my face, and the gravel pressed in my back, and a car came down the road but I kept still. The car came so close everything went WHITE-WHITE, then BLACK-BLACK. Then Rosy Sue potato-sacked me back to the kitchen of the yellow house, where the whole family was eating Gram's apple pie.

I sat in the corner high chair while the others all laughed. Rosy Sue sat in Gramp's lap and smiled across at me with her *never-tell* smile. But I never did see any boy in the sky or lady in the mirror or fairies in the flowers or dead people in the bottom of the popcorn bowl, so of course I didn't believe her when she ran up years later and whispered, *"I know who took Jack."*

THE BOLDFACE LIE

That Thanksgiving was warm, with no snow yet, just a thin coat of ice on the lake. The relatives were gathering at our house, my big brothers and sisters, nieces and nephews, Uncle Bob, Grandma Jane, and the great aunts with their fresh-frozen rolls, relish trays and three kinds of cranberry sauce.

I was out in the front yard doing gymnastics on the brown grass. My niece Little Mary was circling me on her Stick Pony. I was just getting up from a cartwheel when Rosy Sue's boyfriend Stu drove up crooked to the curb. The car was still moving when Rosy Sue practically fell out. She ran to me, her face pale, red hair flying, grabbed my arm, pulled me aside, by the linden and whispered, "I know who took Jack."

She meant Jack Jackoway. Eleven year old Jack was famous for getting taken on Halloween by a masked man. Everyone knew about Jack. But I had my head up my ass about another boy, Kirk King in my Social Studies class. *Kirk with his bronze hair! Kirk with his long bangs! Kirk with his dimple I could curl up in!*

So I asked, "Took who?"

Rosy Sue looked at me like I was an idiot.

"Jack Jackoway! You know who Jack is! And I know who took him!"

Then she whispered the name of someone we knew. Of course I didn't believe her. Thousands of people in Greendale formed a human chain to look for Jack. Yellow ribbons flapped all over the state. Jack was BIG NEWS, NATIONWIDE.

We were not big news. We were just the McClouds gathering

for Thanksgiving dinner, just kids, teachers, construction workers and beauticians. Yes, Dad was an executive at Sweetgood but he wasn't famous, and Mom made blue-ribbon quilts, but she wasn't famous. And the yellow house Gram grew prize-winning roses, and Don died in Vietnam, and John had a purple heart, and Mark championed every sport he played, and Anne was the Best Kindergarten Teacher, and Rosy Sue was Queen of the Blue Moon, and Polly and Molly were twin mutes who together weighed four hundred pounds, and Tammy and Holly were the best looking girls on Little Rose Lake in their bikinis, but none of us was famous. Famous Jack on the cover of People Magazine and our unfamous family did not match. So as I looked at our stucco house and the thin ice and our garage window catching a square of blue, I didn't believe Rosy Sue when she said one of us took Jack.

I also didn't believe Rosy Sue because she stole things, precious things, from my sisters, rings, blouses, slips, and then lied about it. When I was tall as our stair-rail, I saw Rosy Sue and my oldest sister Anne tearing each other's hair out by the doorbell chimes, their faces crunched and hands clutching. Anne was hissing that Rosy Sue wore her best blouse to the Blue Moon then balled it up in a corner of their room with yellow stains under the arms. Rosy Sue hissed back, "I never took your blouse!" "Yes you did!" Then Anne scratched Rosy Sue's face, dragged her to the bathroom and pushed her head in the toilet and flushing, over and over, saying she'd flush Rosy Sue down if she didn't tell the truth. All the while Rosy Sue sputtered, "I never took it, never took it!"

But we all knew she took it. Rosy Sue was a Boldface Liar. Like her Most Embarrassing Secret. The one I'm not supposed to tell. *Cross my heart, hope to die, stick a needle in my eye,* I vowed secrecy. But back then, I didn't know secrets aren't like flat puzzles that you can take apart and put together again without doing any damage. Now I know secrets are living things that plant themselves in our most hidden places. One nests inside the other like fungus on fungus and you can't tear one from the other without tearing the whole thing apart.

That's how it starts, one little secret that the others cluster onto, and pretty soon there's a corpse or two hidden in that cozy nest. *How does this happen in a nice family?*

Like this. That's why I'm opening my mouth. For the kids who never came back and for their families. But also for the kids who did come back and grew up, but are still hiding inside themselves, too scared to breathe, all scabbed over with hearts hard as stone.

The summer I was fifteen I visited Rosy Sue down in Black Oak. We put on her flowered dresses and pastel eye-shadow, stuck petunias in our hair, left Stu playing poker with his buddies and walked to the Black Oak Bar.

It was dark in there, the air conditioning gave me goosebumps, and I was underage, but Rosy Sue winked at the bartender and he mixed us fruity drinks. I drank orange slushies with green umbrellas and Rosy Sue sucked maraschino cherries off frilly toothpicks as she asked me embarrassing questions, like, "How far have you gone with a boy? First base? Second base? Have you had your cherry popped?"

I answered no, no and no. I didn't tell her boys scared me. Even our brothers, Don, John and Mark. Our brothers were so old they were a mystery. Then Don got killed in Vietnam and John was over there forever, and Mark so handsome with his movie star cheekbones, golden skin and bronze hair I was afraid to look him in the eye. Mark was never home anyway, after Dad threw him down the stairs.

And the boys at school, I scared them off with my black mark. And the big neighbor boys and my sisters' dates scared me with their World of Teens, the rough-housing down at the lake, the bulging swim trunks, playing King of the Raft, getting shoved on the slippery surface, getting your skin torn on a rusty nail with no time for a band-aid or for catching your breath, getting dunked by those big boys, coming up for air, getting dunked again. That was not for me. That world belonged to my big sisters.

So in the Black Oak, when Rosy Sue asked me, "have you had your cherry popped?" I kept shaking my head no, and she kept saying, "Oh you will soon enough," then gave me all this advice. Which I would not take. I did not listen. I was more interested in the guys at the bar. With each sip of fruity drink I thought, *maybe it is time to get kissed. If no boy in White Rock would kiss me, then maybe some drunk in Black Oak will.*

I was studying the guys, some old, some fat, some maybes, so I wasn't really listening when Rosy Sue said that when she got her cherry popped she didn't feel a thing, and that it was with some highschooler in back of his whatever car at some homecoming game, and she didn't even bleed.

Then she paused, took a drag and looked at me.

I knew Rosy Sue's pauses. They meant I was supposed to ask her something, but I didn't know what to ask. So I sucked down my drink and asked for another. Then we danced to the juke box, wildly, with each other, not caring what those hick guys thought. Rosy Sue was the best dancer. We slung our hips, whipped our hair and shook our chests. Then a slow song came on, *no peace I find,* and we danced with our bellies and boobs touching. I felt the eyes of the guys on the line where her body met mine.

After the song ended, we went to the Ladies Room to wipe the mascara smears from our eyes. Rosy Sue lit a Tareyton and stared at me in the mirror.

"So, don't you wonder, Cat?"

Wonder what?

"Don't you wonder why?"

Wonder why what?

"Don't you wonder why I didn't feel anything?"

"Feel anything when?"

"When I got my cherry popped. Don't you want to know why

I didn't feel and why I didn't bleed? Don't you wonder why?"

I did not wonder. I'd forgotten all about Rosy Sue's not bleeding and not feeling. Don't some girls not bleed when they lose their virginity? Don't some break their maidenhoods or whatevers on bed posts or monkey bars or climbing trees? Rosy Sue was no tomboy, she never even ran, but all we girls rubbed up against the bed post. *Maybe she broke her thing on the bedpost. Or maybe she was too drunk to feel. Or the guy was too small to feel. Or she was too scared to feel.* I'd never felt it myself, and sometimes I went numb and dumb when I was scared. Maybe Rosy Sue was scared.

I didn't care. I was thinking about the guy at the bar, with the Bobby Sherman mustache, and the guy with the biker biceps, and the one with skinny legs, and wondering, *how would it feel to kiss that? Would those sideburns itch? Would he smell like pork rinds? Would I kiss him with my mouth open or closed? Would he try to squeeze my boob? Would I let him? And if I wanted him to stop, could I just say it nicely, with my eyes? And would it be like my fantasies in bed at night, or slimy and smelly?*

But when Rosy Sue is about to tell a secret, she traps you with her eyes. So I had to ask.

"Okay, Rosy Sue, why didn't you feel anything?"

"Promise not to tell?

I nodded.

"You can't just nod, Cat. You have to promise forever amen to never tell anyone, not even Jill, or your boyfriend when you get one. I'm not joking. You can't even tell this after I die, Cat."

Not after she dies? What was the big deal? She was doing her fantasy-world thing again, making dramas like her shoebox dioramas, dolls in boudoir-poses in castles and gardens, tiny sequined queens attended by glitter-coated, animal-headed servants in frozen coronations and beheadings. This was Rosy Sue's fantasy-party. But she was my big sister, and sweet to me, so I said, "Okay, I promise to never tell, cross my heart, hope to die, stick a needle in my eye, not even Jill or my boyfriend when I get one and not even after you die."

"Okay…"

Smoke curled out her nostrils.

"The reason I didn't feel anything…when that boy popped

my cherry...in the backseat of his car...at the homecoming game...at White Rock High...was because Mark popped my cherry years before."

"Who?"

"Mark."

"Mark who?"

"MARK!"

Rosy Sue looked at me like I should know who Mark was. The name sounded familiar. *Also strange.* Did she mean some goofy Mark? I knew she'd dated a Mark. She'd dated at least one Mark. She dated a string of Marks. I remembered something funny about one of the Marks. *But which Mark was it?* I was trying to put a last name to this Mark. It was right on the tip of my brain, some red-headed Mark at the foot of the stairs, or a doll at the foot of stairs, or a boyfriend who looked like a doll at the foot of the stairs. *Was it Football Mark? Or Motorcycle Mark? Or Convertible Mark?*

"I give up... Did he go to White Rock?"

"Yes."

"Did he live by Dead End Woods?"

"No."

"On Big Rose Lake?"

"No."

"On Little Rose?"

"Yes."

"The other side?"

"No."

"Our side?"

She nodded.

"Not big-nose Mark down the street?"

"Closer."

"I don't know! I give up! Mark who?"

"Mark!"

"MARK WHO!?"

"Our brother Mark."

"Our brother Mark?"

"Our brother."

You know those kids they warned you about, the ones born with no feeling? Their brains aren't connected to their nerves, so they can't feel if they're cutting themselves, and when you broke a rib or sprained an ankle or sliced into muscle, the adults said, *oh you're so lucky you were born with your nerves CONNECTED to your brain, so you can FEEL PAIN, so you know when you're hurting yourself! For you could be like the little girl with no nerves who chewed all day on a piece of metal and tore up her mouth!*

In that moment in the Ladies' Room of the Black Oak Bar, I was the little girl with no nerves. I FELT NOTHING. I was also the Robot on Lost in Space when it gets confused and its vacuum-cleaner arms go up and down and it says, "Does not compute," then its arms go in and its lights go off and its screen goes blank. That was me. Numb and dumb. What Rosy Sue said DID NOT COMPUTE.

If I could roll back time like purple microfiche, I'd ask, *how did it feel, Rosy Sue? Were you hurt? Were you scared?* I'd be the big sister and let her be the little. I'd walk her home, make her a big bowl of popcorn and dump out the yellow house puzzle. We'd spend the whole night putting it together, then in the morning I'd get Dad's rusty old saw and dismember that big brother. But back then, there wasn't any safe place for spilling your guts in front of a live audience. I didn't even know the word for what happened to Rosy Sue. And she was still smiling her never-tell smile. So I just asked, "Where did this happen?"

"Downstairs, in bed, in the room I shared with Anne."

"When did it happen?"

"At night, after we turned off the light. Don or John would knock on the wall, and we'd have to say, 'Come in.' Then John or Don would come in and say, 'Mark wants to do it again.' Then Mark would come in and do it."

"How old were you?"

"A girl. Before I got my period."

I swallowed.

"They tried it on Anne first, but she didn't like it. So Mark did me."

Does not compute.

"And don't worry, Cat! I'm fine! It was nothing. It didn't

bother me. I didn't let it. And I never think about it. I keep it locked in a little box deep inside me and never let it out."

She stubbed her cigarette out in the sink.

I threw up in the Ladies Room. She held my hair. The rest of that night is a blur. I danced with some guy, and felt his bristly mustache, but whoever he was, I didn't let him kiss me. I pushed him away and threw up again back at Rosy Sue's.

Next day I woke on her couch with a headache and my heart pounding. She said, "That's a hangover, Cat. Let's get some food in you!" We made French toast and smoked cigs and joked, and I forgot all about Rosy Sue's secret. Deep-sixed it.

And never told. *Who would I tell? Why pass on a lie?* I couldn't imagine our big brothers doing that to their little sister. Don was in heaven and John a Purple Heart hero and Mark so handsome homecoming queens cried on our front steps at two in the morning for the love of him. No way would Mark need to mess with a little girl! And those words: *Popped her cherry.* What a nasty way to say it! A little girl wasn't a fruit basket. I didn't believe Rosy Sue. Just like I didn't believe her about Jack.

THAT THANKSGIVING

But I kept going back to that Thanksgiving. *What was alike? What was different?* There was no snow yet. That was different. Uncle Bob was telling dumb elephant jokes. That was the same. Dad and Uncle Ned weren't talking to each other since their Halloween fight. That was the same. I was cartwheeling on the lawn and Little Mary was circling on her Stick Pony, skipping round and round on the brown grass, chanting about magical lands, cherry trees and candy mountains, lost in a daydream like I used to be on my Fischer-Price Lawnmower. That was the same.

Then Rosy Sue practically fell out of her boyfriend's car, ran to me, grabbed my arm and whispered, *I know who took Jack.* Her hand on my elbow, her pale lips, going on and on, saying how X visited her for his birthday then drove to where Jack was and *blah-blah-blah.*

That was different. I looked at our stucco house and the garage window catching blue sky. Rosy Sue's words didn't fit with the picture. *X took a kid? No way...*

But she was serious. So I got serious too.

"You really think X took Jack?"

"I know it was him."

"Are you sure, Rosy Sue?"

"Positive."

"Then what should we do? Call the police?"

Who would make the call? Not me. And not in the kitchen, where everybody was running around with the food. We'd dial zero in Mom and Dad's room, listen for the operator, and ask for the White Rock Police...*and then what?* I pictured cops pulling into our driveway, X led out in handcuffs and the cop car disappearing down our street. And where would they take X? To prison? For how long? And what proof was there that X took Jack? None I knew of. How do you call the police on your own relative? Did people ever do that? Call the cops on their own flesh and blood?

Rosy Sue was still pressing her lips together, so I asked again, "Should we call the police?"

I was hoping she'd say, "JUST KIDDING!" Instead, she pressed her lips thinner and said, "Let me think about it." Then she walked into the house.

I wish I could roll time back to that moment. I followed her in, but was instantly surrounded by toddling nieces and nephews with teething rashes, runny noses and new velveteen dresses, kisses on cheeks, sticky hugs and shouts from the sisters, "Come help cut the vegetables!" "Get the bread from the basement fridge!" "Find more butter!" "Stir the gravy!" "Get more chairs!" Meanwhile more relatives arrived, and I lost track of Rosy Sue, and forgot all about her crazy secret.

At the Thanksgiving table, Rosy Sue sliced turkey, spooned gravy and passed the green beans with the rest of us just as if she had never whispered to me an hour before, *"X took Jack."*

One of the great aunts was telling a mashed potato story, another was explaining how much butter went in before mashing, Uncle Bob was teasing Holly about her dress, John was talking about his son's missing tooth, Mom was picking celery from her teeth, Holly was tugging at the hem of her miniskirt, Tammy was nodding in her new haircut, Molly and Polly were stuffing in the stuffing, Grandma Jane was leading a debate over which was better, store-bought cranberry relish that you slid from a can, or homemade with fresh-grated orange peel, and the kids at the kid table were standing up and sitting down in some game about turkey bones, when Rosy Sue lifted her fork and said, "What would you have done?"

I realized what else was different. When Rosy Sue dashed from the car that day, she was running. She never ran. She sauntered, she slinked and she sashayed like Marilyn Monroe. She never ran. That day, she ran. I thought *she must need to pee really badly after that long car ride! Better get out of her way!* But she didn't run into the house, she ran straight to me and put her face to mine, her pale face. Rosy Sue never went out without makeup. For holidays she was always powdered and shellacked, with matching purse, earrings and shoes. When she ran from the car she was wearing old jeans and Stu's big sweatshirt. And her hair lay flat. That's what was wrong with the picture…

But at the table she was hot-curled and glittery as she raised her fork and asked, "What would you have done?"

Nobody answered.

She asked again. "What would you have done?"

One of the great aunts sneezed. Grandma Jane grinned. The kids shook their turkey bones. Mom said, "Please pass the pickles."

Rosy Sue repeated, "What would you have done?"

John cleared his throat and spoke.

"What, Rosy Sue? What would we have done about what?"

"What would you have done if you were Jack Jackoway?"

John didn't reply.

Polly and Molly swallowed.

Rosy Sue said, "If I were Jack, I would've run. Wouldn't you have run, John?"

John was silent.

"Wouldn't you have run, Mark?"

Mark dug into his potatoes.

Rosy Sue said, "I would've run. That's what I tell my neighbor boys: 'If a stranger comes at you with a gun, run!'"

Everybody kept eating as she went on.

"So this man came up to Jack and his friends with a gun. That would be an obvious danger, right? And the man wore a mask. That would be scary, right, even if it was Halloween. A grown man in a mask is scary, right?"

Silence at the table.

She continued, "But when the man said 'stop,' the boys stopped. When he said 'lie down,' they lay down. When he told Jack to stay, Jack stayed. That was stupid, don't you think?"

One nephew poked another with a turkey bone. Holly smoothed her napkin. Little Mary skipped to the adult table and tugged Anne's sleeve. Anne stared at the cuckoo clock.

Rosy Sue went on, "I think it's better to run, and risk getting shot, than get in the car with a stranger, and have who knows what done to you, right? That's what I tell the boys in my building, 'never get in the car with a stranger.' I tell those boys, 'Run! Run like hell if a man bothers you. Even if he has a gun. Especially if he has a gun.' Because even if you get shot, at least you die free, right?"

Silence but for the ticking of the cuckoo clock.

"And wasn't that man middle-aged? That's what the papers said. And didn't Jack play sports? People Magazine said Jack played baseball. Well, if Jack played sports, then he could've easily outrun the guy. And if Jack was stupid enough to stop for the man, and stupid enough to lie down for the man, and stupid enough to get in the car with the man, then I say whatever happened after that was his own fault." Rosy Sue stabbed a green bean.

Tammy picked up the basket of rolls.

"Another roll, Grandma Jane?"

"Thank you." Grandma Jane passed the rolls to Uncle Bob.

Uncle Bob passed to Ned.

"Another roll Ned?'

Ned's face was beet-red. He passed to Dad. Dad shook his head. Dad was as pale as the mashed potatoes. We didn't know then Dad was dying.

THE YELLOW HOUSE

Dad had been sick ever since his Halloween fight with Uncle Ned. After that he just sat at the table getting paler and paler, his coffee undrunk, cigarettes unsmoked and sandwiches uneaten. He didn't even finish his martinis. We thought he had the flu. Just before Christmas, he asked Mom to take him to the hospital. Dad hated hospitals. And he left his cigarettes home.

At the hospital, during emergency surgery, they found a ballooned-out artery in his belly. Then the balloon burst and Dad never woke up. He just lay there full of tubes, surrounded by beeping, blinking machines.

The day they pulled out the tubes, turned off the machines and unplugged the screens, Dad drifted off and we all gathered to say goodbye. Mom asked the nurse to put his teeth back in, so he'd look better, and the nurse put his teeth back in, and he did look better. Then we all whispered I-love-yous and left the room.

I was the last to go. I didn't go. I'd never seen Dad so relaxed. He was glowing like white wax. Something was lighting him up from the inside. I closed the door, climbed on top of Dad, put my head to his chest and listened to the silence. After a while, I heard something in his chest sink. His big heart sinking.

Tammy yelled, "We're leaving, Cat!" I put on my hat, left Dad and stood with the others out in the huffing cold, but I would've stayed all night with my Dad, with the hospital clanking around

43

us, so I could have some quiet time with him, because when he was alive, he was always jumpy, always on edge, about to explode. Like my first trip to the yellow house.

We went in the old blue station wagon with the hole in the floor. You could watch the road go by through that, and you could drop things out, *gone in a blur*, things small as a saltine or a sour grape, or things as big as the three-month old baby.

The boys in the back read Mad Magazines, the girls in the middle cut out paper dolls, Mom next to Dad watched the corn fly by, Dad in the driver's seat smoked Lucky Strikes and I in Mom's lap went nosing for her nipple.

But all I got were mouthfuls of dry cotton. Mom had a breast infection, tender, painful, so she kept her blouse buttoned up, and plugged me instead with a bottle full of Tang, Breakfast Drink for Astronauts. *Sugar, flavor, color, Vitamin C!*

Dad couldn't get the ball game on the radio, just crackles and snaps. Holly kicked the back of Dad's seat, *we there yet, we there?* Anne shushed Holly with a silent *shh*. Noise hurt our dad. Especially kid noises. Too much kid noise and Dad would erupt. *Mount Vesuvius in the station wagon.*

Holly wrestled Tammy for the scissors, *my turn, no my turn, no mine*. Molly and Polly tug-of-warred the box of saltines. Rosy Sue climbed over into the back. The boys back there hatched a secret plan. Anne prayed to keep us kids in hand. I whined for Mom's blouse to open up, and Dad said *simmer down kids, simmer down.*

A paper doll dress got sucked out the hole, Tammy and Holly reached for it, too late, Holly skinned her knuckle on the road, the scissors flew and landed in Mom's lap, Molly and Polly tore open the cracker box, the boys pinned Rosy Sue down upon her back, I whined for Mom's blouse to open up, and Dad said *simmer down, kids, simmer down.*

Holly wiped her bloody knuckle on the upholstery, Tammy

pinched Holly's underarm, the twins bopped each other with the cracker box, the boys began to tickle Rosy Sue, Rosy Sue kicked and bucked and begged for mercy, Anne's mouth turned down into a tight white line, I whined for Mom's blouse to open up, and Dad said *simmer down, kids, simmer down.*

The boys tickled Rosy Sue till she wet her panties, then climbed up to grab another girl, Anne chewed up the inside of her own cheek, Polly and Molly shredded the cracker box, Tammy's best paper doll got sucked out the hole, Holly kicked the back of Dad's seat, *are we there yet, are we there*, and I cried for Mom's blouse to open up.

Just past Swaledale Iowa, Dad exploded. He braked hard.

Saltines, grapes and paper people flew.

"JESUS CHRIST! WHAT DO I HAVE TO DO TO GET YOU GOD DAMN KIDS TO SIMMER DOWN? SPANK THE WHOLE DAMN CARLOAD OF YOU?"

No one answered. The question was rhetorical. The kids got out and lined up by the corn, pants down, skirts up, bent over in the clover. Nine bare white bottoms faced the old highway. A passing semi tooted. Dad slid his belt through the loops and belted all us kids.

Except me. I was too small. I chewed on Mom's blouse while she stared up at a tulip-shaped cloud.

Back in the car everyone was quiet, snuffling down sniffles. Except me. I hadn't learned the Rule of Silence yet. I cried for Mom's breast. Dad gnawed his Lucky Strike. And Mom had two choices: open up her blouse and give me one sore nipple, or pass the crying baby back to Anne, so Anne could *drop the baby out the hole.*

As the boys frowned madly out the back, as Anne tried to swallow her own tongue, as Rosy Sue wiggled in her wet panties, as Molly and Polly thumbed up saltine crumbs, as Tammy palmed her paper doll to pulp, as Holly sucked her bloody knuckle raw, *before* Dad bit his Lucky Strike in half, Mom unbuttoned her blouse and gave me one sore nipple to suck on, for four more hours, until we got there...

When we got to the yellow house, Gram and Gramps stood on the back steps waving, Gram in her blue-flowered dress, Gramps in his striped overalls. Dad flicked his Lucky Strike to the gravel, Mom held me up for show, Tammy and Holly ran to Gramps, Polly and Molly waddled to Gram, Rosy Sue and Anne sauntered out, the boys unfolded their long limbs from the back and everyone turned at the sound of Ned's tires.

Uncle Ned's home from work!

This was a home movie we watched in the living room, with the drapes drawn, us kids in damp swim suits on beach towels, extra chairs brought in for the great aunts, same way we watched the first moon landing. Dad set up the projector, Tammy unrolled the screen, Mom came in from the kitchen with a dishtowel draped over her shoulder and the soundless flicking began.

There's Uncle Ned getting out of his Chevy! There's Uncle Ned's funny grin! There's Uncle Ned holding up that paper sack!

From the sack Ned pulled a stack of sailor hats. Everybody laughed. Ned handed the stack to Don. Don took a hat and passed to John. John took a hat and passed to Mark and so on.

A hat for each kid! Even the baby!

The boys put on their hats and swaggered. The girls put on their hats and posed. Tammy and Holly climbed in the hammock and swung back and forth, laughing and rocking. Polly and Molly squeezed in beside them, then Anne and Rosy Sue. The boys squeezed in too.

There's Dad's gap-tooth grin! And Mom's red lipstick! Look how young Gramps is! And is that blinking pink baby-head me?

Someone set me in the hammock. I was passed hand-to-hand, from Holly to Tammy to Polly to Molly to Rosie Sue to Anne to Mark to John to Don. Don held me gently as I blinked in the sun, so tiny I couldn't sit up.

Every time Mom got pregnant she sent a kid or two down to the yellow house. For us kids, the wide yard, tall trees, yellow barn, flowerbeds and shadowy tangle of fenced-in brambles where Uncle Ned threw old tires and burned old magazines was heaven.

When Mom was a teenager, the yellow house was featured in the American Farmer Magazine with full-color pictures. Gram in her garden pruning a rose, Gramps in his workshop carving a bird, Mom and Ned smiling over a platter of cookies, and Ned so handsome he could be a movie star with his square jaw, dark brows and chocolate eyes. And on the cover, the house in blue leaf shadows on a golden afternoon with Gram's peonies glowing in the background. Gram's flowers were at every church service, funeral and Ladies' Tea in Pearl Pond.

The house went downhill after Gram and Gramps died. After Ned's funeral we found mold in the cupboards, rotten meat in the fridge and the back stairwell littered with dead crickets. Ned had really let the place go. He couldn't keep it up by himself, so he lived in his trailer that was parked out by the barn, or maybe he used the trailer for trash, I didn't know, what did I know, I was just the baby. Tammy and Holly said the trailer was filled with empty mouthwash bottles, but back when Gram and Gramps were alive, the yellow house was a pristine hush of pale pastels. On every shelf sat something of wood, stone or metal that Gram or Gramps had carved, etched or polished, and in the yellow house people talked softly and behaved politely, as Gram hosted in her blue wave-set and tailored suits, with her flower-arrangements blooming on her cherry-wood dining table.

Gram was the queen of good manners. I never heard her yell, scream or curse, except when she was pulling weeds. "Damn weeds," she'd say, "I pull you up one day and there you are the next day, right back again! Damn weeds!" That was the only time I ever heard her curse. And that one time she cursed me.

What Gram made me do in the garden wasn't wicked. She

was teaching me an important lesson. It wasn't till years later I learned what that lesson was.

Gram was in the kitchen singing her pie-making song. I was in the garden wondering what was inside Gram's flowers. I stared at one blue bachelor button bud. The bud was hard and plain, with just a trace of zig-zag. I closed my fingers over it and told myself, *this bud won't feel me pry it apart...*

Gram's garden was a lovely place for a five year old. In her curving beds, butterflies wafted, Japanese cherries bloomed and the sunken bathtub flicked with goldfish in the shade of Candy-cane Carnations, Red Emperor Tulips and Naked Lady Lilies.

When I walked through Gram's garden I turned into the Queen of Light. Every move, step, sigh I made was a move, step, sigh of light, light, light. When I tipped my chin, light wafted. When I waved my arm, light trailed. When I spun a circle, light twirled. I was loveliness personified, kindness incarnate, tender perfection.

When I walked out of Gram's garden and into the fenced-in tangle where Uncle Ned burned old magazines, I became the Evil Queen. All within were subject to my malevolence! I cursed old tires, tore at weeds, enlisted shrubs for my evil deeds and bounced up and down on the rusty box-spring, spitting curses as stormclouds burst from my head!

But in Gram's garden I was always nice, and rolling the bachelor button bud in my fingers, I didn't want to hurt anything. I was just *curious* about what was inside that tight little fist. I wanted to feel it unfold in my fingers, smell the first uncurl to air, and see how intricate it was, how tightly-packed, that origami of eternity.

I snapped off the bud, pried it open and dug my nails in. *What made it flower?*

I couldn't see, or didn't understand. I needed finer fingers. Or a magnifying glass, or to shrink down like Alice in Wonderland. I tore open another. Then another. I stuck my nail in. *Slimy*. The bud was open but still a mystery. I tore open another. Then another. All the bachelor button buds! Then a begonia bud. Then all the begonias! Then a peony. Then all the peonies! Then the marigolds, callas, hyacinths, snapdragons and lilies! And finally Gram's prize roses.

My fingernails were jammed with flower-slime by the time Gram caught me.

"God damnit girl!"

She clamped my wrist. I closed my hand. She pried it open. A mangled rose to the ground. She smacked her own thigh, went to her knees and scrabbled in the dirt, barehanded.

"Do you know what you've done?"

Something bad?

"Do you know what you're going to do?"

Something else?

She handed me a mangled rose.

"Put this back, damnit."

I set the bud on a stem. The bud fell off.

"Try again."

I set the bud on the stem. The bud fell off.

"Again."

The bud dropped to the dirt.

"Wait here. Don't move."

Gram strode to the house.

I waited in the garden, stone-still as the night I lay in the road with Rosy Sue. A bee landed on my neck, walked up my nose and sat between my eyes. Its black buzzing filled my vision.

Finally, Gram came back with a basket, set the basket on the grass and put her hands on her hips.

"Go ahead. Put back every one."

Inside the basket was wire, tape, a pincushion, a ball of string, a spool of thread, sewing scissors and a bottle of Elmer's glue. I looked up at Gram for instructions. Perhaps, like Gramps, she could fix any broken thing. But she marched back to her kitchen.

I scratched in the dirt for the torn petals and tried to match each with each. They were mixed up, red with white, yellow with green, purple with pink. I pressed the scraps into bud-shapes mixed with glue, squeezed gently and opened slowly. The bud fell apart.

Where had my magic powers gone? I threw back my head and wailed at my wickedness.

Gram returned, wiped her hands and bent to help. We taped the bud-balls to the headless stems, we stitched with needle and thread, we wove with wire. The needle tore holes, the wire was hard to bend and the tape wouldn't hold, but we did get the petals back into some sort of buds.

Gram stood and brushed off her knees. "Let's see if this takes. We won't know for sure till morning."

The rest of the day I was too ashamed to go into the garden but I couldn't keep out. I walked past the beds, glancing at my damage, the bandaged heads, drooping stems and dripping glue, then went back to the hammock and swung, my eyes on the sky, the rock in my stomach, the penny in my throat.

That night, when I closed my eyes in the little sewing room, I saw the mangled buds, scattered petals and headless stems. I prayed that the Fairy of Goodness would wave her wand and make all better. In my sleep, an endless row of huge, angry daisies marched toward me, fists clenched, faces contorted, the head daisy shouting, "CAT MCCLOUD, WHAT HAVE YOU DONE?!"

The next morning I stared into my steaming oatmeal bowl with the firm belief that the Good Fairy had tipped her magic wand and made all whole again. I imagined each newly mended bud opening to the sun, as butterflies wafted, goldfish swam and plum trees dappled.

After breakfast, Gram and I filled the enamel tray with the leftover oatmeal, a sprinkle of hard-food and a slosh of milk, and carried the tray down the back steps for the scattering barn cats.

Then we stepped into the horseshoe curves of Gram's raised beds to inspect the garden. Every bud we'd mended was dead.

THE UNSPOKEN RULE

That was at the second yellow house. The second yellow house stood in the same spot as the first, but I never saw the first yellow house, because that burned down back in the Great Depression.

On a winter night when Mom was twelve years old, she woke to an orange shimmer on the walnut tree outside her window. She imagined the shimmer was fairies dancing and made up a poem in her head.

> *Fairies, fairies, flickering light!*
> *Flickering warm and shining bright!*
> *Slender, tender, hard to catch,*
> *Flashing, dashing, lift the latch-*

The light grew brighter-

> *Fairies, fairies, flickering bright;*
> *Fairies twinkling in the night.*
> *Pointed, jointed, flashing stars,*
> *Tiny limbs and tiny arms-*

The light grew brighter-

> *Fairies, fairies, flickering bright,*
> *Fairies shimmer, lovely sight!*
> *Sizzling, snapping, bright and wild,*
> *Look upon the fairy child!*

Mom threw off her covers and ran down the hall to Ned's room. "Ned! Wake up!"

"What?"

"There are fairies! In the walnut tree!"

"What?"

"Fairies!"

"What fairies?"

"Shh! Come see."

Mom tugged him to her room and pointed. "There."

"Where?"

"Those flickers. On the walnut."

Ned squinted. "That's just light on the tree."

"That is them! Fairies disguise themselves. If you have fairy blood, you can see-"

"You're full of baloney."

"Edith! Ned!"

Gram stood in the doorway. "What are you doing up?"

"Fairies!" Ned pointed at the tree.

Gram raised the window, sniffed at the air and ran down the hall with her nightgown flying, shouting, "Wake up! Wake up! The house is on fire! The house is on fire!"

Gramps ran across the road to the great uncle's. The great uncle, the great aunt and little Ben threw their coats over their nightclothes and ran to the yellow house. By then it was just a patch of roof burning. They hauled the ladder from the barn.

Gramps steadied the ladder, the great aunt and Gram yelled directions, the kids took turns pumping and running buckets to the ladder and great uncle climbed up and sloshed the bucket, but the water didn't reach. The ladder wasn't tall enough. Then the ladder broke and the great uncle fell to the snow. He was all right, but the wind picked up and the flames flared. Gramps ran to the barn, for tools to fix the ladder, but Gram said. "Never mind, it's too late! Let's save what we can!"

There was no fire department in Pearl Pond at the time. So they went in the burning house and carried out what they could, dressers, chairs, pots and pans, clothes, linens, the dining room table, even the cast iron stove. All night they carried and dragged. By morning the yard was covered with sooty stuff and the house was a smoking hole. So they went across the road to live at the great uncle's.

The great uncle's was not like the yellow house. At the great uncle's, stuff crept out of place and gathered in corners. In the second floor hall a crate of worn shoes, a bucket of gears and a basket of old blankets sat under a photo of some great-great grandfather, and down in the dining room, brooms, pipes and a box of cracked dishes leaned against the same wallpaper from back when Gram was a kid. One day Mom opened a drawer looking for a fork, and found a used tube of udder cream, a wax elf, some lead shot and sawdust all mixed up with the silverware. Everything was mixed up and out of place.

Great uncle got out of place too. One day when the great aunt and Gram were down in the kitchen, and Gramps was out in the barn, and the boys were out with the dogs, Mom was up in her cousin Ben's room folding a stack of white clothes. Mom was just developing then, her new buds aching under her t-shirt. She didn't know the great uncle was in the hall watching her. But as Mom folded, she got that feeling of someone's eyes on you, and looked up, and there was the great uncle with his private part sticking right out and up at attention. But Mom knew what to do. She knew without being told. She knew the Unspoken Rule.

Next spring, when the snow pulled back from the road and the road became a river of mud and the crocuses pushed up, Mom, Ned and Gram and Gramps tromped back across to the yellow house. But there was no house, just the burn-hole round the chimney. So they slept in a canvas tent, and dragged the cookstove from the barn, and Gramps built a lean-to for Gram to cook in, then they hired a crew of men to help build the house back up again.

All that summer, Mom said, Ned slept in a slap-dash shed with one of the hired men, and the family and the hired men sawed, pounded, roofed and framed, through rain, heat, and hurt backs, and finally they got the yellow house back up again, with special built-in nooks and crannies for Gram.

On the August day when everything was back in its place, clothes in closets, cups on saucers and sheets on beds, that was the day the car came down the road and broke everything apart again.

IF ONLY

At first Mom never told me about Uncle Ned's accident. She just walked me across our yard to the mailbox and said, "Stop here Cat." I stopped at the curb and looked down at my scuffed shoes. "Listen carefully," she said. "When you go outside by yourself, this is where you must stop, where our yard meets the road. Do not ever step off until you are old enough."

Every day I walked to the curb and stared down at my shoes, until one day Mom said, "Now you are old enough to cross by yourself, but you must never step off without looking. You must first look both ways. Look right. Now look left. Don't step off yet. Now listen. Listen with both ears. Don't step off yet. Listen to the right and listen to the left. Then feel for a rumble. Do you feel a rumble? Only if you do not see a car, hear a car or feel a car, then you may step off and cross to Jill's house. And do not daydream, Cat. Never daydream while crossing the street."

There was very little chance of me getting hit on our street. The only cars were dads coming home from work, the milkman, the bookmobile and boyfriends of the big sisters.

But I was a daydreamer. With my Fischer-Price Lawnmower. Yellow wooden handle, clear plastic dome, and inside the colored balls that went pop-pop! The mystery of the universe was in that clear dome. Not the mystery of what made the balls inside go pop, that mystery was solved when Tammy turned the Lawnmower over and showed me the wire connecting the wheels to a gizmo on the underside. I confirmed this by wagging my own warty finger on the wheels.

Slow pushing, slow pops. Fast pushing, fast pops. Mystery solved.

And not the mystery of the balls inside, I could tell by their look and sound those balls were made of wood, and painted in the hard, bright colors of childhood, like the neighbors' pool table and croquet balls. But unlike the pool and croquet balls, the balls inside the plastic done were different sizes, small, medium and large. And though they had no distinguishing numbers, I knew with certainty the personalities and proclivities of each:

The green was a pesky boy down the street, the yellow a girl in a buttercup skirt, the red a big-chested church lady, the navy blue a man skinny as his brief case, the purple a fancy man in a ruffled shirt who ate fried parakeet wings with his fancy friends, the black a lady who lived under the earth and knew everything, the orange a gum-snapping cheerleader, and so on…

No, the mystery was in the pattern of the popping. *What made which pop when? What made the red pop before the green and then the yellow?* As I circled our dining room, living room, kitchen, with the powers of my toddler mind I slowed down time. *Red then green. Black then white. Purple and orange. Pop-pop…*

Meanwhile, Dad sat at the head of the table asking me politely to stop. The King of the House should not have to repeat himself, but I was lost in the mystery of probability. *Red, blue, yellow, white, purple, orange, green, black. Was there a pattern? Did it repeat? After how many times round the dining room? Red, yellow, blue, pop, pop…*

Dad's hand came from nowhere.

"GOD DAMNIT STOP THAT RACKET RIGHT NOW!"

I flew across the dining room. A cartoon character. Unable to change my trajectory. But I could look around. Mom at the open fridge, her hand round a milk carton. Tammy at the counter spreading mayonnaise. Dad standing red-faced, his big arm in retrograde, a ball game on the radio. *Three and one at the bottom of the seventh.*

I hit the wall by the doorbell chimes. The chimes softly donged. I slid down the wall. Holly ran from our bedroom to see who was at the door. *No one. Just the baby sister on the floor. And she's fine. There are no bones poking. And no blood showing. She just got the wind knocked out of her. This time.*

In that bubble of breathlessness, I realized it was not safe to daydream in our house. At any time, a hand could come and send me flying. I couldn't protect my outsides, but I could protect my insides, so I turned my heart hard and small as a stone.

Jill and I dug those stones up from the hot asphalt in our street on summer afternoons. *Agates*, we called them, the small rocks with curving stripes and a blood-red translucence when you held them up to the light. Those agates that we unearthed on sweaty days with a shared flat-edge screwdriver from the tar of Little Rose Lake Road reminded me of my hard little heart, a rare-find, bright-red, hard-to-dig-out. But by the time we turned thirteen, Jill and I had lost interest in digging up agates and my heart was no longer translucent, fancy-striped or worth digging up. My heart had turned into a hard gray pebble suspended in emptiness.

Mom was a daydreamer too. That's why she never told me about Uncle Ned's trouble till years later when I asked, "Why is Uncle Ned different?" And she said, "Because he was hit by a car when he was just a boy."

That was back in the Year of the Terrible Accidents, same year as the house fire and Gramp's electrocution, when Mom was a girl of thirteen. They'd just finished the new house and everything was in place, oatmeal in bowls, steam rising and Gram calling everyone in to breakfast...

"Edith! Put down that book! Find your brother. And put on

your apron."

Mom yelled out the mudroom door. "Ned!" She went down the back steps. "Ned!"

Hot already. Going to be a scorcher...

Ned wasn't in the garden. Or the barn. Or the orchard. *There he was.* Spinning circles in the front yard. "Ned, breakfast!"

Ned fell to his knees, and ribbons of green and yellow spun round him.

After breakfast Gram oversaw the cookie-baking. "You should get three dozen out of that, Edith. That's too much. Pinch some off. Hands off, Ned! Spit that out! What did I tell you? Don't eat raw dough! You'll get worms! And don't pack them warm, Edith! Let them cool fully before you put them in the bucket. I'll finish up here. You go get scrubbed up. Wear your apricot pinafore. I got that stain out. Ned, polish your shoes. Edith, make sure that he does. I'm not feeling well today. I won't be able to attend the picnic. You and Ned bring the cookies, with my regards, and Edith, you carry the bucket this time. Don't let Ned carry it. Remember what happened last time!"

Last time, Ned swung the bucket, and by the time they reached the church, every cookie was in crumbles. So this time, Mom hugged the bucket to her chest as she squinted in the sun.

Before they got a quarter mile down the dirt road she'd sweated through her clothes and Ned was grabbing for the bucket.

"No, Ned! Don't grab! And don't scuff your shoes."

"I'm not scuffing."

"Yes you are."

"No I'm not!"

Ned was being an airplane again.

Headgear? Roger! Fuel tank? Roger! Full speed ahead! To the statue of Liberty! Over the mighty Atlantic! To the sunny coast of Italy!

Mom couldn't tell Ned anything. He was handsome and smart and could stand up in class and add three-digits out loud while all the other kids' mouths hung open.

Mom gave up on Ned and studied the clouds.

That cloud is a rabbit. That cloud is an elephant. That cloud is a mermaid. I'm the mermaid! I'm captured by pirates! The swarthy crew is keeping me caged below-decks, tangled in fishnets and bestrewn with seaweed and nipped by crabs and bruised by the thrashing seas. I'm all alone, away from my merfolk, and hungry, and at twilight a deaf-dumb shipmate with red hair and sea-blue eyes sneaks me bits of dried beef, and though he cannot speak, he looks in my eyes and sees the depths of the salty sea, and oh, the sailor falls in love with me, deeply in love, and oh, he cannot look away, for in my eyes he sees the burly sea, and at night, when I cannot see, and can hardly breathe in that crank of a place, the mute sailor sneaks down to feed and water me, and comfort me with songs of the sea, and untangle my seaweed locks, and all the while, my mermaid heart yearns, please, oh please, ship-boy, set me free! Unlock this unholy cage and carry me above deck into the fresh air and starlight, where I can smell the sea and not the filth of sick animals on this endless crossing, and oh, sailor boy, kiss me!

Meanwhile a car headed down the road. Mom heard the car and snapped from her daydream. Ned stood spinning in the middle of the road.

"Ned! A car! Run!"

Ned stopped spinning, got his bearings and ran. The car swerved to avoid Ned. Ned swerved to avoid the car. Both swerved in the same direction. The car hit Ned. Up Ned flew. Up past the cloud shaped like a rabbit. Up past the cloud shaped like an elephant. Up past the cloud mermaid. Up so high he could see the shining gold dome of the Iowa State Capital.

Then he came down, down. He hit the road both hard and soft, like a hay bale landing. His eyes rolled to whites. His legs trembled. His arms shook. Spit foamed at his lips. On his pants a wet circle.

"Ned?"

No answer, just eye-rolling, twitching and frothing. A white-faced man got out of the car, walked to Ned, took off his hat and stood over him as if standing over a grave. Mom set the cookie-bucket down in the clover. The man knelt, touched Ned's chest, put two fingers to his neck and asked, "Where your folks live?"

Mom pointed down the road.

"They home?"

She nodded.

"You got a telephone? Don't move him. Stay right here."

The man left in a tail of dust. Mom chewed her finger as she stared down at her brother. *There's no blood coming out of you, Ned, and no bones poking. You're all in one piece. But where are your socks and shoes?* She studied his bare feet, then turned in a circle. Far down the road was a hover of bumblebees. After a while, an ambulance came and drove Ned to the Brownmound hospital. The doctor found a tender spot at the back of his head and said, "We'll keep an eye on him…"

Keep an eye on him…

As Ned lay unconscious in the hospital, Gramps stood in the corner of his room carving a bird, Gram sat darning socks and my mom imagined an eyeball on Ned's cheek, watching for movement. *Wake up Ned.*

Gram said, "Don't lean on the bed, Edith. Stand up straight. Get your finger out of your mouth. Stop fussing. Stand here. Bring a book next time, or your beading."

Wake up Ned. Mom traced the words on paper, in her head and on the hospital window. *Wake up, wake up.* But Ned did not wake up. Not that day or the next. His eyes sunk to brown circles, his chin drew to his chest and his hands fisted. Ned slept while bees filled the garden, the windfall apples fermented and the pumpkins fattened. While everyone else in Pearl Pond got ready for the Iowa State Fair, Mom snuck a hand-mirror into his room, held the glass to his lips and wrote in the fog, *WAKE UP!*

"I know where your shoes and socks went, Ned. They went down the road quite a ways, with your socks still in them, and the laces still laced. The Doc says he'd heard of, but never before seen, a force so hard it knocks off a person's socks and shoes, with the laces still laced."

Ned slept through the corn harvest, the start of school and the leaves turning. Leaves turned and fell, leaves skittered over the lawn, yellow, red, purple, spinning circles, rising, landing, circling the barn, corncrib and henhouse, curling round the flowerbeds, getting caught in the wrought iron fence, huddling together, piling up, as Mom lay awake in her bed and stormclouds gathered in her room, gray shapes of the car coming, Ned flying, Ned landing and Ned trembling.

Just before his eleventh birthday, as the hospital orderly wiped his lips, Ned opened his eyes and said "ah gah."

The orderly told the nurse. The nurse told the doctor. The doctor phoned Gram and Gramps. Gram and Gramps told the relatives across the road and they all drove to Brownmound Hospital, piled into Ned's room and spoke at once.

"Open the window!" "Close the door!" "Prop him up!" "Leave him be!"

Ned said "ah-gah."

Everyone stopped to hear what he'd say next, but all Ned said was ah-gah. Mom kept quiet while everyone else babbled, "What's he saying?" 'Call the doctor!" "What's he want?"

Mom held up a picture book and pointed to an apple. "You mean this, Ned?"

"Ah-gah."

She pointed to a glass of milk. "You mean this?"

"Ah-gah."

She pointed to a picture of an airplane. "This?"

Ned said "ah-gah," but instead Mom heard, *I'm so thirsty!* And instead of an airplane, she saw a dripping orange slice.

"Ned wants juice!" she said. "He wants orange juice!"

The whole family laughed, the nurse squeezed the juice, Gram held the glass and Ned sputtered most of it down his gown, but no one cared. Ned was awake. He was alive. He could come home.

But back home Ned couldn't do anything. He couldn't make words, walk or sit up. They had to teach him everything all over again, how to wash his face, hold a spoon, chew and swallow. Every day someone sat in his room with a lesson. "This is the letter A. This is the number one. This is a knife and fork." Again. Again.

Next spring Ned was well enough to go back to school, but he was never the same. He had hard white headaches and sound hurt him. All sound, any sound, people chatting, glasses clinking, forks scraping. Some noises sent him into a red rage. One night Mom was stringing glass beads down in the kitchen. She picked up each bead from an enamel tray and set each down quietly so as not to upset Ned. But to Ned up in his room each bead touching the tray was like a giant slamming a giant tankard down on a metal bar in a giant tavern. BOOM! BOOM!

"OP!" Ned yelled.

OP meant STOP.

Mom startled and upset the tray. Beads scattered everywhere, under the icebox, under the stove, under the counters. *Shh. Whisper, everybody whisper.*

Putting together a sentence, adding numbers, buttoning a button, Ned lost his way, his hands balled into fists, he pounded the table, and whatever was there, salt shaker, cream pitcher, fell over, rolled off and smashed to the floor, and Mom lay up in her room listening to the crickets and the silence of the oncoming winter as the IF ONLYS clustered in her head.

If only Ned had run the other way. If only the car had swerved the other way. If only we had walked to the picnic earlier, or later, or not gone to the picnic at all. If only I'd let Ned carry the bucket. If only I hadn't been daydreaming! I was looking up at the clouds. I wasn't looking after my baby brother. That's why Ned was hit by that car. That's why he went in a coma. That's why he woke up so different. The whole thing is my fault. IF ONLY.

THE WANTED POSTER

I know how Mom felt, the guilt that won't go away, the copper taste at the back of your throat, the boulder in your gut. You try to be good, but how can you be when you can't see the whole picture? Like that Halloween I became a murderess.

Yellow leaves were zig-zagging, the Johnsons were out raking, Jill's brothers were tossing a football, Little Mary was galloping her stick pony in her Sleeping beauty costume and Uncle Ned was visiting for his birthday.

His cake was in the basement fridge, chocolate with blue frosting, and it was so warm Little Mary and I took off our shoes and went wading in the lake. *In October!*

Then Mom called us up for lunch. I carried our shoes and sock and Little Mary galloped up on her pony. I was in the kitchen spreading mayonnaise and Little Mary was making her magic circles, chattering around the living room, dining room and kitchen in her make-believe land of cherry hills, strawberry fairies and blooming hearts, purple hearts blooming from purple hearts, humming and daydreaming into infinity like I used to do with my Fischer-Price Lawnmower.

Our cat Marshmallow sat on the floor with her tail twitching. She felt the bad thing coming that day, the dark undoable. Dad was nervous. Ned was nervous. Mom went back and forth between the fridge and sink. Dad sat at the head of the table trying to watch the game. Ned sat kitty-corner from Dad, smoking, drinking spiked coffee, cringing at the game, getting up and sitting down. Ned kept saying, "Why don't you kids go outside? No kids should be inside on a day like this!" But we didn't go out. We just kept doing what we were doing. Little Mary circling. Me spreading. Mom going back and forth between the fridge and sink, Dad smoking, the game blaring, the cat twitching and Ned standing up and sitting down.

Each time Little Mary galloped past Dad, he jabbed his cigarette, touched his ear and leaned forward, smashing his Lucky Strike into the ashtray...

Three and one and the bottom of the seventh.

Finally, Dad's arm flew out towards Little Mary.

"STOP THAT GOD DAMN RACKET RIGHT NOW!"

Before his hand reached her, I planted my feet and opened my mouth. A GIANT VOICE came out.

"STOP!"

Dad stopped. Marshmallow clawed up the drapes. Little Mary scampered away, unharmed. But I broke something! The Rule of Silence! Dad stood. Ned stood. Their cups clattered to the floor. Ned grabbed Dad. Dad pawed Ned. *What were they doing? Hugging? Dancing? Goofing off? Oh they were fighting!* I'd never seen two old guys fight before. It was funny. Then over. Dad fell to the floor. Ned tromped downstairs, stomped up with his bag, grabbed his smokes and left. He drove away in a red-faced rage.

We didn't cut his cake. We forgot all about Ned's birthday. After lunch, we were going to go to the Mini-Mart for ice cream. Ned, Little Mary and I were going to lean on his car, feel the hot metal through our backs on that warm afternoon, lick our cones and watch the boys do wheelies in short sleeves in the parking lot, but we never did. Instead the cups lay sideways on the floor, the pools of spilled coffee spread, the sandwiches curled and a gray stillness filled the house after Ned left, a gray dread.

I wiped up the coffee, wrapped up the sandwiches and picked up the cups, but soon after, out in the world beyond my reach, where I couldn't smell the blood or hear the screams, I became a murderess.

There's that saying, a butterfly flaps its wings in Florida and a volcano erupts in China, or a kid laughs in Egypt and a family drowns in Lake Whatever. Or whatever. I can't remember that saying exactly, but the tidal wave had begun.

A week after Thanksgiving it finally snowed. I was crunching through the glittering crust to the Mini-Mart for some Hubba Bubba Bubble Gum, wondering, *why doesn't Kirk ask for my telephone number? Why doesn't Kirk ask me to Winter Wonderland? Why doesn't Kirk talk to me after Social Studies Class?*

I was also wondering how I was going to buy presents for my whole family with just thirty-six dollars and fifty-seven cents of baby-sitting cash. Then I saw the poster taped to the Mini-Mart window and almost fell over.

WANTED. FOR THE ABDUCTION OF JACK JACKOWAY. HEIGHT. WEIGHT. EYE COLOR. DEEP GRUFF VOICE. And the face. A pencil sketch. Of Uncle Ned.

I'd forgotten all about Rosy Sue's Thanksgiving whisper, her hand on my elbow and her pale lips saying, "It was Ned, it was Uncle Ned! I know it was him! He was visiting for his birthday and he wanted to go hunting with Stu, but I said, 'No Ned, you're too drunk to hunt!' Then he wanted to take the neighbor boys hunting instead, but the neighbor boys said that Ned was 'weird,' you know, *weird*, so I said, 'No Ned, you can't take the boys hunting, you're too drunk!' Then Ned drove off so mad, and so drunk, and he drove right to where Jack was, and took Jack. I know it was him! Ned was the one who took Jack Jackoway!"

Of course I didn't believe the Queen of Secrets! Why would Ned take a kid? Yes he was weird from his car accident but not that kind of weird. And yes he talked in a gruff voice and made up funny rhymes and lived his whole life in the yellow house, but that didn't make him a kidnapper...

But that wanted poster.

Kirk King flew out of my head. I forgot to buy Hubba Bubba Gum. I didn't even go in the Mini-Mart. I crunched home and dialed long-distance. Rosy Sue answered in her sleepy cotton-candy voice.

"Hello?"

"Rosy Sue, have you seen it?"

"Seen what?"

"The Wanted Poster."

"What Wanted Poster?"

"For Jack Jackoway-"

"Jack's face is all over. So what?"

"No, of the guy who took Jack. It looks just like-"

Her voice went rock-hard. "Don't tell me Cat. Average height. Average weight. Like every middle-aged guy in America. That could be anybody. Drop it."

Drop it.

Dial tone.

Rosy Sue never said another word about Uncle Ned.

And by next summer she was dead.

When someone dies a door opens. People think death is an end and cry and tell themselves they've lost a loved one, but death isn't an end, death isn't a big pink eraser, death isn't a bottomless hole. Death is an open door. Whoosh, the wind comes in and new things appear and people you knew your whole life stand in doorways backlit so you can't see their faces and turn into brand new strangers. And the rules change, things get rearranged, *who's the secret-keeper, who's the secret-teller.*

By the time Dad died the lake had frozen hard enough to skate on, and at the church cross the lake, we blew our noses in the Grandmas' flowered hankies and stood outside as they slid Dad's bronze-colored coffin into the hearse, then rode to Soldiers' Hill, where he got to be with all the other thousands of white crosses for fighting in the Big One. After the however-many gun salute we stood looking into the hole and watched as they lowered the coffin, down, down.

After the pastel-mint, ham sandwich and black-coffee lunch, we had our own meal back at home, just us sisters. Mom escaped to some *Quistmas Quilting Quest* so we had the whole house to ourselves. And we had a feast. Black licorice, spaghetti and meatballs, dill pickles, pickled herring, mashed potatoes and gravy, jumbo Hershey's bars, macaroni and cheese, T-bones, circus peanuts, cheeseburgers, hot dogs, Swedish meatballs, cherry vanilla ice cream. Dad loved to eat.

We used every pot and pan in the kitchen, and in the center of the fondues, platters and casseroles we put Dad's Employee of the Year Award, his bowling trophies and a three-olive martini, then we feasted in honor of Dad who wasn't there to yell at us anymore.

Molly and Polly got silly and tossed a meatball back and forth until splat, it hit the wall, slid down and left a greasy smear, then Grandma Jane's cuckoo clock struck the half hour, a slow koo-koo because the weights were running down, and we stopped laughing, wiped our mouths and started cleaning up.

After the dishes, the serious partying began. We lit candles, made a fire and told stories of how Dad used to take us on drives into far neighborhoods to see the Christmas lights and how he did *this fun thing and that*, stuff from before I was born, stuff I don't remember.

I sat off to the side and played with the melted candlewax. I didn't believe in ghosts, visions or candy-land shoeboxes, but I kept seeing Dad in the house that night, Dad in his easy chair, Dad at the head of the table, Dad passed out on the living room floor, Dad who taught me *it's better to die for the truth than live with a lie.*

After seeing the Wanted Poster, I'd asked my other sisters about Uncle Ned, but they shut their mouths, held their breath and turned to stone. I'd rather be backhanded across a room than stare at that row of stone faces, so I stopped asking…

But I kept seeing the Wanted Poster in my head that night of Dad's funeral, so I devised one simple question to ask, without speaking the name of Uncle Ned. My question: *do you remember any weirdness in our family?*

While the others were up making popcorn, Tammy and I got our skates from the laundry room nails and trudged down to the lake. I was wobbly at first. Tammy knew all the tricks. I let her get warmed up then asked my question.

"Tammy, do you remember anything weird in our family?"

She glided in an arabesque. "Weird like how, Cat? You mean

weird like hitting? Because, if you mean weird like hitting, no, there was none of that. None that I remember. No hitting to speak of. Not by Dad. Dad had calmed down these last years. So no..."

She scraped backwards.

"Except that one time, Cat. That time with Mark. When Dad threw Mark down the stairs. I do remember that. Dad almost killed Mark that time...

"Oh, and Dad would punch out Don and John quite a lot. Like the time Don tried to sneak a watermelon in his bedroom window. Dad really punched Don out for that...

"And Dad bloodied my nose quite a few times. He'd knock my head against the fireplace, just to shake me up... But no hitting, Cat. None that I remember. And Dad didn't hit us girls. Not with a fist. He'd make a fist."

Tammy fisted her red mitten, "Then just before his fist landed, he'd open it, like this, and hit open-handed."

My skate caught a bump. I aimed for a snowbank, turned onto my back and stared up at the night sky. Tammy shooshed to a stop beside me, raising white lace.

"But not you, Cat. Dad never hit you...Except spankings... And that one time, I do remember..."

She put out her mittened hand to help me up.

"You were a toddler. Just old enough to walk. You kept pushing that toy lawnmower. Remember that, Cat? That Fischer-Price? You loved that toy so much! You just kept popping and popping, and Dad kept saying 'stop,' but you were in another world, pop-popping...so finally, Dad backhanded you...and you flew across the dining room."

Three and one at the bottom of the seventh.

Tammy wiped her nose.

"You probably don't remember that. And nothing bad happened, Cat."

She dug into the ice with her blade.

Chunk.

"You just hit the wall, slid down and lay there. You were fine. You just had the wind knocked out of you."

Chunk.

"That's not why I remember Dad hitting you. Dad hit us all the time...Dad hitting us was not unusual...What was unusual was that time, Mom said stop. Real quiet. So quiet I could barely hear, but I heard, because I was right there spreading mayonnaise. That was the one time Mom said stop in all those years of Dad hitting. And I wondered, why say stop when Dad hit you? Why didn't Mom say stop when he hit the rest of us?"

Chunk.

"But it was just that one time, Cat. And nothing else bad happened... Not to you... Is that what you mean by 'weird'?"

Tammy spun in place as I stood silent.

"And afterwards... Rosy Sue took care of you. She carried you down to her room, wiped your tears and washed your face. You were swelled up pretty good by then. You looked like a baby Uncle Fester!"

She cracked a grin. "So Rosy Sue got a mirror and told you not to look in. She made up some story about an old lady in the mirror who'd eat you alive, so you wouldn't look in and see your own busted face."

"Don't look in here, Cat. Not till I tell you it's safe."

As a kid I believed everything Rosy Sue said. I believed fairies lived in flowers and each unpopped kernel in the bowl was a trapped soul and a boy flew over the corn and an old lady lived in the mirror. And I never looked in till Rosy Sue said it was safe.

That day Mom had a migraine. Her door was shut. I knew Mom was on her back in the bed with a cool washcloth over her eyes. We weren't to disturb her. Even if we did tiptoe in and lift a corner of the washcloth, Mom wouldn't be there, because Mom's migraines took her someplace far away where strangers repaired moms while putting them through GREAT PAIN.

So Rosy Sue took care of me that day. She led me to the basement, paused on the middle step for the halfway poem, walked me to the basement bathroom, lifted me into the sink,

held up a white tube and said she was going to make me pretty.
Make me pretty?
I was a toddler. I didn't care about pretty.
"Hold still."
She unscrewed the tube, pulled out an antenna and waved it
at my eye. I flinched. "Don't move, Cat. You have to be a stone
princess. Your head is stone, your neck is stone, your whole
body is stone."
I turned to stone.
"And this is a butterfly landing on your lashes." She waved
the antennae. "Now blink."
Stone princesses do not blink.
She put her eye close to mine. "When I touch your shoulder,
your eyes will come to life. Just your eyes."
She tapped my shoulder and my eyes came to life. She
brushed the antennae on my lashes, and with each blink, my
lashes got heavier. Then she brushed softness on my cheeks and
stickiness on my lips and turned me to face the mirror. "Now
look at yourself."
But the old lady!
"It's okay, Cat, the old lady is sleeping."
I looked in.
A green-eyed Munchkin!
"Aren't you pretty? Now, Mommy's going to take you
shopping!"
Rosy Sue dressed in the plaid dress, wiped her glasses clean,
carried me upstairs, folded me into the stroller and wheeled me
into the sunlight. I squinted. My lashes stuck to my cheek. My
hand rose.
"Don't touch! You'll ruin your eyes!"
Ruin my eyes? Like the tiny onion Mom pulled from the garden
then tossed on the compost heap? When I picked that onion up
it smeared into a putrid paste in my hands, *and the same thing would
happen if I touched my eyes?* I sat stone-still, gripping the colored
wooden beads on the hand-hold as Rosy Sue pushed me to
Sunnyvale Shopping Senter, chanting, "Call me Mom, call me
Mom…"
That's how it was spelled, Senter, with three big red esses

hovering like snakes about to eat the other letters. Sunnyvale was a huge square with shops round the edges, high rectangles of stained glass, echoes of shoppers bouncing off the far ends and a shallow pool in the middle with colored lights underwater. I wanted to splash in that turquoise pool.

But stone princesses do not splash.

At Oscar's Office Supply Rosy Sue got felt tips in the colors of Gram's flowers, and at Pete's Pets we looked at cages of whining puppies, crouching kittens and painted turtles clawing their cages, stinking of sawdust, pee and ground-up bones. I knew that those turtles didn't care for their plastic palm trees and would rather be down at the lake. I wanted to stand up in the stroller, grab those turtles, take them home and set them free.

But stone princesses do not reach.

At Helen's Hobbies, Rosy Sue collected packets of beads, sequins and rhinestones and stuffed the packets between me and the stroller. At Teddy's Toys we walked past puzzles, board games and plastic dinosaurs, and stopped in front of the boxed dolls. The boxes had clear windows so the dolls could look out, and the dolls had puckered mouths about to kiss, and eyes wide with fear at seeing a monster sneak up behind you. Rosy Sue picked out a strawberry blonde in a white dress specked with red flowers and set the box in my lap.

I didn't move, or all the sparkle-packets would fall to the floor and echo up and down and the shoppers would turn their heads and look at us and say, did you pay for those?

She wheeled me to a round table stuck to the floor with a fat silver column and held a chocolate-vanilla cone to my mouth. The cold wet my nose.

Stone princesses do not eat!

Rosy Sue wiped my nose, finished the cone, turned the stroller on its wheels and pushed me home.

When we got home she ran me a bath, and in the warm water I melted back into a real girl. Then she set me in the high chair so I could watch her use the new markers and sequins to decorate the insides of a shoebox, one of her miniature captured-fairy moments with tiny dolls dressed as Egyptian princesses, dark-skinned servants and animal-headed gods performing ancient rites, coronations, funeral marches, beheadings, an angry queen with an upright blade made from one of Dad's plastic cocktail skewers.

Rosy Sue kept making those boxes her whole life. Years later, when she was grown up, and had an apartment of her own, she was still making those magical boxes. Her Black Oak apartment was covered with sparkling wonderlands and she had an unfinished box on her kitchen table surrounded by glue bottles, Q-tips and sequins that summer that she kicked the bucket.

THE SNAKE

It wasn't suicide, or she'd have left a goodbye note in her endless daisy-chain crammed with sensational secrets, and she'd be sitting up in bed with a satin coverlet, hair curled and mouth frosted like a queen in one of her shoeboxes.

Stu came home from a fishing trip and found her passed out on the couch in his t-shirt with a Curse of the Mummy matinee on TV and a sink-full of dirty dishes. No way would Rosy Sue be found dead like that. It was just too many tranquilizers and Red Devils washed down with Royal Rum Colas. An accidental overdose. Stu called an ambulance and it came with lights blaring and siren screaming, but she never woke up.

We sisters knew she wanted to be buried in her gold mini dress, gold pantyhose and gold shoes with the soles nearly worn through from dancing at the Blue Moon, and we knew the undertaker wouldn't do her makeup right, so we brought her whole beauty kit to the funeral home.

They'd already sponged on some sun-kissed orange grease-for-the-dead, so before the mourners came we told the mortuary guy, let us grieve in private, pushed him out, closed the velvet curtains, wiped off the grease and started over with the cover stick.

I climbed up and painted on each individual lash, Tammy glossed her lips, Holly penciled in her beauty mark and Polly and Molly did her nails. We made Rosy Sue breathtakingly alive, just like she was in real life.

Her whole class of White Rock came to the funeral, all the boys anyway, who'd survived Vietnam. Some had missing arms, some missing legs, but they all filed past her coffin and left flowers, and a bunch of people I never knew came crying with stories of what Rosy Sue did for them, how they'd never forget her, how she inspired them or taught them how to laugh again and see the world in a new light, and Rosy Sue shimmered against the emerald lining of her coffin, her hair a river of lava, her mouth a never-tell smile, her body buried in flowers.

Our oldest sister, Anne, did not come to the funeral.

Back home, we took down Mom's quilts, hung up the sparkling shoeboxes, and set out the death feast. Rosy Sue wasn't crazy about eating, so we just had popcorn, potato chips, chocolate-covered almonds, chocolate-covered cherries and a cut-crystal bowl of her pills, pink lozenges, white crosses, green zingers. Then we dumped out the yellow house puzzle.

I didn't feel like doing that, so I picked a green pill and went out to the deck. Past the Anderson's cottonwoods, the clouds opened over a full moon. I rolled the pill in my fingers, thinking of all the drugs Rosy Sue took in her wild days, the LSD and psychedelics she'd swallowed like mystery-candy, the speed she'd popped to keep on truckin', the downers mixed with booze that finally did her in.

I thought *everybody else just talks about living, but Rosy Sue really lived.* She was the QUEEN OF PUZZLES and the QUEEN OF BLUE MOON and the QUEEN OF SECRETS and she saw the mystery in everything, and if only I could pull my head out of my ass and think like Rosy Sue thought, and see what Rosy Sue saw, and dance like Rosy Sue danced, then I'd really be living. I brought the pill to my lips, then remembered the poster in my sixth grade science class, the bright array of red devils, pink hearts and magical surprises, one hundred full-color pharmaceutical gemstones laid out on black velvet with their side effects: Nausea, Dizziness, Disorientation, Paranoia, Hallucination, Death. I dropped the pill to the grass as Tammy popped her head out.

"Want to go for a swim, Cat?"

"Yes!"

We peeled off our clothes, grabbed beach towels and ran down the hill naked. We had the whole lake to ourselves. No light but the moon, no sound but our breath. Out in the middle, Tammy turned on her back. Her breasts floated silver-lit. I sucked on my question.

There was a lot we didn't talk about in our family. We didn't talk about feelings. We didn't talk about fears. We didn't talk about hopes or dreams or anything but the food on the table and the dishes in the sink and the grease spots on the counter. But I swallowed the penny stuck in my throat and asked.

"Tammy, do you remember anything weird from when we were kids? Not hitting, but really weird?"

She spit a silver arc.

"What do you mean by really weird, Cat? Do you mean the big brothers? Because no, there wasn't any of that... Not for me.... I was too young... But why don't you ask Anne."

She swam further out, towards the far shore. I followed.

"But don't you remember anything, Tammy?"

"No."

She treaded water. A cloud passed over the moon. Her face went dark.

"Oh, I do remember one thing, Cat... Back when I was little. The brothers' teenage friends would come over and ask me to lick their things. They said if I licked their things, they'd give me a marble... I was only seven. And I liked marbles. So I'd give their penis just one little lick down in the laundry room. Then get a marble... It was no big deal. I'd lick a penis, get a marble. They didn't hurt me. And ever since, whenever I see a marble, I remember my first taste of penis."

I turned on my back and looked up at the night, imagining Tammy from her second grade picture, a bird-necked kid in the plaid hand-me-down with two missing teeth.

"So no, Cat. The brothers never did anything weird... Not to me."

The moon cleared. Tammy turned on her side and stroked silently.

"Oh, I do remember one time, Cat. With the yellow house Gramps... He and I were alone in our living room and he said, 'Come give your old Gramps a kiss.' You know how he'd say that, 'Give your old Gramps a kiss', no big deal, and we'd give him a kiss, and that would be that. But this time, he slid his tongue in my mouth and French-kissed me, then grabbed my boob and squeezed. I was sixteen, I didn't think much of it, just figured, *poor old man, probably doesn't get much from Gram*, you know? I thought it was funny. No big deal...Is that what you mean by weird, Cat?"

I went under and opened my eyes to black nothing.

My yellow house Gramps? My sweet, funny Gramps? My Gramps who could fix any broken thing?

I resurfaced to Tammy's face next to mine.

"Oh, Cat, I do remember one time. I was asleep in bed and someone's hand came from under and felt me up."

"Felt you up?"

"You know. My breasts."

"Where?"

"In our old room."

"How old were you?"

"I don't know. Just developing."

"Whose hand?"

"I don't know. Just someone's. That's all, Cat. There was nothing else."

We swam back in silence. In the shallows, Tammy moon-walked to the shore.

"Oh, one more thing, Cat, I do remember. Afterwards..."

On our small strip of sand she twisted her hair and moonlight dripped down her torso.

"Afterwards..."

She picked up her towel and buffed dry.

"Afterwards, when Rosy Sue was a teenager, she'd do anyone. Afterwards, all a boy had to do was look at her, and she'd spread her legs anytime, anywhere. In the driveway, down here at the lake, in bed next to me. I'd wake up to her humping some guy she brought home from the Blue Moon, with me lying in bed right beside her. By the time I got to high school, all the boys expected me to be just like her. They thought I'd spread my legs for anyone at the drop of a hat."

She swatted a mosquito.

"But I wasn't like that Cat. I had to live down her reputation. That filled me with so much shame. So no, there wasn't much weirdness in our family. None to speak of... But why don't you ask Anne."

As Tammy and I climbed towards the house we met Holly descending.

"Hi."

"Hi. How's the water?

"Good."

Tammy continued up. I sat with Holly on the hill. We watched the moon chase the clouds and slapped mosquitoes as I gathered my courage.

"Holly, can I ask you something weird?"

"What, Cat?"

"Was there ever any weird touch in our family?"

Holly shrank into her towel. Her voice went high. She turned five years old. "No, Cat. Not for me. But why don't you ask Anne."

As I headed up, I spied Molly and Polly under the deck, wrist-deep in the bowl of chocolate-covered almonds.

Anne knelt by the hearth in the living room. She wore an

oversize sweatshirt, sipped a wineglass and held a Virginia Slim. "Hi, Cat."

"Hi Anne. How are you?"

"Fine. How are you?"

"Fine."

"How's the water?"

"Good."

"So, Cat, what are you up to?"

"Just swimming. It's warm. If you want to-"

"Maybe later."

Smoke snaked from Anne's cig. The fire snapped.

I heard Mom and Tammy murmuring over the Yellow House Puzzle in the dining room. It wasn't the real yellow house, just a puzzle Rosy Sue bought years before at Sunnyvale where she got me velvet dresses, fancy dolls and gold-edged storybooks. Rosy Sue was good to me. Anne hated Rosy Sue, hated to be in the same house, sit at the same table and breathe the same air. At holidays, soft-spoken Anne would purse her mouth, sling back drinks and hiss nasty cracks about Rosy Sue's clothes, her hair, her boyfriends. I wondered if Anne was happy now that Rosy Sue was dead. She took a drag, sipped her wine and smiled at me. *What are you up to Cat?* I smiled back, *nothing. See you later,* and headed for the dining room.

Mom and Tammy stood over the yellow house puzzle. They had most of the outsides done and were working on the insides.

Mom crunched a celery stick. "Hi Cat."

Tammy bit into a chocolate-covered cherry.

"Hi. How's the puzzle?"

"Good."

"Want to help?"

'Sure."

The puzzle lay in the circle of light where Dad had kept his coffee, martinis and ashtray, where we had our family meals, where Dad would explode if the milk spilled or a word peeped, where I sat in the high chair with the whole family. But when I tried to remember the faces from back then, they went blank, flesh over flesh.

Mom snapped in a piece. "There!"

Tammy snapped in a piece. "There!"

I studied the pieces. The puzzle blurred, the colors paisleyed. I shut my eyes.

"You okay, Cat?"

"Would you like to lie down?"

"Yeah, maybe you should."

Mom said, "I'm going to lie down," and headed to her room with the celery stick. Tammy stared at me, candied cherry at the corner of her lip. I picked up another piece, held it to the box and went cross-eyed.

Red with red, blue with blue, green with green. Dancing clouds, whispering corn, screaming flowers!

"What are you up to, Cat?"

"Nothing. Just trying to fit-"

"No. I mean, what are you up to?"

"What? Nothing. Sleepy."

I rubbed my eyes, adjusted my towel and walked toward Mom's room. But something tugged me back to Anne.

Anne was curled on the love-seat plucking potato chips from the bottom of the bowl, sipping wine and eyeing the fire.

"Hi."

"Hi."

"Chip?"

"Thanks."

I fingered up a last salty bit, picked up the poker, jabbed a flimsy cube and watched the ashes topple. Orange sparks rose. Blue flames wavered. A city in there, an untouchable kingdom, like one of Rosy Sue's-

Was that one of her boxes? That gray slumped rectangle in the fireplace?
"Anne, did you-?"

"What?"

I nudged the slumping ash.

"What's that?"

"Nothing. Cardboard. Junk."

I glanced round the living room. There was a blank spot where one of Rosy Sue's glittery shoeboxes had hung. *The small queen brandishing an axe.*

"Anne, may I bum a cig?"

"You're too young."

"Just for tonight?"

She sighed and lit me up, her slim fingers flicking the Bic. A log shifted. The sound of Dad's late-night coughing. Dad's chair was empty. Dad was six feet underground, but his pale legs extended, his martini ice chunked, his smoke rose, saying, ask, Cat. I wanted to open my mouth and let my question fall out like a chocolate covered cherry with the chocolate sucked off, shiny, embarrassing. The smoke from Anne's cigarette filled my lungs, the smoke stung. It felt good to feel something, because I wasn't feeling anything that night, not sorrow for the loss of Rosy Sue, not love for my other sisters, not wonder at the moon shimmying on the black water. But asking was dangerous. Especially if you asked the right person. Especially if that person knew the truth.

When I'd asked Rosy Sue about the Wanted Poster and she had said drop it, I felt like someone left me alone in a room with no windows waiting to be questioned, but no one ever came to ask me anything. I didn't even get a glass of water, and the only person I saw in the glass was me and me, back and back, smaller and smaller, forever and ever amen. And I couldn't ask the brothers, because we never said anything to them except hi, how are you, fine, how are you. But this was my moment. Rosy Sue's death opened the door. I took a deep breath and swallowed the penny in my throat.

"Um. Anne?"

"Yes?"

"I'm going to ask you a question."

She sucked on her Virginia Slim.

"And you don't have to answer."

"I know what you're up to Cat."

"I'm not up to anything-"

"Yes you are. Go ahead. Ask."

She tapped her ash.

"Okay. Do you remember anything weird in our family?"

She drew her arms into her sweatshirt.

"Because you don't have to-"

"I want to, Cat. Just give me time."

Anne's big eyes went soft. She drew her legs and chin in too.

"Rosy Sue and I...she and I... First we'd turn out the light."

"Where?"

"In our room, downstairs, when we went to sleep. Sometimes I turned out the light. Sometimes Rosy Sue. We took turns. Because we didn't want to. Turn off the light. Because then they'd come."

"Who'd come?"

"The brothers. Don or John. Don or John would stand in the doorway and say, 'Mark wants to do it again'."

She drew further into her sweatshirt.

"Then Mark would come in and do it."

"'It?'"

"It. They did it to Rosy Sue. Not me. I didn't like it. They tried it with me first, but I squeezed close to the wall as I could, so they did it to Rosy Sue. And afterwards, there'd be that spot."

Her nose wrinkled. A log shifted.

"When was this?"

"When we were little girls. Before we got our periods."

Little girls? Before their periods? I couldn't get my head around it. The boys were teenagers then. *Why didn't she cry out? Why didn't they tell Mom? Why didn't they run and hide?*

Anne popped her chin out. "I know what you're thinking, Cat. *Why didn't we yell? Why didn't we scream? Why didn't we run tell Mom and Dad?* That would be the normal thing to do, right? But this was a different time. Things were very different. We didn't know what was happening to us. We didn't even know what sex was. And we were scared, not just of the boys, but also of what

Dad would do if he found out. We were afraid of what Dad would do to us, and afraid of what he would do to the boys. And we were ashamed. And the worst thing was to upset Dad."

Don't upset your father.

She drew on her Virginia Slim. "Once, when I was four years old, I was out in the field with Dad at the farm in Iowa, just he and I, and he was driving the haywagon, and I was down below, and so happy to have Dad all to myself. And he drove the wheel over my foot. It was an accident. He didn't even know he'd done it. He just kept on driving. My foot hurt so badly I had to cry out, but I didn't. Instead, I shoved my fist in my mouth and swallowed my tears, because I knew crying would upset Dad."

She tipped her glass, set it down empty.

"And that was the worst thing. To upset Dad. That was drilled into us, Cat. By Mom. But Dad did find out somehow. About Mark and Rosy Sue. But not from me."

I felt sick. *Somebody. Somewhere. Get me something.*

"You okay, Cat?"

"Yeah. You okay Anne?"

"Yes."

"Me too." *I don't feel a thing.*

I left Anne curled in her sweatshirt and bee-lined for the bathroom. Tammy cut me off in the hall. Tammy had been listening. She brought her face to mine and hissed. "Cat! That's when Dad almost killed Mark! That's why Dad threw Mark down the stairs! After he found out what Mark was doing to Rosy Sue! That's why he picked Mark up by his hair! That's why he dragged Mark up the stairs! That's why he held Mark up and-"

Enough!

I backed away from Tammy, into the bathroom, locked the door and stared in the mirror.

Where was I when all this happened? How old was I?

I was a baby. I didn't remember being a baby in that house. I didn't remember crying, didn't remember crawling and didn't remember diapers, patty cake, faces, voices or smells. I did remember Rosy Sue taking care of me, making the bathwater just right, not too hot or too cold, soaping my hair into bunny-ears, holding the mirror and wiping the steam away so I could see the pink-faced elf, then folding the washcloth into a rectangle and telling me to hold it tight to my eyes so no soap got in. I held the cloth so tight I saw red stars dancing in the blackness, an infinity of red stars marching from the center. I did remember that.

But I didn't remember Rosy Sue getting called to help with supper, didn't remember lying on a towel up on the pink-tiled counter, waving my arms and legs at the lights above, and didn't remember a male voice, not Dad's, some other male, cooing at me. I didn't remember his hard-heat on my cheek, the taste of salt, the scent of copper, and the feeling not being able to breathe, the feeling woken in me, too big for my little body. *I didn't remember any of that!*

A knocking at the bathroom door.

"Cat? Is that you in there?"

"Yes, Mom."

"Are you alone?"

"Yes."

"What are you doing in there?"

"Nothing. Do you need to come in, Mom?"

"No, but when you're done, come to my room. There's something I want to tell you."

Mom was propped up on pillows in a circle of light on Dad's old side. She held a book in her hand. She patted the blanket. I sat next to her. She smelled of milk and Jergen's hand lotion.

"Hi Cat."

"Hi Mom. How's your book?"

"Interesting." She set the book down. "I hear you're asking questions. About Mark and Rosy Sue."

"No. I'm not asking questions about Mark and Rosy Sue. I'm asking about Uncle Ne-"

"Yes you are asking about Mark and Rosy Sue. I've heard you asking. And I've been thinking. And I thought I should tell you." She scrunched her face. "I think that started at the yellow house."

"What started at the yellow house?"

"What happened with Mark and Rosy Sue."

"What happened with Mark and Rosy Sue?"

"You know."

"What, Mom?"

"You know!"

"Why do you think that started at the yellow house?"

"I just do."

"But why?"

"I JUST DO!"

She picked up her book and read.

I pulled a book from her headboard and read.

> *When the men reached the northern peak, they had a magnificent view before them, the sky below, the clouds yellow-lit, and the vista so wondrous they knew that they could go on, even blistered by cold, even with broken bones, even with three of their party gone, so they mustered what strength they had left, took stock of their supplies and vowed not to give up until all members of their party were topmost or-*

Mom put her book down. "Alright, Cat. I know you've been asking your questions, about what happened to the girls when they were young, and it got me to thinking about when I was a child, and something came back to me. A memory. Would you like to hear what I remember?"

"Yes."

"Alright then I'll tell you."

She stared at Dad's suits hanging in the closet. "That winter the house burned down, well, for a time after that, we lived across the road at the great uncle's, and one day I was folding clothes up in cousin Ben's room, and your great uncle stood in the hall and exposed himself to me. But I knew what to do."

Mom raised her chin, "I knew the Unspoken Rule!"

"What was that Mom?"

"The Unspoken Rule!"

"What was that?"

"The Unspoken Rule!"

"I know, Mom, but what was it?"

"The Unspoken Rule!"

"What was the Unspoken Rule?"

"You don't know about the Unspoken Rule? I thought you knew! You ought to know! I can't believe you don't know! The Unspoken Rule is 'IGNORE it'! So that's what I did. I didn't say a word. I put my chin in the air and behaved as if he wasn't there. I just kept folding. I was a farm girl. I'd seen penises before. His was no prize. I ignored him, and eventually he went away."

I imagined Mom, twelve years old, strand of hair in her eye, and the great uncle's eyes on her, as she kept folding and refolding the stack of clothes until finally he went away.

Mom scowled as if reading my mind. "Farm life wasn't like life now. It wasn't simple or easy. That was the Depression. In one year our house burned down, Ned got hit by the car and your gramps got electrocuted."

She crossed her arms over her chest. "Did you know about that? About your gramps getting electrocuted? No? Well then I'll tell you. Your gramps was helping your great uncle with the threshing, and there was a downed electric line from a windstorm the night before, and your gramps thought the downed wire was a guy line, not a live wire, so he went to move it out of the way. He touched the wire, was thrown thirty feet, landed with the wire still in his hands and shook like a holy roller. Your Uncle Ned thought quick, grabbed a branch and knocked the wire from your gramp's hand. Otherwise, he would have died right then. As it was, your gramps was bedridden for weeks, with a black hole in his leg where the electricity went into the earth, and a black hole in his hand where it entered him, but he lived, thanks to Uncle Ned."

She twisted her mouth and scooted up in bed. "Things like that, they just happened, and you kept one foot in front of the other. You couldn't stop and mope, because the cows didn't stop making milk, the hens didn't stop laying, and the crops didn't plant themselves. You kept your head down and your mouth shut, or you didn't eat."

She nodded at her own words, settled back into her pillow, took off her glasses and refocused on a point just past her nose. "But that's not what I meant to tell you. What I meant to tell you was this. What I remembered when you started asking your questions. It's strange how memory works. You're aware of one thing, one scent or sensation, and that one thing, that smell of medicine, or the texture of a fabric, or the way the wind moves a branch, will cause you to remember an unrelated thing, and that will spark another memory. One small piece brings back the whole picture.

"Well, that happened to me. This also happened at the yellow house. I was a girl, and I had a fever. I was delirious for days. *'Het up',* we called it. And while I was het up, I remembered something that happened before, but I didn't understand it the first time it happened, because I had no frame of reference, no way of knowing what was happening to me till years later, when I was a grown woman, and only then did I discover what had happened to me years before. At that time, as an adult, I had an infection, that made being close with your father painful, scratchy and dry. When I felt that sensation as a grown woman, of dry tissue rubbing on dry, it came back to me. Suddenly I was a child again, up in my old room in the yellow house, and a big snake pushed into me. That's what it felt like, a snake pushing into me. I thought of it as a snake back then, but it was the identical sensation I had with your father, of dry tissue on dry, and in that moment, as a grown woman, I realized that what happened to me, when I was a girl was someone trying to enter me when I wasn't ready for it. I realized that what I remembered then, as a snake, was a rape."

Mom sniffed. "And I'm not sure who did it, or when, or where, but I do know it happened. So. There. I told you."

She picked up her book and read.

I picked up my book and read.

> *When the men reached the northern peak they had a magnificent view before them, the sky laid out below, the clouds yellow-lit, and the vista so wondrous they knew they could go on, even under duress, even blistered by cold, even with broken bones and three of their party-*

> *When the men reached the northern peak, they had a magnificent view, the sky laid out, the clouds yellow, the vista so wondrous they knew they could go on even with-*

> *When the men reached the northern peak, when they reached the northern peak, when they had a magnificent broken-*

The vowels squirmed out of place, the paragraphs turned into tail-eating snakes. I put the book down and stared at my sleeping mom. Her mouth slowly opened. The book slid from her hands. I picked it up and replaced the bookmark, not sure if it was the right place, then tiptoed to the kitchen for the chocolate-covered almonds, *if there were any left.* The lights were on, the kitchen was empty, and no one left in the living room. *They must be down at the lake, taking in gulps of coolness, stroking through the black water, letting the heat slide off them like snakes shedding their skins.*

I wasn't going to run down the hill and join my sisters naked in the dark water, because there was something I had to find in the house. The old red Wilson's College Dictionary or the new blue Word-King. I needed the definition of that unspoken word. But neither the Wilson's nor the Word King were anywhere upstairs so I started down, thinking maybe they were in Mom's quilting room. Halfway down, I remembered John's old ditty.

> *"Wine is fine,*
> *Candy is dandy,*
> *But SOMETHING is best."*

How'd it go? Wine is fine, candy is dandy, but *something* is best. *Hmm.* Childhood has all sorts of hiding places, in closets, under beds, between sheets. *Find me, hold me, I can't breathe...*

Halfway down the stairs I remembered something I'd buried. A memory of the night John called me down. I was twelve years old, up watching TV, with my new buds aching. John was a grown man, home from the war, down in the basement drinking beer. No one home but him and me.

John called up, "Cat, come down here!"

I pretended not to hear. I felt the boulder in my gut, the bad-thing-coming. But I loved my big brother. All those years John was away in Vietnam, while he parachuted into machete-sharp jungles with centipedes big as baseball bats rearing up on their hind legs and an orange chemical-spray that stripped bare all living things and Viet Cong hiding behind the jumbo leaves with knives in their teeth, we waited for him to come home with only his striped airmail letters, so light they shivered in our hands, and the heavy packages he sent to Mom, ivory elephants, enamel goldfish swimming black depths, and snapshots of skinny GI's with white chests and brown necks, one arm reaching out to feed a scrawny monkey a fruit slice. *Mango,* John wrote. *They call it a mango.*

Mango, mango. Saying that new word out loud in our kitchen with John's letter shivering in my hands made my mouth feel like a woman's. *Mango, mango.* All those years of waiting, I hoped he would come home in one piece, and not dead like Don, or wrapped in bloody bandages like the soldiers on the cover of Life magazine.

When John came home the first time, he brought a bundle of bamboo sticks and tissue paper, sat down at the dining room table, and made the sticks and paper into a kite. He and I waited for a windy spring day, and walked together to the Little Rose Lake playground. The wind turned our ears red, made our windbreakers slap and took my breath away, but John said it was, "A PERFECT DAY TO FLY A KITE! Run, Cat, run!" I ran against the wind hard as I could, and we got that kite up! I was so happy to have John home in one piece, and that kite up, I felt it was me up there, looping with a view of the whole neighborhood.

The second time John came home, he woke me before sunrise and we dragged his small sailboat down to the lake, unrolled the sails, uncoiled the ropes, and before the sun broke, John taught me all the knots, the fore and aft, then we slid her into the water and spent the whole morning chasing diamonds. That was the happiest day of my life so far.

The third time John came home, he brought red sores on his legs, a bottomless thirst for beer, a wrap called a sarong that he wore all day with his shirt off in the basement, and the black-and-white basement TV blaring game shows, with his stump resting on the old couch's armrest.

John got his arm blown off when he saved a bunch of other soldiers from getting their heads blown up. He got a purple heart for that. Right after he came home, he and I posed for a Polaroid at the dining room table, my arms round his neck, our cheeks touching, his sleepy smile. In that flash you can see how alike we were, our same nose, hair and eyes, and you can see in my eyes that I loved John so hard it hurt.

"Come down!" he called that night with my buds aching.

"What for?" I shouted back.

"Just come down."

Bad thing coming. I wanted to stay upstairs in front of the TV but couldn't disobey my big brother. I walked to the head of the stairs. "What do you want, John?"

"Just come down here."

I went halfway down. He wavered at the foot in a haze of cigar smoke.

"What?"

"Just come here Cat."

"What for?"

"Just come."

"Why?"

"Come give your big brother a kiss."

Oh, just a kiss! That was all! No big deal. In our family, kisses were common, kiss-hello, kiss-goodbye, kiss-great-aunt-on-the-cheek. *No big deal.*

I went down. I walked to John. My head barely reached his chest. I saw the damp end of his cigar, the pink nub of his arm, the few hairs growing from the scar, and felt the heat through his t-shirt, the ache in my buds.

John licked his lips. I went up on tiptoe and gave him a quick peck. I tasted bitter cigar, felt his bristly moustache, his moist lips. His mouth parted. His tongue pushed out. I stepped away.

"Wait, Cat-"

Wait for what?

"I mean a reee-all kiss."

A Reee-all Kiss? What did that mean? One with tongues? With moans? With shared saliva? Where the line between brother and sister blurred?

I couldn't look John in the eye, but I said, "no." Then turned and walked towards the stairs.

I disobeyed my big brother! I knew when I stepped on the first step, thunder would crack. And when I stepped on the second step, the earth would open. And when I stepped on the third, the stairs would crumble in and I'd be sucked under, and the broken steps would close over me, and my mouth, nose and eyes would fill with dirt, and my screams would be muffled and my body covered by a ton of debris. And no one would hear me. I would cry but make no sound. And life at the McCloud house above would go on as before. People would eat and watch TV, the great aunts and Grandma Jane would visit, Little Mary would gallop her stick pony and play with all the other nieces and nephews, and people would laugh, tell jokes and celebrate the holidays and birthdays, Christmases and Thanksgivings, and no one would hear me. I would be stuffed with dirt, stuck under the house, and the nieces and nephews would grow up and have kids of their own, and Mom and Dad would die, and the sisters and brothers would die, and the other White Rock girls my age would get jobs and get kissed and go to college, grow up and get married and have kids of their own, and their kids would have kids, and I would stay thirteen in my training bra stuck under the house, forever amen.

But I said no anyway, turned my back on John and went upstairs.

After Rosy Sue's funeral, I found both dictionaries, the Old Wilson and the new Word-King in Mom's quilting room under layers of old clothes and looked up the unspoken word. INCEST. Then remembered John's ditty.

"Candy is dandy,
Wine is fine,
Liquor is quicker,
But INCEST is best!"

Then he'd laugh. "Heh heh heh…"

Remember, remember, what do you remember? Do you remember anything weird? …Don or John would come in and say, Mark wants to do it again then Mark would come in and do it… He was just an old man… It was no big deal… I did it for marbles… We were too scared to tell… Don't upset your Father… Give your big brother a kiss… He exposed himself… We didn't like it… There was a wet spot… It was dry on dry… It was no big deal… It was funny… It was nothing… I don't remember… I knew what to do, ignore him! …I think it started at the yellow house...

Connect the dots. Fill in the blanks...

Once upon a time special moments happened in our family, small touches, here and there, each tucked away from the other, now and then, out of sight, nothing much. If all the pieces are hidden, who sees the whole picture? The great uncle opens his fly. Mom says nothing. *If I ignored him, he would go away.* No more said. *I didn't say a word.* It wasn't much, just a touch, where a person wasn't touched before, in a way that felt new. *Is this bad? Is this good? How am I supposed to feel about this?*

It wasn't dangerous, was it? It was passed down, generation to generation, the touch and the silence. Someone crept into Mom's room and pressed into her. *It felt like a snake, but I didn't know who it was.* No harm done, right? It was just a memory, coming back. My mom wasn't raped, was she? Can you rape someone who remains silent? Who doesn't say stop? Who doesn't know what's happening?

Then the little kisses scattered through time. Gramps slides his tongue in Tammy's mouth. *No big deal, he's just a lonely old man.* Tammy was a hot teen. *Give the old guy a break.* But what if Gram did that to her grandsons? That would be another story. We went easy on the men, hard on the women...

Another kiss, big brother to little sister. *Give me a real kiss.* No big deal. No law broken. I don't say a thing. *No need.*

And the big brothers breaking into the little sister, *taking Rosy Sue's cherry.* No big deal. Rosy Sue said *I didn't let it bother me. I keep it locked deep inside. I'm fine...*

Maybe these touches confused us. Maybe they hurt us. Maybe they scared us. *So what if they did?* We kept it to ourselves. *Don't worry, big brothers, we won't tell. Cross our hearts. Hope to die.* So what if it ate up our insides? So what if it made us numb and dumb? So what if it made us hide inside ourselves? So what if we kept the best of ourselves hidden from the world? No big deal right? *We're just the sisters...*

But what if that chain reached a weak place? What if that little *nothing* got into a broken head? What if that sent the pattern outside the family, out in the world? *Then maybe someone would get really hurt...*

I opened the old red Wilson.

> ***In´cest*** *(ĭn´sĕst), n. [L. incestus, incestum,*
> *unchastity, incest, fr. incestus unchaste, from the French*
> *in- not + castus chaste.] 1. The crime of cohabitation*
> *between persons related within the degrees wherein*
> *marriage is prohibited by law. Prohibited by Law.*

And the new blue Word-King.

> ***Incest*** */insest/ n. sexual intercourse between persons*
> *regarded as too closely related to marry each other. [ME f.*
> *L incestus (as IN-¹, castus CHASTE)] Incest. See*
> *UNCHASTE…*

> ***Unchaste*** */úncháyst/ adj. not chaste. Impure,*
> *wanton, immoral, promiscuous, loose, dissolute, immodest,*
> *indecent, unclean, obscene, licentious, debased, lecherous,*
> *lewd, impure. See IMPURE…*

> ***Impure/*** *impyoor/ adj.* ***1*** *mixed with foreign*
> *matter; adulterated.* ***2 a*** *dirty.* ***b*** *ceremonially unclean.* ***3***
> *unchaste.* ***Impurely*** *adv.* ***Impureness*** *n.* ***1*** *mixed,*
> *admixed, alloyed, base, debased, cut.* ***2 a*** *see DIRTY…*

> ***Dirty*** *adj.* ***1.*** ***b*** *unclean, unhallowed, forbidden.* ***3***
> *immoral, sinful, wicked, evil, vile, corrupted, defiled,*
> *degenerate, depraved, loose, wanton, lustful, promiscuous,*
> *libidinous, dissolute, licentious, obscene, prurient, filthy.*

FILTHY.

No wonder we kept it to ourselves. No wonder we couldn't talk about it. *We were dirty.* It wasn't so much the act as the shame around it, not so much the touch, which could have been pleasure or pain or numbness or confusion or all of the above. It was the *silence* around the act that bred the shame that bred more silence that bred more shame…

We fell asleep in different places that night after Rosy Sue's funeral, Anne on the loveseat, Molly and Polly in Holly's room, Holly and Tammy in my bed, me with Mom.

Next morning we stretched awake from our various nests. Tammy whispered, "Morning." Molly and Polly shook cereal boxes. Anne rubbed her eyes. Holly sipped orange juice, Mom wiped her glasses clean, and before breakfast, we slid from our nighties, wrapped up in towels, filed out the deck and tracked down through the dew to watch the sun rise over the water.

As we descended, one fish leapt up from the still lake, then another, then one after the other, breaking the surface, flipping up and slapping down, sending ripples to the far shore.

At the little strip of our beach we let our towels fall, stood naked and toed the edge. The water still held the warmth of the day before. As we walked in, and as we tossed round the soap, and tossed round the emerald shampoo, and lathered our faces, necks, heads, arms, breasts, legs and crotches, and as our splashes rippled to the far shore with the rising sun spilling diamonds on the water in a blaze of dots and dashes too bright to look at, too bright to see, we laughed and laughed, as if all our splashing, scrubbing and laughing were an unspoken song, sung over and over. *Wash us clean, wash us clean, wash us clean, so we can speak.*

Part Two

BILLY & BECKY

AFTER THE FAIR

I thought the stories would spill out after that, like a baby horse slipping from its mama, wet to the hay on the Wonderful World of Disney, or like the blind kittens in our garage. But no more secrets came out after Rosy Sue's funeral. The mouths that had snapped open snapped shut. BAM SHUT. We all went back to our lives as usual. No more secrets were revealed until after Uncle Ned's funeral.

So I'm stepping aside with my puny life to let Billy Bell tell his story. You remember Billy, the kid who ran away from his sister Becky at the 1969 Iowa State Fair. On the Midway on that hot August night, with the barkers calling "Win a Bunny!" and the Tilt-a-Whirl screaming and the onion, mini donuts and sizzling oil, Billy Bell got into a tug-of-war with Becky Bell, tore a dollar in half, ran behind the Pronto Pup stand and got taken by that Smiling Man.

Let's roll back to that moment Billy stood on the straw bale out at Redtail Rise with Smiling Man behind, the Ruger warm in Billy's hand, five bullets in the target, and one bullet left.

An' this is for Smilin' Man!

Billy twisted, jabbed his elbows and bolted from Smiling Man's grasp.

Smiling Man barked, "Hey!"

Both struggled for the gun-

BAM!

Billy jerked in a frozen tango pose, and got the itchy tingles, like when you almost wipe out on your bike an' your ghost flies ahead an' itches when it lands back in. His belly bloomed black.

Boy'm I tired! Wired! Fired! Hey! Them Pronto Pups are catchin' up with me!

A breeze blew, and Billy slipped between the layers of the night. *Hey! I'm One Big Spinnin' Thing! I'm the Big Number One! I'm a big fat knock-knock joke. What was that joke? Oh yeah!*

KNOCK-KNOCK!

Who's there?

ORANGE!

Orange who?

KNOCK-KNOCK.

Who's there?

ORANGE.

Orange who?

KNOCK-KNOCK!

Who's there?

BANANA-

Wait! DO-OVERS! I GOT IT BACKWARDS- I meant to say-

The ground pushed Billy to standing.

Whoo-hoo! Beam me up Scotty!

He was no longer sleepy. He was wide awake. *Ready for action!* But that other kid on the ground, that kid looked wiped out. Billy never meant for that kid to get hurt. *Not my fault.* Smiling Man was trying to wake the kid, shaking him, and the kid's limbs were flopping. *Beam me up, Scotty, I'm outa here!*

Billy meant to hide behind the big maple and wait for his gramp's friends in their pickup, but no need. The August night sucked him up. *Warp speed!* He'd never been so close to the stars, and there were knock-knock jokes up in the cosmos. *BIG FAT KNOCK-KNOCKS! An' spinning gyroscopes with colors instead a' black an' white, an' the stars were janglin', an' how come I never heard that sound before?* The motions of the planets made a symphony, layers of glass-violins. *An' what was that other sound? That low BOOM-BOOM behind all that?*

Then he was heading down, dive-bombing nose-first through a race-track of black nothingness, till his face pressed against a window pane. The woman on the other side sat at a table with her face in her hands. Her head was heavy. Billy could feel that weight, lead on a fish-hook. The woman's sadness drew him through the window, over the tabletop and into her chest. *Warm, warm an' dark...*

All night Billy curled into the sad woman's chest, and drunk on her grief, he took off his skin and became another boy, a running boy, running barefoot over grass, down dusty paths, beside school buses, running home to chug down a glass of milk, smile a white mustache, then back outside, ever-running inside the sad woman.

Then Billy went deeper, threw off the running boy and became a bell tolling so low it was inaudible, and the woman so weary she did not have the strength to draw the sides of her throat together to swallow.

When pale color came into the sky, her head bobbed off her fists, her grief slipped out like a cat to its bowl, and Billy came to himself again.

Shit! How late is it? Shit! I been away all night! Shit-canned for sure!

He zipped home, but by the time he reached the screen door, he saw things weren't as before. *Yeah, a night, yeah, adventure, who knew what would happen? Maybe I got beamed into another dimension. Maybe Smilin' Man was part of some Twilight Zone Fourth Dimension shit. Or maybe one of the carnies slipped some LSD in my Froggy's Frosty Lemonade, but home should be home!*

And it *was* home when he got there, but it *wasn't*. He was quiet with the screen door, but it didn't make its familiar squeak, and he was in. The walls whispered a dead-water sound as Billy headed for the front hall closet.

Yeah. Hide in there.

He'd hidden in that closet after his mom had belted him, hidden in there as a toddler, tallying his fingers and toes, his nose thick with mucous, his cheek numb, and he'd hidden in there from his sister between the jackets, breathing in mothballs and old perfume, but now the front hall closet smelled of *nothin'*.

Then the walls softened, and gave way, and Billy was pulled again, into some *dark beatin' heart. Yeah!* That was the sound behind the bell-stars, *ONE SUPER-DUPER MAGNET, JUST FOR ME.*

But what was that down the hall? Somebody crossin' a line! Somebody breakin' a rule! The Bitchster crossed the Forbidden Tape! You are dead Bitchster!

Billy *zzzt!* to his room. Becky was poking her finger into his bed. She opened her mouth. Brown worms slid out. She went to the kitchen. Billy hung at her back. Becky shook boxes, his mom coughed up gray worms, his dad waggled a black worm, then Becky slapped the screen door and biked to the Turn's and the Dern's and finally to the fair.

Billy rode her shoulder as Becky eyed the morning crowd, the sleepy faces, the crabby carnies and the twisted mouths. She turned her head in all directions, looking for someone.

Hey, she's lookin' for me! I'm right here but she don't see! An' hey! Where's the smells? Where's the onion an' donut smells? An' hey! Where's my dollar? An' hey! Where's my pocket? There it is!

All Billy had to do was THINK *pocket* and there it was.

But where's my half-dollar? An' what could you buy with half a dollar anyway? Half a jackrabbit? Half a bulldozer? Half a freak's ass? Ha!

Billy's laughter wheelied him up over Becky and through the crowds, past the shoulders, elbows and ball caps, on a jangle he couldn't stop. *Dragonfly! Bumblebee! Whirligig!*

He jimmied through the shooters at the Bag-a-Bunny, over the pop-rifles, snow-cones and beer-bellies, screaming with the roller-coaster, dropping with the Death-Drop. *Wheee-heee! Smilin' Man, now just try an' catch me!*

At the thought of the Smiling Man, Billy was sucked through a tunnel of silence-

Whoosh

-to an old barn, and there was Smiling Man, standing by a small fire.

Hey! I'm gonna get you for rubbin' on me at Redtail Rise!

Then Billy was at Redtail Rise, and there were last night's

bullet holes in the morning light, with butterflies lazing, the wildflowers bending and the dew-drop rainbows, and there was where Billy took his fair-food dump, and there the straw bale where he yanked away, and there the patch of earth turned over, with no thistles, crabgrass or clover, just bare dirt humped. Billy knew Reflection Boy was buried under that hump-

Then he *xipped* back to the hall closet and rested in the beating arms of the dark heart that lurked behind everything.

Becky awoke atop her bedspread. She was still wearing her pink seersucker shirt and shorts set from the night before, and still had the torn-in-half-dollar bill clutched in her fist. She dropped the bill into the empty glass jar on her dresser.

That jar had sat empty for months. She'd planned to dig some dirt from the yard, press in a scrap of moss, tweezer in a bubble-gum machine troll and bury a sprig of her mom's houseplant for extra credit in her Seventh Grade Science class. She'd imagined a ferny paradise in there, mist condensing on the glass, and her teacher giving her an A and a red-pen note: *let's meet after school for a nature walk to find more plants for your fine terrarium, Becky...*

And on their walk, he'd slip his hand in hers, and she'd feel that cool TEACHER'S hand-

But she'd never gotten round to putting anything in that jar. Then Plant Biology was over.

Then Seventh Grade was over.

An' now summer's almost over...

The half dollar reminded Becky of something. *Somethin' about last night. Oh yeah. I got my period! An' that THING with Doug Douglas.*

She tugged at her shorts, picked out an eye-crumb and slogged to the bathroom to change her sanitary pad.

The sticky blood, tug of pubic hair and off-sweet scent already felt familiar. She squinted at her reflection, the same wolf-face as Billy, the same sharp chin and dirty blonde hair. *But no boat-shaped scar under my eye. Morning, Becky Bell! You got kissed last night. With Doug's tongue! An' what are you gonna do next time you see Doug? Stick a garter snake down his throat!*

She inspected a new blemish, fingers poised to pop, then froze. *Wait a minute. Somethin's not groovy. Somethin' 'bout last night. Oh yeah. Billy ditched me. By the Pronto Pup Stand. An' tore that dollar in half.*

She tromped to his room, crossed the masking tape into the Forbidden Zone and stood over the boy-size hump. Sometimes Billy ended up at the foot of his bed, sometimes half on the floor, and one morning she'd looked all over but didn't find him until his favorite cartoon, Scooby-doo, was over. He'd been stuck like a leech between mattress and wall.

Becky spoke to the lump. "Fart-head, where'd you run to last night?" She poked the bed. Her finger pressed to mattress.

Not here. An' what's my excuse for comin' in late? Oh yeah, we was late, Mom, 'cause Billy lost his shoes, then we biked home, an' he was right behind...

Mrs. Bell sat at the kitchen table in a haze of menthol smoke. "Mornin' Beck-a-boo."

"Mornin'."

Becky rose on tiptoe and shook the cereal boxes.

Cap'n Crunch, Fruity Loops, Cocoa Puffs...

As the brown balls jumped in her Charlie's Angels bowl, her dad shuffled in, holding up a single black sock.

"You seen this?"

Her mom answered, "Morning to you too. It's right there."

"No, I mean the mate."

"No, I have not seen-"

Mrs. Bell began her morning coughing fit as Mr. Bell shook the sock in her face. "Stop that! Beck-a-boo, you seen Billy?"

Becky concentrated on the cereal-box knock-knock jokes. *Knock-knock! Who's there? Fred. Fred who? Fred I can't tell you! Knock-knock. Who's there? Angel. Angel who? Angel jealous of my golden wings? Knock-knock! Who's there? Ben. Ben who? Ben thinkin'-*

"Becky! Where's Billy?"

She shrugged. "He sleep at Turn's or Dern's?"

"So where is it?" Mr. Bell still waggled the sock.

Mrs. Bell waved it away. "You look in the dryer?"

"It ain't in the dryer."

"Well if you look BETWEEN-

"Well if you FOLDED the DAMN-"

"Well if YOU HELPED with the DAMN-"

Becky pushed away her bowl. "Be right back."

"Beck-a-boo, where you off to?"

"BE RIGHT BACK!"

Mrs. Bell resumed her coughing, the cereal popped as if to say *right behind, right behind*, and the screen door swung shut with a whine as Becky hopped on her bike. Turn's was five houses down. Billy's bike was not against the Turn's garage or in their backyard. *But it could be stashed in the weeds by the creek.* Becky pressed the cracked doorbell.

Ding dong!

A small face appeared behind the screen. *Timmy Turd.* A larger face appeared. *Rick Turd.*

"What the hell you want?"

"Billy here?"

"Hell no."

"He didn't sleep over last night?"

"Hell no."

"He at Dirt's?"

"Hell if I know."

The little face echoed, "HELL NO!"

"Well if you see him, tell him COME THE HELL HOME!"

Billy's bike wasn't outside the Dern's either. Before Becky could press the bell, the door opened and a hairy arm reached down for the morning paper. *Mr. Dern with his shirt off!*

"Morning, Becky."

"Mornin'. Billy here?"

"Uh-"

"He sleep here last night?"

"Not that I know of. Wait a moment, Becky. I'll check."

Mr. Dern backed in with the Brownmound Bugle covering his chest.

Becky leaned against the stucco and squinted at the tiny houses across the street thinking, *Mr. Dern looks different with his shirt off an' his face all stubbley, like a movie star cowboy...*

Maybe Billy's with some new kid over the freeway, with a smooth driveway an' a basketball hoop, an' bet they stayed up all night playin' UFOs an' now they're eatin' waffles smothered in whip cream-

Mr. Dern returned with his shirt on. "Sorry Becky. He's not here. Why don't you try the Turn's."

Becky mounted her bike and headed for the State Fair.

The sun was not yet over the barn as Smiling Man poked the fire, lit another Chesterfield and stared into the flames.

He'd driven home early that morning, before the sunrise hit the rearview mirror, before the white wall in his head came down. No headache. Not today. But something had gone wrong at Redtail Rise...

And he'd prepared so carefully for his day at the fair! He'd lathered with minty soap, toweled all the cracks dry, shaved close, patted on aftershave, put on a new short-sleeve shirt, freshly unpinned from department store cardboard, and belted his khakis high, *the Ioway, like respectable crop-planting men, not down around the hips like some drunken scalawag cowboy.*

Before departing, he'd asked his mother if she needed anything, she'd said no thank you, his father said buckle up for safety son, and out the door he went with a smile.

His mother had taught him to smile and to behave in a civilized manner. And he had behaved at the fair. He'd asked politely for a bratwurst, asked politely for a cone, asked politely for miniature donuts, brushed the powdered sugar from his chin with the small napkin provided and stood up straight, watching the crowd for a friendly face. He'd seen numerous boys, some yelling, some somber, but none quite right.

Then he spotted the boy. By the farm machinery. Slender as a barn cat, in overalls, with no shoes or socks, and with that look, both transparent and opaque, as on a partly-cloudy day, when the sun shines through everything, flowers, trees, leaves, then clouds over, shady and sun, shady and sun. The boy was that changeable. When he'd argued with his sister, his face darkened, when he bent for a nickel, his face brightened, and when he leaned in to buy another corn dog, Smiling Man leaned in and got a whiff of that neck.

Milk and apricots.

But he hadn't butted in. He hadn't tapped the lad's shoulder. He hadn't spoken out of turn. He'd waited for an opportune moment; he'd followed him to the Hog Building, where he'd teased a nursing sow, then to the radio booth, WMEC Best In Country, where he'd gotten a free balloon, then to the Midway, where he'd lost the balloon, stuffed himself, argued with his sister and ran off behind the concessions, where Smiling Man waited patiently, looking away while the lad did his business. Only afterwards had he stepped forward to say how do you do.

And while driving towards Redtail Rise, he'd kept his eyes on the road. He had spoken only once during the drive, to offer the lad a stick of gum. Because if he'd engaged the lad in conversation, then he may have become distracted, then his eyes may have left the road, then he may have crossed the yellow line, and if the Redtail County Sheriff happened to be driving by-

If we catch you driving under the influence one more time.

No, there must be no more arrests, no more nights in county jail and no more suspended licenses. And the car had not swerved, and the boy had kept quiet, and the drive had been without incident. But something had gone wrong at Redtail Rise.

Smiling Man tossed his cigarette into the fire and studied his hands. Dirt under the nails. One nail torn. Fresh blisters on both palms. Those would heal. He emptied his pocket of the few things he'd saved from the boy's pockets, three pennies, a nickel, a dime, the silver triangle of gum wrapper and the half dollar bill. He set the bits on the chopping stump, stepped from his clothes and tossed them in the flames. The fire smoldered. He poked at the pile with a fallen branch. The fire bloomed. His mother would ask about his clothes. But no use trying to wash those stains out.

He crossed to the barn, felt for the extra pair of overalls hanging just inside, and stepped into them as barn-cats scattered

and swallows swooped. No cows in the barn anymore, just feral cats, empty stalls, an overturned canning jar opaque with time, and a desiccated bird caught long ago up on a dangling loop of rafter-wire, flitting back and forth, disturbed by the daredevil swallows.

Smiling Man adjusted the overall straps, returned to the fire and nudged the burning hump. As the sun broke free of the barn he closed his eyes against the light. *No headache. Not today.*

His mother had taught him to count to ten when the white wall in his head came down. But when the white wall of steel came down, it was all he could do to count to three. If he was driving he had to pull over, take deep breaths and palm his eyes. If he was eating, he had to excuse himself, lie down and grasp the sides of his bed. If he was at work he had to put down the wrench and rest on the old Chrysler seat. One, two, three. But counting did not take the pain away. Aspirin did not. A cool washcloth did not, a hot washcloth did not, a nap did not, eating did not, sleeping did not. Even drinking did not take the pain away. Well, drinking did if he drank till he passed out, but when he woke the pain was greater. And now they said he must stop drinking or destroy his liver.

Well to hell with them! He drank mouthwash instead. *That took the edge off.* But mouthwash did not take the pain away. He glanced towards his vehicle. The Ruger sat safe on the passenger seat. Yes, there were guns, there were always guns, and how wonderful each gun was, wonderful to touch, wonderful to hold, wonderful the way the parts fit together, so intelligently, so particularly. A gun was a gun but more than a gun. A gun was a tool, a motion, a method, a mode, an action, a way of life, the way the bullets slid home, slid home, the feel of the ammo, the rounded, the smooth, the phallic, the pointed, the flat, the clicks, the resistance, the kickback. *Come home to me.* A gun was a key to adventure, to a man's world, to silent walks, dead leaves, cold hands, huffing steaming puffs of air, and game thudding, kicking to the frozen earth and the warming of chilly hands on a thermos of hot coffee with a brandy squirt. When everything else went to hell, there were always the guns, steady, loaded and commanding obedient silence.

And there were books. There were always books in the house, educational books, safaris books with zebra covers, books on rose-pruning, civil wars and ancient Greeks, the poetry of the ages. But never books like those that needed to be hidden. When he first picked up such a book, passed on by friend with a whisper out the side of the mouth, his cheeks went red. He thought, *who crept into my head? Who sees my private thoughts? Is there someone who thinks as I do?* This was a revelation of pain and pleasure, both at once, to be discovered, to be not alone. With books like those he could have a bit of fun and never leave home.

And yes he was red-blooded! Yes, he'd had gals. Gals were fine, with gals he had a good time, gals with rounded hips and swelling chests or gals lean as barn cats. Now Betty, there was a gal, what a gal Betty was! And Patsy, there was a gal! What a gal Patsy was! And Sandy, she was a gal if there ever was one! But gals wanted witty chatter and an easy chair with him always in it. And gals wanted more or less than he wanted to give. And gals wanted a ring before they could do anything, and gals got impatient with his jokes, and with gals his smile froze.

But lads, oh lads! Lads tugged at his heart like gals never could. Lads could go hunting, and lads could go fishing, and lads didn't mind a bit of grease under your nails, or a day's beard, and lads laughed at his jokes. Lads were never a problem, never a problem. The boy, the boy, he needed the boy, and the boy was out there everywhere, at the gas station, playground, shopping center. And lads, oh lads, could take the pain away, with that one sweet, that one deep, that one sweet deep dark forbidden.

Becky dismounted, leaned her Schwinn in the corn and sweated through the tall stalks. Billy's bike, crisscrossed with fresh spiderwebs, was leaning in the same row as he'd stashed it the night before, and there were his sneakers, dew-sequined. *Just where he left them. So stupid, that dare, to go barefoot at the fair!*

As she snuck under the fence, her shirt caught again, and the wire scraped her shoulder. *Ow! Dang Billy!*

She ducked between the gargantuan tractors. The fair looked different in the day. The colored lights barely showed, the barkers mumbled, "Win a bunny, test your luck," the Lemonade Man was a grizzled geezer, the I-Scream booth stood empty.

But the Ferris wheel guy is the same as before, same purple circles under his eyes, same pale face an' greasy hair, but he looks worse today, like a Walkin' Dead. Bet he lives in the Freak-trailer an' has hippie parties an' smokes marijuana cigarettes.

The smell of cotton candy turned Becky's stomach, the feeble cries from the Tilt-a-Whirl made her jaws clamp, and the thought of biting into a corn dog brought a cold wash of saliva into her mouth. *Maybe Billy got sick an' threw up behind the stands. Or what if-*

She looked at all the faces, seeking something suspicious, an evil glint, a pointed fang, a matted coat of hair beneath a sleeve.

Everybody looks normal. An' everybody looks suspicious. The dried-up by Froggy's, the rotundo at Candy Lane, the weasel at the heliums. They're all dressed like normal an' act like normal, but I bet they turn into gypsies an' LSD freaks at night, an' steal innocent kids an' sacrifice 'em to a horned god...

Don't let your imagination run off with you, Becky Bell! Billy prob'ly just got sick behind the stands, an' slept there all night in a pool a' hot dog vomit.

She stepped behind Pete's Pronto Pups and caught herself before she stumbled on a black electric cable. Her nose wrinkled. Back there was the stink of soured citrus, a scatter of smashed cups and sodden, discarded napkins. Becky picked up a Chesterfield butt and studied the fine line wavering round the filter. Her gaze shifted to a small footprint in the fine sand. *What idiot would go barefoot at the fair? An' where's this lead?* Becky swung open the gate and followed the car-wide path.

His clothes were a lump in the fire ring, blue flames riding the spine. As he tapped the lump with his stick, a blue jay flew from corncrib to the barn roof, slicing the morning with its nagging scream. The sun hit the west windows.

Folks'll be up soon.

Smiling Man went in through the mud room and turned the shower taps on hot in the back-hall bathroom. As the previous night's misadventures washed down the drain, his impending headache eased. He rubbed his crew-cut, squinted against the strong blue shampoo and inhaled deeply.

Everything's going to be fine, he told himself. Last night was fine. The Ruger was fine, the lad was fine. Then the lad squirmed away! With a loaded gun! Then he was in his lap, a puddled sand-sack with a broken belly. And his own bile rose, and fresh heartburn had flooded his chest as the lad's belly-juice steeped his clothing.

What to do? He could have driven back to 119 and waved down a truck. But who'd be passing at that time of night? Even semis would be few and far between. He could have loaded the lad in the Blazer, driven to one of the nearby farms and roused the sleepers. But this was a gut shot. Too late for an ambulance. No, a shame, a damned shame, and no use getting the Sheriff mixed up in this.

He had wiped his nose, slid the boy from his lap and counted his blessings. Luckily, he had the Trunk Buddy with him, *handy little travel shovel*, always ready for an emergency or an accident.

This was an accident. This was a shooting accident. A tragic shooting accident. Hadn't there been a boy like this? Years back? Yes there had. He'd heard the stories at Dinah's Diner. Running Boy, they called him. Lived on a farm near Redtail Rise. Ran like crazy, that lad, ran just for the hell of it. Ran alongside the bus to school, ran barefoot after school, ran through the paths at Redtail, ran summer and winter. And folks would look up, see a trail of dust and say, there goes the Running Boy! And hunters would say, what the hell is that? Oh that's Running Boy! Helluva lad! Runs with his feet bare! Can you beat that! Then the tragedy. One fall morning, two hunters unfamiliar with the area saw a brown flash. One raised his rifle and BAM! The lad was dead. And that was that.

These things happened, and you took care of them, and got on with life. No good looking back. No use upsetting the folks. Better to *leave well enough alone.*

Smiling Man rinsed the lather from his head, gave a shake to his privates and stepped from the shower, refreshed and clean, and certain he'd made the right decision.

The road beyond the chain link led round the fair and out to Highway 119. Other than the one barefoot print, Becky found only tire tracks, cigarette butts, a few lost lone shoes and a pair of trampled panties.

She biked home, hot, thirsty and hungry.

Mrs. Bell was leaning on the counter, phone cord dangling between her legs, Kool on her lip, Fone-O-File in hand.

"Becky! I been phoning since you run out! Where the hell's Billy?"

Becky ducked. Her cereal was sunk in the milk, her mom's feet, in turquoise flip-flops, were edged in grime, her dad was coughing down in the basement and the pad between her legs was sodden. "Just a sec, Mom."

She opened the fridge, pulled out the Kool-Aid and drank straight from the blue aluminum pitcher.

"Becky! What the hell!"

"Sorry, I was, ah, thirsty."

Becky drooped against the counter.

"Mom. Last night. Billy was right behind. An' I felt sick cause-" *Pause for effect.* "I got IT."

Mrs. Bell lowered the Fone-o-File. "You got WHAT?"

"IT."

"Fer Chris' sake, young lady, speak English. You got what?"

"My first you-know." Becky dropped her eyes toward her hips.

Mrs. Bell's eyes followed. "You got THAT?"

"Yeah."

"Oh Becky!"

Mrs. Bell fumbled for her lime-green lighter. "You find the pads?"

"Yeah."

"You all set then?"

"Yeah."

"You got the cramps?"

"Not anymore." Becky cracked a grin.

"Well then, you're old enough for the Extra Strength Excedrin!" Mrs. Bell gave her a one-armed hug.

"Hey lovebirds!" Mr. Bell stood in the stairwell, holding up three dust-coated socks and a dust-smothered bra. "Look what I found in the Land of the Lost Socks."

Becky and her mom pulled apart, laughing.

"So, what's for lunch?"

After bologna sandwiches, ripple-chips and raspberry Kool-Aid, Mrs. Bell made more phone calls, to the second cousins, the Brownmound Hospital and the Redtail County Sheriff. The Deputy said twenty-four hours need to elapse, ma'am, before we put out a Missing Persons.

So they waited. Mrs. Bell called every number in the Fon-O-File, Mr. Bell drove the neighborhood, and Becky pedaled East Brownmound looking for signs of Billy, but she knew she wouldn't find his bike ditched in the creek-weeds or at the playground because it was still hidden in the corn. *An' which was the twenty-four hours? The REAL twenty-four? Or the LIE twenty-four?*

By suppertime Mrs. Bell didn't feel like grilling the chicken, so Becky made herself cinnamon toast, Mr. Bell cracked more beers and they all sat in front of the Six O'clock Nightly News. There were no reports of train-mashed boys, drowned boys or mangled boys. After Marcus Welby M.D., the phone rang, but it was only Grandma Bell, asking could she get a ride to the Pie Picnic, and did they want her homemade potato salad this year, because last year's was, well, she wouldn't say soggy, but could she get a ride? Mr. Bell said, sure Mom, you can ride with us, an' do call if Billy shows up okay?

After Laugh-In the Bells turned on every light in the house, the front hall closet, the kitchen fluorescents, even the bare bulb in the basement crawlspace. The ten o'clock news had the same stories, flooding along the Raccoon River, a tornado up in Minnesota and the local softball champs lifting a gold trophy in a sea of upraised arms. But no Billy.

At Ed McMahon's call of, "Heeeeeeere's Johnny!" Mrs. Bell lit a fresh Kool and coughed to the kitchen. Mr. Bell turned the sound down. Johnny Carson laughed silently as the starlet Goldie Hawn drew her legs up into the guest chair, and the Deputy on the other end took Billy's details: age, weight, height, and was Billy the type to run away.

Mrs. Bell said into the phone, "No, Deputy! He never run off! Not this time. An' how tall? Becky! How tall's your brother?"

An empty beer bottle rolled towards the picture window as Becky walked to the fridge and fingered the fridge marker lines.

67, 68, 69. Stupid Billy! I warned him, didn't I? That day last summer when it was so hot our legs stuck to the seat, an' we rolled down the windows an' stuck out our heads an' Dad yelled, HEADS BACK IN! BEFORE YOU GET DECAPITATED, an' at the hardware store, we waited outside, an' that rusty pickup pulled up an' that guy said them nasty things to me, an' when he drove off I grabbed Billy an' I said-

"BECKY! HOW TALL'S YOUR BROTHER?"

"BECKY! YOUR MOM'S TALKIN TO YOU!"

"Uh." Becky touched the 1969 mark. "Four ten."

"Four-ten, Deputy. An' seventy-five pounds. Thereabouts. Blue hair an' blonde eyes. Yeah, ha, that's what I meant. An' a scar under his right eye. Boat-shaped. Okay."

Mrs. Bell covered the receiver. "Becky! Deputy wants to know, you see anything suspicious on the road last night?"

Becky took the phone. "Yeah. 'Bout ten thirty. Not that I could see. Yeah. He was right behind. Bluebird an' Fifth. Okay."

She walked the phone to the living room and handed it to her dad. "He wants you."

Mr. Bell hunched over the receiver. "No, Deputy, nothing like that. No, no. Yeah, yeah. We'll do that. Thanks. You too. G'bye." Mr. Bell turned up the volume and Goldie Hawn's giggles filled the living room.

"Becky! Come hang this up!" He pulled on his beer. "Deputy says don't worry, he's likely a runaway. Says he'll prob'ly turn up tomorrow, tired, thirsty an' hungry. Says wait till morning."

"Wait till morning?" Mrs. Bell stood in the kitchen doorway, sending smoke rings up with her chin.

Mr. Bell repeated, "Wait till morning."

Wait till morning. Becky slipped down the hall to her bedroom, lay on her bed and stared up at the ceiling. She traced the crack back to the light. *Back to the light. Nearly back but never quite...*

The crack led her out the screen door, across the back yard and to the railroad tracks. *An' there was Billy!*

He was gliding down the silver track with skill and grace, like the sequined skaters in the Ice Capades. Billy glided all the way to the Midway, behind the Concessions and into the Freaks' trailer. In that smoky haze, he sat down on the Fat Lady's lap. The Fat Lady smiled at Billy and licked his cheek, then licked an immense lollipop in her outstretched hand, then licked Billy's cheek, then the lollipop, then Billy's cheek-

AH!

Becky woke sweating. Her room was dark.

Hey. Who turned off the lights?

"Mom, did you-?"

She felt Billy close. In the corner. By her chair.

"Billy? That you?"

Yeah! It's me, Bitchster! An' I'm not on some Fatso's lap! I'm right HERE in your prissy room!

An' I!

Am watchin'!

YOU!

STICK TO THE LIE

Next morning, Becky's parents were both asleep on the couch, her dad face-down, his fingers dangling over the full ashtray, her mom face-up, her snores rising along with the organ chords of Pastor Paul's Power of Prayer. As Becky gathered last night's empties she dropped a bottle. Both parents jerked awake.

"Billy?"

"Just me."

They threw water on their faces, got in the Ford and headed towards the small town of Prairieville. The Redtail County Sheriff's was a dog-yellow brick one-story on the corner of Main Street, down from Dave's Donut Hole, the ladies' wear shop and the Post Office, and across from the robin's egg blue-and-white Dinah's Diner.

They pushed through the heavy door with the small pane of chicken-wired glass and stepped into the dimly-lit entry tiled with chipped black-and-white hexagons. In the haze beyond the tall counter sat several empty desks. Mrs. Bell hit the bell beside the dusty potted violet. A blank-faced woman emerged. "He'll be awhile."

The red hand on the wall clock ticked. Mrs. Bell combed her fingers through her hair. Mr. Bell chewed his nail. Becky eyed the clock and hoped her sanitary pad would hold till after breakfast.

He was right behind. I looked back an' there he was...

Becky resolved to stick to her lie. *When Billy comes back, they'll believe ME, not HIM. He lies 'bout everything, 'bout the size of fish, an' turtles an' where he runs off to at night.*

A door opened down the hall. A giant in a butterscotch uniform ducked under the doorframe and extended his hand.

"Morning, folks."

Sheriff Giant led the Bells into the dim interior, where they all sat round a large desk and repeated the answers to the previous night's questions, as blank-faced Sandy typed. *Name, age, height...*

"Miss Bell, I understand you were the last to see your brother?"

Becky nodded and shifted her hands in her lap.

Like fish floppin' over each other-

"You'll need to speak out loud, Miss Bell, so Sandy here can get your answer."

"I said on the phone. You want it again?

"Yes."

"Uh. I was feelin' sick." Becky put a hand to her belly and looked at her mom. Mrs. Bell nodded.

"With a stomach ache. So I hurried home. An' Billy was right behind."

"You see any suspicious person or persons on the street that night?"

"No."

"Any evidence Billy came home and left again? Any food missing? Or clothes, sleeping bag, fishing pole?"

Becky shook her head. "Just his bike."

"We'll need a description of that. Now Miss Becky, yesterday morning, you checked on your brother's whereabouts. Correct? You went to his friends' homes, the Turns' and Derns' to see if Billy slept there?"

"Yeah."

"You actually go inside those homes to ascertain your brother was not there?"

"Ass-sir-tane?"

"You actually go in and see for yourself?"

"No."

"You did not enter the Dern household? Or the Turn's?"

"No."

Becky squirmed around her pad. Her shirt-tag scratched her neck. The shoulder-scrape stung. *An' how long was the giant going to ask these dumb questions?* She felt as if she was in the witness box on Perry Mason. Next the Sheriff would be calling the blank-face Sandy *Della*, that scary theme music would play, *dum-duh-duh!*..

After the Sheriff's, the family crossed the street to Dinah's Diner. The bell rang as they entered. Mrs. Bell ordered coffee and a glazed donut, Mr. Bell asked for two sunny-side ups with hash browns, and Becky got her usual ham-and-scrambled, but no one ate. Mrs. Bell took one bite and set her donut down, Mr. Bell forked his hash browns into a field, and Becky dragged the ham-cubes through her eggs then picked up the sugar dispenser, poured a long white stream into her orange juice and stirred, stirred. The only sound at the Bell's booth was the clang, clang, clang of Becky's spoon on the glass.

Two booths back, Smiling Man sat in his own booth and tried to ignore the clang-clang of metal on glass as he chatted with the regulars about his upcoming retirement. The old fellows joked about how he would fill his days, (*hamburgers, women and beer, ha-ha*) and warned that retirement was not the paradise it seemed, it was all about how to kill time!

He laughed them off. The tragic accident was behind him, and he had a plan, a way to spend his long-awaited retirement and not piss it away, as one of the regulars had so crudely phrased it. And Dinah's Early Riser Special was as satisfying as ever, the sausage a lip-smacking balance of salt and fat, the eggs creamy, the hash browns crisp-edged. When the waitress asked, slice a' pie? he smiled, just coffee please, and when she refilled his cup, he added a slosh of something stronger from his flask underneath the yellow formica tabletop, thinking, *now that I'm nearly retired, the rules are changing…*

Mr. Dern was miffed to get a call from the Sheriff on a Sunday morning, but not surprised, as the Bell girl had come to his door the morning before. *Awkward girl*, he thought, but one day soon she'll be a looker. He told his wife not to worry, it's just an inquiry into the whereabouts of Billy Bell, who's probably off on some fishing trip, and no, I won't miss the Pie Picnic. Then he put on a tie and headed for the County Sheriff's.

Sandy sat at the typewriter with her hands in her lap. Mr. Dern watched the clock, marveling at Sandy's ability to remain motionless. He was wishing he'd had more than just a cup of coffee for breakfast, and thinking he might miss the Pie Picnic after all, when there was a flushing sound down the hall. Sandy poised her hands above the keys. Sheriff Giant emerged.

"Hello, Mr. Dern. How're you?"

"Fine, Sheriff. You?"

"Fine. Thanks for coming in."

"Certainly, whatever I can do."

"Well, just a little thing to clear up. Corner of Bluebird and Fifth."

"Yes?"

"That the location of your home? Five-oh-one Bluebird?"

"Yes."

"Your son Dickey and the Bell boy are friends?"

"Yes."

"Billy Bell often sleep at your home?"

"Sometimes."

"Mr. Dern, Sandy here needs full sentences."

Mr. Dern nodded. "Alright. Yes. Okay."

"So, Miss Becky Bell came to your home yesterday morning and asked had Billy Bell slept there?"

"Yes she did."

"And what did you tell her?"

"I told her he had not. Slept there. Well, first I checked with Dickey, because I wasn't sure-"

Sheriff Giant raised his eyebrows.

"Well, you know, these boys often make last-minute plans, Sheriff, and often Billy will be at breakfast, and it's only then we discover he's slept over. You know how kids are."

"You're saying you did not know for certain whether or not Billy Bell slept at your home on the night of August second?"

"Correct. I did not believe so, but I did check, and I found he had not. Slept at our home."

"I see. And how did you ascertain that?"

"I ASS-CER-TAINED by looking in my son Dickey's room, then by waking Dickey and asking him."

"And what did Dickey say?"

"That Billy was not. At our home. May I please have a glass of water?"

"We're almost done here, Fred, if you don't mind. So, your son Dickey said, Billy is not here. Did your son also say, 'Billy did not sleep here'?"

"I believe so."

"You believe so?"

"Yes."

"Did you ask your son, 'Did Billy *sleep* here?'? Or did you simply ask, 'Is Billy *here?*'?"

Mr. Dern brought his hands to his mouth. "Uh."

Sandy's hands hovered over the keys.

"Uh... I said, both."

"Meaning?"

"I asked Dickey, 'Is Billy HERE?' And when my son said no, I asked for confirmation. I asked, 'Did Billy SLEEP here last night?'"

"You sure of this?"

"Yes."

"And what did Dickey say?"

"No. He said no to both."

"Got that Sandy?"

Sandy drew in her lips.

"Your son always speak the truth, Mr. Dern?"

"Pardon me? "

"Your son ever tell a lie, a little fib? You know how these kids cover for each other, fabricate, sneak around. Could your son Dickey be protecting Billy Bell? Any possibility of that?"

"I don't believe so."

"Well, Fred, we'd appreciate it, just to rule it out, if we could come by your home and have a look-see."

"Yes of course, by all means."

In the initial search of the Dern home, the Deputy found one pair of pee-stained underwear in the toe of a basement sleeping bag, a bloodied boy's striped pullover in the back of Dickey's dresser drawer and a girlie magazine tucked up in the garage rafters.

All the young women on the cover of the girlie magazine, holding pom-poms, wearing cheerleader skirts and baring the lower halves of their buttocks, appeared to be under the age of sixteen, and when the Sheriff showed the bloodied pullover to Billy's mom, she said that is Billy's, where the hell didya find it?! And though none of the Dern boys laid claim to the underwear, and Dickey said the pullover was stained by one of Billy's nose-bleed months before, and Mr. Dern said he knew nothing of the girlie magazine, Mr. Dern was held at the Redtail County Sheriff's for further questioning in connection with the disappearance of Billy Bell.

That same day, a warrant was issued for a more thorough search of the Dern home. A section of basement paneling was removed, three porch boards ripped up, and the yard examined for signs of recent digging.

As Becky biked past on her way to the fair, she saw the Deputy parked in the Dern's driveway, two men with shovels in the garden and little Donnie Dern on his training wheels by the mailbox, sucking back tears.

"My dad's been thrown in jail!"

Becky biked directly to the Sheriff's.

Sweaty, panting, she rang the bell. Sandy emerged from the dimness, tucking her blouse into her waistband.

"Ma'am, can you please get the Sheriff? It's a 'mergency. I

forgot somethin' important."

Half an hour later, Becky sat across from Sheriff Giant with a kleenex in her fist.

"Now what's so important, Miss Bell?"

"Well, we was fightin', me an' Billy. At the fair. We always fight, so I didn't remember at first, but I just remembered. Billy run off an' ditched me, an' I said I'd kill him."

Becky looked into the Sheriff's flat brown eyes then down at the balled tissue in her lap.

"I mean, I didn't kill him, but when we biked home, he was scared I would, an' he was behind me, on his bike, but not by the Dern's. He was headin' for the bridge, an' shakin' his fist, like, 'catch me now Bitchster!' Sorry, but that's what he called me. 'Bitchster'."

Becky gulped, un-balled the tissue and began tearing it into strips. "So he musta gone over the freeway. That way. Not to Dern's."

"Not to the Dern's?"

"No."

"And why didn't you tell us this before, Miss Bell?"

"Um, 'cause I was scared. Of my mom. 'Cause she'd be so mad if I let Billy bike over the freeway. An' I didn't mean to get Mr. Dern in trouble! An' Billy wasn't even goin' that way." She wiped her nose. "He went the other way."

"You sure of that?"

"Yeah," Becky sniffed. "Positive."

"And how are you so sure of that, Miss Bell?"

"'Cause I saw him go over. But I wasn't worried, 'cause he made a new friend at the fair, some kid from the other side, an' went there, to his new friend's. To hide. From me." She zombied her eyes and dropped her voice. "Cause me an' Billy, we fight. *Hard*. Once we fought so bad I hurt him bad. Cut his cheekbone. Right here." Becky touched her face. "Seven stitches. That boat-shaped scar. So no wonder, right? No wonder he was scared of me."

"Why didn't you tell us this initially?"

"Initially?"

"Right away. Why didn't you tell us this right away?"

"Like I said, Mom woulda whacked me good. For lettin' him go over."

"Okay." Sheriff Giant leaned back. "Sandy, you got all that?"

Sandy compressed her lips.

"Miss Bell. Would you swear this on the Holy Bible?"

"Yes sir."

"And you know you've made a big mess? And you're going to have to suffer the consequences?"

"Yes sir."

"And you're not to lie to the Law again? Or you'll be thrown in jail? No questions asked, right into Girl Town, lock and key. If you lie to the police one more time. And things in Girl Town aren't pretty. Understand me?"

"Ye-es sir."

The tissue in Becky's hands was completely shredded.

"One last thing. This new friend of your borther's. He have a name?"

"Um..." Becky concocted a boy. *Crew-cut, pale, wimpy.* "Uh, Dan."

"This Dan have a last name?"

"No. Sorry."

Becky's bike ride home was blurred by tears. When she got home, her mom was stubbing out a cigarette and hanging up the phone. "I know all about it."

Then Becky got really whacked. By her mom. With the paddle. She'd had to take off her panties and the pad, stand by her bed and take it. *Like to die!*

Becky hadn't been whacked, *not like that*, not since she'd put that scar on Billy's face.

Afterwards, she laid on her side, fingering the welts, her eyes on the ceiling, following the crack.

I hate you, Mom! I hate your ugly face! An' I hate you Billy! I hate you for gettin' Mr. Dern in trouble. An' I hate you for messin' up my life! I hope you're rottin' in some ditch someplace! An' I hope you NEVER COME HOME!

GET OUT OR EXPLODE

Every day after that Becky snuck into the fair. First she stopped in the corn rows to wipe the spiderwebs from Billy's bike and shake the dew from his shoes. One morning rain had spattered his tennis shoes with mud. Another morning, a gold beetle crawled out from under the tongue. Another morning, a spit bug was stuck in the eyelet. Every day she shook the shoes off, and every day she crawled under the fence, and every day the wire scraped her shoulder until the cut was raw, infected, though her mother wiped it each night with rubbing alcohol, asking, "Why don't this heal? Are you pickin' at it again?"

And every day Becky wore the same pink shorts set, until the outfit was rubbed thin and her mother made her wear *some stupid shorts an' blouse.* That didn't stop Becky. She carried the pink seersucker shorts set in a knapsack and changed in the corn. As she dressed, she felt the cool leaves brush her skin like tender handmaidens. *Everythin' must be the same as when he run off...*

Every day she sat on the same bench. The cone had long been washed away, but the flies still licked the spot as Becky shut and opened her eyes on the crowd, watching for signs of suspiciousness. *Eyes open, everybody's innocent. Eyes closed, everybody's suspicious. Now normal. Now a kidnapper. Now normal. Now a werewolf. Now normal. Now a vampire!*

The footprint in the dusty road beyond the fence was smeared by other footprints, the old garbage replaced by new,

125

and every day the faces changed.

But Doug Douglas, *her crush*, stayed the same. Doug kept reappearing at the Popcorn Stand, the Sweet-Swirl and the Bag-a-Bunny. He sneered at Becky out the side of his eyes as he aimed a popgun, bit into cotton candy or licked a cone. And he was always alone, not with his cluster of buddies. And never with a girl, *cute or otherwise*. But Becky avoided Doug, scowled, turned away.

By the last day of the fair her blood-time had ended. There were no more reddish spots on her underwear. She searched Doug out. She found him at the Fantasy Fountain, dared him with her eyes to follow her, then ran. Doug ran after. She zig-zagged through the Midway, behind the I-Scream, put her hand on the wood and waited. He caught up, panting, wiped his mouth and passed her a silver flask. She sipped. Fire for her belly. *Pepper-minty.*

Becky felt her knees soften, eyes roll and belly swim. Together, as night descended, she and Doug walked the Midway. He bought her caramel corn. She shoved in handfuls and laughed wildly, spitting out kernels through her pink-glossed lips. She screamed on the Tilt-a-Whirl and spat on the crowd below, and on the Death Drop, laughing, she vomited upon the passing fairgoers, and in the Spook House, scared silly, she screeched into Doug's ears, dug her nails into his arm and breathed her sour breath on his cheek. Doug didn't flinch, cringe or pull away.

On the way back, in the dark, before showing Doug her sneaking-in place, she pushed him up against the corrugated metal of the 4-H building and stuck her tongue in his mouth. Doug tasted of schnapps, sweet cigars and iron.

Becky took his finger and guided it under her pink seersucker shorts, into the place where the blood had been, and showed Doug how to push his finger in and out, in and out, again and again, until she forgot all about Billy.

The Deputy found many boys named Dan on the other side of the freeway, Dan Smiths, Dan Johnsons, Dan Supinskis. After narrowing the search down to a one-mile radius west of the fair, the Sheriff had eight young Dans to interview. One was wheelchair-bound, one out of town, and all the others claimed they didn't know Billy Bell. Except one. Twelve year old Dan Yellowbird.

On the phone, Dan Yellowbird said yes he knew Billy Bell, they saw each other often, and were blood brothers, and planned to build a raft, pack survival kits and float down the Raccoon River. In person, interviewed at his home, Dan Yellowbird told of the many adventures he and Billy Bell had had. Some trips, he said, were sworn-to-secrecy, but some could be revealed, including a trip to Yellowstone, where they trained to be Forest Rangers, and to Niagara Falls, where an old man with a white beard taught them how to build a fail-proof barrel for a death-defying drop, and to the Shortcash Ranch in the great state of Texas, where they lived for one summer on the Four Bar X and roped longhorns, polished saddles and got stinking drunk on rotgut whiskey with the wild-romping cowgirls. But, Dan Yellowbird said, he hadn't seen Billy Bell since their last trip down Skunk Creek, when they'd caught a snapper this big, cracked the shell open with a boulder and roasted the meat over a blazing campfire.

Mrs. Yellowbird stood on the other side of the couch and smiled into her hands. As she walked the Deputy to the door, she explained, in a quiet voice, that her son had a creative imagination, and sometimes had trouble discerning lies from truth.

Becky had no trouble discerning lies from truth. She'd become adept at both. *How to keep them separate?* She'd taken to keeping two journals, in two Five-Year Diaries, that both aunts had given her for her fourteenth birthday One was brown, the other red, and both had a gold lock and key and the too-small space for each entry. *One for truth, one for bullshit!*

Becky kept the brown under her pillow, where she knew it would be found if she met with sudden death, and where her mom could sneak peeks, if she wished to, and kept the red on her bookshelf, inside a rectangle she'd hacked in a Trixie Belden mystery, *another stupid birthday present.*

Dear Diary, Momll' kill me bout Billys' bike.

Dear Diary, probly hes' hidin at Dans'.

Dear Diary, I let Doug finger me again.

Dear Diary, Ill' never do more than hold hands!

Dear Diary, we drew Math Teachers' butt like monkey with poop comin out. Then he eats it. HA!

Dear Diary, LOVE the NEW MATH!!!

Dear Diary, Racoons eatin food I leave by Billys' bike.

Dear Diary, spozed to write modern fairy tale for craetive writin. Goodie!

Once upon a time a Fat Lady GREW MOLD IN HER BUTT CRACK!!! HA!!!

Dear Diary, Modern fairy tale for Craetive Writin. Once this girl lives in high rise an looks down at World. But shes' all alone till this kid comes on elevater. Up buttons only work for him. So this kid plays Chinese Checkers with this girl but one day he says Im' just a ghost! HA!

Dear Diary, Halloween! Me an Doug gonna egg houses an steal fat kids candy! HA!

Dear Diary, Mom in closet again. WHATS' SHE DOIN IN THERE??? BITCH DEAD BITCH.

Dear Diary told Doug Im' pregant. He said how can you be? We didnt' do it yet. I said your' gunk swam up me, DUMB ASS!!!

Dear Diary, Went to Grammys' for Thanksgivin. Wore nylons. Ate alot. FUN!

Dear Diary, what my spozed to do with shitty ENCYCLOPEEDEEYAS???

Dear Diary, Got cool presents for XMAS. Bubble bath from Grammy shaped like Sleepin Baeuty. Wow. White Bible from Blue Gram. Wow. Encyclopeedeeya's from Mom. Wow.

Dear Diary, Happy 1970! Bleck!

Dear Diary, why the eff dont' I have freinds???

Dear Diary, had dream bout Billy. He sat in hall an stares at me. Then were' at Fair but its' a giant forest an we ride dinosaur's backs. FUN!

Dear Dairy, Im' a woman now. We did it. Me an Doug. Why? CUZ! Where? Dougs' rec room. When? WE SKIPPED math class! SO GROSS!!!

Dear Diary, deckorated Easter eggs with Mom.

Dear Diary Dad is a eff ass...

Dear Diary Doug is a eff ass...

Dear Diary Mom is A EFF ASS!!!

Dear Diary, la la! Ggot a JOB at Dinah's Diner $$$!!!

Dear Diary, SHIT-SHIT!

Becky was confused. Which was the true diary? Which was the lie? She wasn't sure anymore, and was no longer concerned whether her mom read either. Her mom was always drunk and her dad rarely home.

Dear Diary, they YELL. Dad slams door. Then peels out. Moms' plastered ALWAYS. HATE IT HERE with DEAD BITCH. WHAT MOM??? WHAT DID I JUST SAY??? I SAID YOUR A FICKIN ZOMBIE!!!

Dear Dairy. Doug wasnt' at fireworks. Where was he? Went by my Self. Then see Billy on blanket goin ape-shit over Fireworks. Then hes' gone...

Dear Diary, nother kid went missin. From Blue Winds Camp Ground. Some Strait A Egghead. Why would a smart kid go with stranger? Maybe Jimmy Moon an Billy both got taken by UFOs'. Yeah. WHY WOULD UFOS want STUPID BILLY? What a LOAD a CRAP!!!

Smiling Man rolled over on his bed, parted the curtains and looked out the window. He could see across the yard, to his cousin's house, and see the leaves were falling silently, covering the lawn below with yellow. A year had passed since the tragic accident at Redtail Rise. One whole year had passed without incident. The fair came and went with no misfortunes. He'd filled his time with guns, with guns and books and gals, with buying guns and trading guns and shooting guns, and reading books and buying books and hiding books and charming a few of the local gals.

But with books and guns and gals, there was only so far he could go, then he had to put the book down, go down to the sitting room and suffer the long evenings of educational programs with the folks. Even up in his room, he felt the house grow smaller, the trees press in, his ribs close round his lungs.

Then he must get out–

OR EXPLODE!

Books and guns and gals were not enough! Perhaps he'd meet the perfect gal who'd laugh at his jokes, and perhaps he'd find the perfect book to fill his mind with imagined delights so potent that he'd never need to go seeking true-life adventures, and perhaps he'd find the perfect gun or set of guns or collection of obscure firearms–

And perhaps his new retirement would not drive him mad! Before retirement, he'd thought, planned and imagined all that he'd do, how he'd relish each moment, filling up his days with reading, collecting, perusing catalogues and visiting old friends. But the newness of retirement quickly flattened. He missed the garage, missed using his hands, missed cleaning an engine, the smell of oil, the sounds of tools zipping, the camaraderie. And he missed getting up in the morning with a purpose, with a place to go where he knew the folks, where they turned their heads and said, how are you.

He visited work often, at least twice a week, but they were always too busy to set down their wrenches and chat, or go for lunch at the local diner.

And he visited his cousin across the road. His cousin would certainly have time for him, they'd been best buddies since boyhood, but his cousin was busy with his crops, his animals and growing kids.

Even the gals were too busy with women things, hairdos, knitting and flower bulbs. It was becoming difficult to find a friend. Either folks were grown up with lives of their own, or too old and feeble, or too young, or not young enough! Like his nephews, now grown up, with kids of their own. When his nephews were boys, they were eager to listen, learn and go adventuring. At least until their faces clouded over and they said *no more uncle…*

But now! Everyone was too busy, or too old, like his folks, like his mother's poor bones and his father's feeble nagging! NAGGING, NAGGING!

He heard them now down in the sitting room, disagreeing over a television show. And when it wasn't a TV program, it was the weave of a fabric, or the price of a jacket, or the amount of butter on a slice of bread!

Whatever was in front of them.
ARGUING OVER NOTHING!

Yes, these days were driving him MAD! He had to get out and find a friend. FAST.

He pressed out his Chesterfield, adjusted himself in bed and turned the page in the book he'd been reading. A slip of paper fell out, a pamphlet for Bluewinds Campground.

VISIT BLUEWINDS
YEAR ROUND BEAUTY
WILD WILDERNESS WATERWAY!

Not so wild, those rapids. Pretty damn tame. A picturesque place for scouts of all ages to enjoy a little nature before snow fell. Perhaps a trip to Blue Winds was just the ticket. Smiling Man imagined the plashing waterfalls, bubbling rapids, turning leaves and quiet walks along the creek, and the well-kept campsites located conveniently close to the modern new Restroom Facility.

THE SILENT PRINCESS

Jimmy Moon was excited. Gathering fallen wood, stacking fuel and setting the pyramid alight was one of his *favorite things,* along with catching frogs, toads and butterflies, then looking up the species in his Golden Guides. Jimmy was always careful not to injure his Lepidopteron catches. His grandmother had taught him how to trap gracefully, to bring the net down swiftly, with no wing-damage, but there was always some velvety dust lost. *So challenging to catch a butterfly with ABSOLUTELY NO DAMAGE.*

And Jimmy wasn't a wimp. Just because he was gentle with Lepidoptera didn't make him a milksop. He could climb trees, catch fish and worm a hook as well as any boy in West Brownmound. Just because he didn't dynamite bullfrogs, pull the wings off flies or torture stray cats didn't make him a pushover. Jimmy was, in fact, a kind of soldier, a soldier of knowledge, *a soldier of learning, a soldier of questions.* That's what his grand-poppy called him. *HELLO THERE, MY SOLDIER OF QUESTIONS!* What is the Question of the Day?

Because if you didn't ask, how would you ever learn? And if you didn't learn, how would you ever grow? And if you didn't grow, you'd become a black hole and fall in on yourself instead of expanding like the ever-expanding universe. Jimmy knew every planet in the solar system, and the paths they moved across the sky, and could decipher, just by looking at an astronomical map, what time of year it was in the western hemisphere.

And what time of year was it today? TIME FOR FIRE-BUILDING! There was plenty of fallen wood near Campsite Three, not only branches, but also insects roused by his passing and a wide variety of leaves, *serrated, smooth, lobed,* and numerous species which he could identify. Jimmy held an aspen leaf, studied the vein pattern, cast it away, then identified a green damsel-fly on his forearm as *Erithemis simplicicollis,* before the insect breezed off.

As he pulled up another branch, Jimmy was sure the fire would be a one-match success, and with the fire blazing, he *WOULD NOT BE AFRAID,* because he knew every planet in the solar system, and knew the black holes were far away, and that emotionally-disturbed characters like Marvel Granger were locked up in high-security sanatoriums for the criminally insane.

When Jimmy first heard about Marvel Granger he didn't believe it. This was comic book horror, not reality, *just a tale dreamed up by my imaginative buddies.* But the tale haunted him, he took it to bed, the visions of Granger's unwashed kitchen, the ceiling hooks, the clotted stove. *Could it be true?* Jimmy had gone to the West Brownmound Library and studied the microfiche from the 1940's, and there it was. In bold headlines.

CANNIBALISM UP NORTH.

And that twisted nursery rhyme-

Granger, Granger, Iron Ranger!
Nothing weirder, nothing stranger-

The retired bachelor, living alone in squalor, unwashed pots in the sink, stained wallpaper and sticky floors, was discovered by a neighbor to have been digging up graves, and-

Jimmy shooed away a black fly. The details of the kitchen floor were horror enough, *not to mention what was on the shelves, in the freezer and in the cupboards.*

Jimmy stacked the twigs, then the thicker branches into an expert teepee, stroked his Strike-Light on the rough bark and touched the kindling.

Whoosh.

How could anyone dig up human corpses? And how could anyone

not only exhume rotting flesh, but also gut the bodies, scrape muscle from bone, and use the remains to fashion household objects, lampshades, couch covers, hollowed-out skulls for bowls, and then refrigerate the hearts, kidneys and livers for stew? *Stranger than fiction!*

The flames jerked over leaf-edges, hopped twigs, snickered in the pine needles and bloomed. *A one-match crackler!*

Night was coming fast. Jimmy went to the tent for his hooded sweatshirt. The other boys were rough-housing, throwing clods of dirt, falling to their knees, hugging each other's necks and getting caught up in each other's limbs. But as twilight descended, they sobered, parted, stepped back and crawled in their tents for more wraps, then gathered round the fire for their post-beans-and-weenies treat, marshmallows on sticks sharpened with pocket knives and the ritual ghost-stories-with-hot-chocolate.

Jimmy burned his tongue on his first marshmallow, which he'd pulled from the fire a rolling torch, laughed with the others and jumped at the scary punch-lines in The Golden Arm, The Hook and The Swamp-Drenched Bag of Bones Coming up the Stairs. When his turn came, he told his true-terror of *The Man Who Dug Up Graves,* and chuckled when the other boys joked about dancing in human skins, slurping from human skulls and cooking human-soup. But Jimmy silently questioned the motivation of such grisly acts.

How could a person sit alone in their home in the long winter and cut up corpses, then coax skin from bone and sew tiny stitches into a lampshade, a leather pillow and a couch of human skin? That took time. That wasn't blind rage. What was that? Loneliness? Jimmy felt lonely sometimes, but that was offset by his probing curiosity. Perhaps, despite his solitude, Marvel Granger wanted to be seen. Perhaps somewhere in his old bachelor brain, Marvel knew what he was doing was SO ATROCIOUS, that one day human beings would think on it, ponder, and repeat the tales of the grotesqueries out loud, saying his name over and over. Marvel Granger, Marvel Granger. And perhaps, in that way, Marvel Granger was not alone, *perhaps Marvel Granger had sewn up his slot in eternity with each stitch,* Jimmy thought, as the others laughed round the flames, waving their burning marshmallows.

$$\text{ʕ•ᴥ•ʔ}$$

Smiling Man was glad, not only for the pamphlet falling from the book just as he was itching for an adventure, but also for Blue Wind's nearness to the highway and its popularity with young scouts squeezing in outings before snow fell, those jolly scouts with their uniforms, blue and yellow, green and red, black and tan.

Smiling Man was also glad because he had happened on a campsite adjacent to a small pack of unstructured boys, seven rousing lads without uniforms and just one adult chaperone.

He parked in Campsite Number Five near the Modern Facilities, unpacked his gear, poured lighter fluid over the precut firewood, shook a swig of rum into his thermos, cut a fat slice of summer sausage and proceeded to enjoy the scent of smoke, the fading light and the boys' nearby laughter.

As late afternoon slipped into evening, he set his eye on one particular lad off by himself, who paused to pick up a leaf, stare at an insect and study the undergrowth. The boy reminded him of his eldest nephew when he was a youngster, sharply observant, thoughtful, withdrawn…

After darkness fell, he kept watch on their glowing circle, particularly the lad with the dark hair, pale skin and shiny-hole eyes. When the lad stepped from the fire and headed for the Modern Restroom Facility, Smiling Man was ready. He got there before the lad.

$$\text{ʕ•ᴥ•ʔ}$$

Jimmy was not afraid of the dark. How could you be, when you knew what the darkness consisted of? Elements, dancing atoms, electrons, protons. *And beyond that? Who knew?* Jimmy confidently stepped into the blackness. He knew his eyes were designed to adjust to light changes, and that artificial light caused night-blindness, so he walked with no flashlight, trusting his ears, night-eyes and the feel of the path beneath his genuine deerskin moccasins.

Boldness is rewarded. And there are no bears, bobcats or wolves in this part of the country. And no ghosts of Marvel Granger's dug-up corpses. His skinned ghouls are not wavering in the overhead branches. And I am boldly striding forward...

Smiling Man waited in the last stall of the Men's Restroom. He waited with patience and confidence. He'd thought this through. How to make a sudden friendship. There was the benefit of surprise. Not to attack, but to engage, get close up, survey the skin, the curve of the chin, the slope of the neck.

Milk and apricots.

Smiling Man had been indoctrinated early in the Facts of Life. The farm had sex on every surface, behind every swinging door, mating animals, snipped testicles and cow-babies dropping wet to the hay, hot-fresh from their mothers. He'd been instructed by his uncle in how men and women made a baby. "They do it this way; he lifts up the skirts and puts it in while she's on her back with her legs wide open."

Once instructed, though far too young, he'd tried it with his own sister under the shadowy trees on the wide lawn. This is how it's done, he'd said, you lie down. He had pushed his sister to the grass, pried her legs apart, lay between them fully-clothed, and began the jerking motions. But his sister was a fighter. She'd have none of it. She kicked his shin, punched out and ran to hide in the henhouse.

Later, there was the cousin's bed, where he and his cousin invented pleasing games with their boy parts. Those secretive moments, in the basement, the barn, the pond and the cluttered upstairs rooms were steeped in the smells of living things, drying corn, aging wood, sweating stone and the sweet-nutty scent of their own boyish prepubescence.

After his family moved back home, there was the purple-eyed Hired Man. That Hired Man had constructed a shed for himself out of scrap and slept alone, away from the others. The Hired Man would pause in his working up on the roof, or bending for the nail-bucket, or walking to the pump, and stare at him with that bruise-colored gaze. That stare was bitter, poison, a snake bite, and made his guts drop into his shoes. *Delicious.*

One day the Hired Man invited him into his slap-dash shed, saying, yer far too old to be sleepin' with yer ma, pa an' sister. Why don't yer sleep in here with me? Come look-see. Yer'll fit right there. An' there's room fer yer cup. An' we can stay up late an' tell tales. I can tell yer 'bout what it was like growin' up down south. But yer cain't tell one word a' my stories to no livin' soul. For if yer go tellin' I'll be thrown in prison fer knowin' what I know. An' they will hang me till my tongue stick out, like this. The Hired Man stuck out his tongue then drew it slowly back in and went on. But if yer man enough to come in an' sleep with me, he whispered, an' keep yer ears open an' mouth shut, an' yer'll learn what no sister nor ma could never teach yer.

So he went in, and the stories he learned were not made of words but of movements underground, of grunts, sighs and a pain so sharp it slid into panicked pleasure, sunrise slicing in after darkness.

When he walked out of that shed the boy who'd played skin-games with his cousin in the cornfields and hideaways was gone. That sweet act had soured and the sour was intoxicating, the word of god to a zealot, and had to be spread over the land.

After that his boyhood was heavy with hidden fervors and his manhood drove those fervors underground. There were books of all kinds, with stories of men and boys in sailing ships, and space ships speeding through the depths of time, in war-cockpits, lost caves and polar wastes, on horseback, on trains, in ancient Greece and sunny Italy. And there were the commoner tales of men and boys in public restrooms, intricate, hearty, but private, best kept to oneself.

Did he dare live out such a story? In the Men's Room at Blue Winds campground? With that dark-eyed lad?

Perhaps not. Perhaps it was best to just talk to the lad, engage him in conversation, pick his brain and find a shared interest. Perhaps he could befriend the lad slowly. Wasn't that how friends were made, gradually, over time? Perhaps this new lad would invite him to their campfire. Perhaps they'd lunch together next week, perhaps go on a hay ride or target-shoot at the Rise. There was always hope. The hope of a perfect friend.

When he heard the boy's moccasin-scrape on the concrete pad outside the Modern Restroom Facility, Smiling Man made a quick decision. He'd wait in the last stall while the lad did his business, and as the lad washed his hands, he'd step out, wash his own hands at the adjacent sink, and engage the lad in friendly conversation.

Jimmy made it to the Men's Restroom without being attacked by corpses, ghouls or dangling ghosts. There was an impressive spider, an *Araneus diadematus*, in a large web over the door, and common Daddy-long-legs in the sink, but no stinking horrors in the trees.

Jimmy ducked under the spider web, used the toilet and shooed the *Pholcus phalangioides* to safety before turning on the taps.

COLD WATER! Jimmy clenched his fists.

Someone behind me. In the mirror. Ruddy skin. Wide grin.

The man spoke. "Hey you."

Jimmy held down his startle reflex. Predators could smell fear and weakness. This man had a predator-scent: alcohol, sweat and cinnamon.

"Hello there. How's your campsite?"

Jimmy didn't answer.

"I have a high-powered flashlight."

Jimmy glanced up.

The man waved a big silver Eveready.

"Where is your flashlight? Did you leave it at your campsite? Aren't you afraid of things that go bump in the night? Can you see in the dark? Do you have night vision? Do you have the eyes of a cat? Do you have the ears of a bat? What is your name? Hey. I'm talking to you. How do you do?"

His hand came into view, thick and red, waiting to be shaken.

"I'm your neighbor. Next site over. Number Five. I don't see your uniform. Are you a Cub Scout? Or are you a Boy Scout? Are you an Eagle Scout? Do you have a Deer-hunting badge? Do you have a Leather-working badge? Do you have a Life-saving badge? What kind of scout are you?"

Jimmy held his hands under the cold tap as the man went on and on. *Why would he not stop talking?* There was a fairy tale his mother told him long ago, when he was small enough to curl close and feel her chest reverberate as she read. *The Silent Princess.*

The Silent Princess sat alone in an oval room. She sat without speaking, while beyond her windowless oval, the townfolk carried on. They talked as they walked arm-in-arm, children scampered, tradespeople hawked their wares, vegetables, flowers, blocks of cheese, carriages and wagons clomped by, people threw back their heads in laugher, snapped good-naturedly at the misbehaving children and went on their noisy, bustling way, as dogs barked, donkeys brayed and hens cackled.

But the Princess sat alone in her room, never speaking, because she knew that if she spoke, she'd break the town's spell of happiness. If she let out one single word, the bell in the church tower, and the bells in the court tower, and the small bells in the gardens, and on doors, and the bells around animals' necks would begin to toll, and when the bells tolled, the walls of the town would begin to crack, hairlines at first, then wider, then cottages would fall, and the church fall, and the tower, the stone wall round the town, all would crumble, and the horses would die kicking, and the dogs would die spewing black vomit, and the children would burst, the men's stomachs rupture, and the ladies' unborn children would spill out as the town fell to ruin if the silent princess spoke even one word.

Was that the fairy tale this moment reminded Jimmy of? Or

was it the tale where a small tailor killed seven flies with one flick of the coat that he was mending, and the story grew, to where he'd killed seven giants with one swipe of his sword and was made head of the army? Anyway, the Man was still talking.

Finally, because his hands had wrinkled into white prunes, Jimmy cleared his throat, turned off the tap and said, "Excuse me, sir, I need to get back to my troop."

Then squeezed round the Man and out the door.

Smiling Man had forgotten the most important part of his plan! He was going to wash his hands beside the lad at the next sink. This would've set up an instant camaraderie. But he'd forgotten, in the excitement of being so near that pale skin.

Then he was miffed, just *a little*, that the lad hadn't replied to his questions. Then he was angered. How rude, not to reply, not to engage in friendly conversation! He had tried to bring up any subject the lad might be interested in! Scouting! Hunting! Echolocation!

Then he became enraged. How blatantly impolite, not to shake the outstretched hand! How purposefully rude! How impudent, to stand there, washing his hands and say not one word in reply to his elder, except finally, excuse me, I have to get back to my troop! My troop! Absurd! The lad had no troop!

Smiling Man knew this for a fact. The lad was just one of those rag-tags watched over by one skinny man round a puny campfire. There were no troop leaders! No uniforms! And no badges! No earned manhood of any kind! JUST BLATENT RUDENESS! *Just that little group of know-nothing smart-ass civilians.* The lad was not only a mocker, a rude, impudent mocker. He was also a liar, a bold-faced liar. *And must be punished.*

THE BIG IF

Life was becoming beautiful for Becky Bell. She lay on her bed and traced the ceiling crack with her eyes, drawing it back to the light. *And you are a most becoming girl. Be-coming.* That's what her science teacher said. *Oh yeah? What am I becoming, Mr. Eyebrows?*

Well, for one, she had a new set of C-cups upon her slender figure, though she'd long outgrown her pink seersucker shorts set. That threadbare thing had been torn into rags.

And her bedroom was spinning. Sloe Gin made her belly warm, the edges soft and life grand. With booze she could flow in and out of herself, from shy to loud to bossy to mysterious. And she had the boys round her pinky finger. Doug mostly, but she could glance at the other boys and set them sweating, put her hand on her hip, move her spine a bit and watch the beads pop out on their upper lips. HA!

Her heart was broken when Billy disappeared, so no other boy could hurt her, and each night she took the torn half dollar from under her tip change in the jar on her dresser and traced the edge, then hid the half dollar back under her waitressing tips. *Keep that hidden.*

She'd become adept at juggling the hidden parts of her life, booze, cigs and hickies, with the unhidden, kitchen sink, school subjects and her part time job at Dinah's Diner. It was all about the *who, where and how.* With her grand imagination, new good looks and the lubrication of liquor, white lies came easy.

An' if you tell a lie enough times, even you start to believe it. Like Doug was her true love. *Lie!* And things were fine at home. *Lie!* Truth: her dad was shacking up with the blonde from the Cootie Factory, *but what the hell. Let the chips fall where they may.*

Truth: Doug had soured on her. Truth: Doug was whiny. *How in the HELL could she have had a crush on Doug Douglas?* Truth: There were older boys, boys who'd been watching her, boys who went to parties downtown and had cars and jobs and hair down to their shoulders, and she was just about ready, one day soon, when they came in to order burger and fries, to look down from her order-pad and meet their eyes.

Dear Diary, Moms' in closet again. ZOMBIE- FREAK! Wish she'd be her old self an BITCH AT ME AN MAKE HER CRAPPY MACRONI AN CHEESE!

Billy liked his mother in the front hall closet. He could feel her hurt in there, how much she loved him. Sometimes she fell asleep under the hanging coats, one leg imprinted with fallen hangers, sometimes she pushed her way out in the morning and fell asleep on the couch, but most nights she rocked back and forth in the closet, tipping back beer after beer.

Oh yeah she loves me all right.

Being in the closet with his mom was better than tagging along behind Smiling Man. At first it was fun, riding his shoulder, making faces behind his back, trying tricks. Billy tried to slide the Man's smokes off his bedstand, douse his lighter, grind his hips against his back: *See how you like it!*

But Billy couldn't move solids, air or fire, and couldn't press into the flesh of another with whatever he was made of. *Flyin' Handkerchief! Buzzin' Dragonfly! Zippin' Bumblebee!* He could dip and dive, but couldn't be seen by the hard-folks and couldn't move anything except himself.

Well he could do one thing. He could make Becky drop

things. He could get into the muscles of her hands and squirm there, so a spoon, glass or cup would PLOP! CRASH! BOOM! *To the floor!* This was especially fun at Dinah's Diner, seeing dishes skitter as Becky dropped the order, seeing her face redden as the burger skated over the linoleum and the customers scowled and the cook pawed his hips, *not again!* Ha!

But the trick only worked on the Bitchster, or Billy would have played it on Smiling Man, to distract him when he went out boy-shopping. At the gas station, the library, and the ball park, Billy rode the Man's shoulders, and could tell by the hardening of his back, the tucking of his chin, and the feel of him thickening, when the Smiling Man was aiming for a target.

Oh yes, *THE BIG IF.* If only Billy could have affected objects, then he would have torn the steering wheel from Smiling Man's hands and torn his throat open and ripped his privates out. But Billy could only stand by and watch. He saw it coming, saw the new boy look up, pause and decide, *this guy's not dangerous...*

Billy tried to get into Smiling Man's head before he left the house. *Stay in your room. Don't go out. Read your book. Smoke another butt. You're too drunk to drive. It's too cold to leave the house. It's too hot, too much snow!* But the Man had a burning, so Billy followed, as he descended the stairs, checked his reflection and went out to the Blazer. *Don't get in! You forgot to brush your teeth! You forgot to wipe! You forgot to put your ass back in bed till you rot to death!* Smiling Man never heard. Instead he got in, buckled up and turned left.

The next boy was that egghead from the campground, the Jimmy. *STUPID, STUPID. How could anyone so smart be so stupid?* Billy would NEVER have stood washing his hands till the cows came home. Billy would have kicked backwards, jammed his heel in the guy's balls, sped through the spiderweb and grabbed Jimmy's dad from the campfire while the Man was still bent over in pain, then watch as the dad pinned his arms behind his back in a Citizen's Arrest.

Well, first he had to disarm the guy. Smiling Man never went out without his weapons. Always a gun on him, one in the glove compartment, a few in back. And always loaded. Billy couldn't stop what happened to the Jimmy. He could only watch, then zip to the boy's ear, whispering, *it'll be over soon, an' then he can never hurt you again, an' you can come learn tricks with me, how to dip an' dive, an' one day we'll ram a brontosaurus up HIS BEHIND.*

But Billy could not turn back time. He could twist, dip and change his own shape like a squid, but he could not go back and tell the Jimmy to stay in the tent till morning. *Don't go out! Or just pee outside the tent, an' if you have to go number two, do it in the WOODS! WIPE WITH LEAVES! Don't be a pussy!*

But the time was set and the boy ran out and the sky was high and the Man was waiting, and the shower was where he took the boy, the blasted shower, the bloody shower. And the shower was where the water ran, ran, down the drain with the shot-out brains of twelve-year-old Jimmy Moon.

THE RED-HEADED GIRL

Smiling Man had lost his temper again. He had set out NOT to lose his temper. He had set out to have a good time, make a new friend and not raise his voice. Not unless absolutely necessary.

This was, after all, the prime of his life. No telling, after retirement, how many years you had left. So he enjoyed the night, the camp-smoke, the summer sausage, the stars coming out, the fresh air, the cold coming, the autumn returning, the seasonal change always rising up, a new beginning, a new chance to shine, to be our best selves, outshine our past, do good turns and turn around the dark and hold all that is dear and ignore that fire in the gut.

But this lad, oh no, not another tragic accident! Why couldn't the lad just relax and have a good time, as he had done in his time with the Hired Man? But no, this lad had to wiggle and plead. GOD DAMMIT LAD! *Don't irk me! I have a short fuse!*

Then the gun to the small, dark head, not as a threat, just as a tool of negotiation, to calm the lad, as any smart person would know to stop squirming with a gun at their temple, but the lad was A FOOL with his squirming, and before anyone came to ask what the matter was, he had to be shut up.

Then there was the clean-up, and having to leave the campsite before sunrise. Good thing, good thing the camp-host was out when he pulled into Blue Winds Campground. Good thing, good thing he put cash in the box and not his name or license number.

Good thing the next campers over were sleeping as he packed up in the dark, set towels on the seat, maneuvered the dripping lad in and drove home.

And perhaps, he thought later as he stood at the fire, a big fire this time, fueled by kerosene, raging high as the barn, perhaps the folks in Site Number Three were too busy tale-telling and marshmallow-roasting and guffawing to take note of me.

This time the smoke got to the cousins. They came out in their nightclothes. Why a fire so early, they'd asked, what are you burning up, a body, ha-ha. Just some old magazines, he'd answered, and that trunk the mice got to, you remember that trunk in the basement. Well you're making one big stink over to our house, they said, one big black cloud. We had to shut all our windows, on a nice morning like this. Maybe not such a good idea to burn now, I'm sure your folks don't want that smoke. Sure, just let me get the hose. Get the shovel, that's what you need. Sure, sure.

Billy and Jimmy stood watching the smoke rise. Jimmy wasn't angry; he was shaken, pondering, pulling himself together. The pain back at Bluewinds was at first an unbearable explosion, then Jimmy rose above the pain as a wave of Novocain began at the screaming boy's head and descended, numbing the boy.

Jimmy hovered over the showerhead looking down at the man, red-faced, and the boy, cringing, and the act, appalling, animals in a zoo, caged beasts. That made Jimmy sad, sad. This would ruin the camping trip. The boys would come out of their tents in the morning scratching their heads, asking, where's Jimmy? Didn't he sleep with you last night? Yeah. Well, where is he? Don't know. Did he go off chasing some dumb butterfly? Don't know. Worse would be his mom and his dad, sad, sad, and the grandparents, sad, and the teachers at school.

But there would be hope too, because there was his body in

that conflagration, the scent of hair, flesh and fat disguised by burning rubber, and teeth do not burn up. Maybe one day his jaw would speak.

Billy was glad for a buddy. Now that the Jimmy could see him, in that underwater kind of way, Billy could take the kid with him, *zip*, to another place, and they'd have a blast!

But the Jimmy just frowned into the fire. He wasn't a flipper or a zipper. Billy tried to engage him in conversation.

That's you in that fire there, right? An' you're here too, by me? See? So how can you be two places at once? Funny ain't it? An' if that's you in the fire, then how come you ain't screaming? Ha!

The Jimmy didn't answer. Both boys stood by as Smiling Man shoveled out the coals, broke apart the pieces and pushed glowing bits back in.

Not done yet.

Billy cracked a joke about a barbeque, but the Jimmy didn't laugh. He tried to shape the joke again, swing the punchline, but the Jimmy still didn't get it. Billy rose, did a few spinning tricks to cheer the kid up, and distract him, show him what fun could be had in this Triple X Dimension, but the kid wouldn't take his gaze from the flames.

Forget about that kid in the fire! You're with me now! An' there's so much to see! I know, kid, fire can hypnotize. I get it, but look!

Billy rose high above the barn.

He's not so big from up here! Come see!

The Jimmy didn't move. Billy zipped back down.

Hey, kid, I get it! You're in what they call A STATE A SHOCK. That's not like the state of Wyomin' or the state of North Dakota or any of the United States. That's what they call STATE A MIND. But where's your mind? Is your mind in that fire? Or in your head? Then where's your head? Your head's in the fire! So where's your mind? Maybe you ain't got no mind! Maybe your mind's all burnt up! So how can you think? Ha! Like I said, don't think about it! Cause pretty soon you'll see whatever you

THINK is where you GO!

Okay, okay, stare at that fire all day! WHAT DO I CARE? But that Smilin' Man? He hunts boys like us. What you gonna do about that? Just stand there? Well, if you're gonna just stand there why not push him in while you're at it? Burn him up. Like to see you try.

The Jimmy wavered, a heat-mirage.

Too scared ain't you? Well I don't care if you kick him or not. An' I don't care if you come with me or not. I got plenty to do without you. I can do whatever the hell I want. I bet you're just gonna stand there till the cows come home an' there's nothin' left but a little smoke, then you'll be starin' at ashes while I'm off havin' fun an' he's messin' with some other kid. Suit yourself. I'm outa here. Scottie, beam me up!

And Billy was gone.

Jimmy gave the flames more time to crackle, then focused on Smiling Man, felt what was left of himself, slowly unfolded his ghost-leg and gave Smiling Man one sharp kick in the shin. But his foot went nowhere.

Jimmy waited till the fire cooled and the Man left, then pushed his hands into the ashes to feel for his mandible, but the ashes weren't disturbed by his hands, and Jimmy couldn't scratch his jawbone from the ashes or pick up the smoking morsels of himself.

Later, after the Man came back with a wheelbarrow, shoveled up and reburied what was left under a hump of composting weeds behind an empty henhouse, Jimmy couldn't pick up the shovel and dig himself up. He could THINK shovel, and FEEL shovel, but that didn't move dirt.

And now he had to think of what to do with himself.

He returned to the split-level in West Brownmound, to the boxes of the rooms and made the rounds, his folk's room, living room, his room, but the rooms were boxes and his folks had become boxes and their grief was in boxes they held close. He tried to lift the lids, pry an opening and get in, but something told him *not time yet.*

And that other boy, the one who kept trying to get him to play, that boy was a *lightning bolt! Buzzing too fast to see!* Jimmy was glad the boy was gone. He needed to keep everything slow, in order to navigate the physics of his new realm. *Up was up and down was down, but not always,* and if Jimmy wasn't careful, he'd zip like the zipping kid.

He imagined home, and there he was. Then thought of school and was at school, then in the tropical land in his open geography book, gazing at a sapphire sea, his toes buried in white sand. It was dangerous to think, especially quickly, and Jimmy had always been a quick thinker, so he pulled his toes from the sand and slowed his thoughts then erased them. When he formed a new thought, he thought *slowly,* so he could travel at a more manageable pace.

The zipping kid hadn't seemed to care what he thought. He'd zipped to Jimmy's side, then atop of his head, and then gone. Jimmy wished he could have reached out and grabbed the kid, balled him up and pocketed that battery-pack, but he seemed to have no control over anything.

He could observe. He could think of a place and be there. He could travel at the speed of thought, but he could not put a hand on his mother's shoulders or cup his grandpa's chin or worm his way into his dad's fist as he sat holding a fishing pole with no worm on the hook, just his red eyes on the bobbering water.

Dad, I'm right beside you, and perhaps you can feel me, even if you can't see me. I'm like wind or water but without form. Fire can't burn me. Water can't wet me. I can't be seen but here I am. How does that work? There are radio waves. They can't be seen. There are television waves. They can't be seen. There are atomic particles. They can't be seen with the naked eye. That doesn't mean they don't exist. They make up everything!

So what am I? A product of my own imagination? How long will I be like this? Is this a stage, like an insect pupating? And what comes next?

Jimmy grew hot with wondering, and the heat drove him straight to his mother. She collapsed round Jimmy, got into his bed and covered herself with his boy-smelling sheets.

As his mother slept, a redheaded girl in kitty cat glasses and a plaid dress slid unseen into Jimmy's room and watched and waited.

THE OPAL CADET

The new guy's hair was greasy, but otherwise *he was perfect. An' his eyes ain't really brown,* Becky thought, as the sun shot through Dinah's window and lit his face. *His eyes are amber. An' he got a bad tattoo on his hand.* Under the arm of the undiscernible tattoo sat the Brownmound Bugle.

JIMMY MOON
ONE YEAR
STILL MISSING

Becky sniffed and glanced up at the ceiling. *Maybe Jimmy an' Billy are together, lyin' at the bottom of Orangevale Creek, or maybe they're Russian spies, or on a flyin' saucer, or maybe this guy with the amber eyes will look up from his menu, like what he sees an' date me.*

Becky licked her lips, flared her nostrils and lengthened her neck. Smoke snaked out the guy's nose. As the smoke cleared Becky saw. *One eye's amber! The other's blue!*

She felt her bra-straps cut into her shoulders. She wanted to unhook herself, get out of that sling and shake her breasts in this guy's face, *yeah!* After bringing his order, she leaned against the far counter, smoking Kool after Kool as he bent to his food, held his BLT close, and snuck glances out his eye, *like a mouse afraid someone'll steal his cheese. He eats like he hasn't had a decent meal in weeks. Bet he's hungry for somethin' else too...*

153

When Becky brought his bill she picked up the matchbook with the black words over a yellow smiling sun, *HAPPY DINERS MAKE DINAH HAPPY*, wrote *IM' OFF AT 7*, added a smiley-face and leaned forward so the new guy could smell the heat rising from between her breasts.

He stood like an old man, stacked the tip, gimped to the door and got in the tangerine Opal Cadet with black lace designs spray-painted on the sides.

How cool's that! Two-Tone Eyes got a two-tone car! Becky wiped the yellow counters clean, flicked bits of egg from the red booths, refilled the napkin-holders and felt her guts falling with that scared feeling, *UP ON TOP OF A FERRIS WHEEL!* She hummed a tune she'd made up, *hmm-hmm*, till the glasses were spot-free and the booths shiny, *hmm-hmm-hmm*, and when the hand on the clock hit seven, she got her jacket off the hook, checked her purse for cigarettes, her lighter and the slippery feel of the packet, *hmm-hmm*. The wind caused her to gasp as she opened the door, and small oval leaves scattered under her feet.

Two-Tone was still there in the tangerine Opal. Becky swiped her index finger along the driver's side window, opened the passenger door, and spoke as if she knew him. "Let's get out of here."

Past Dave's Donut Hole, she pointed left towards Redtail Rise. There'd been bulldozers up there that summer. *Some kind of wild-life thing*, Becky had heard.

When they got to the Rise, one yellow dozer sat crooked atop a mound of dirt, and two others were parked off to the side near the spreading maple. Becky slid out of the Opal to watch the sunset. *Hot pink through deep purple.*

As the colors intensified, Two-Tone leaned out for her wrist. Becky let him tug her back in. Then she was on her back. Then his face scratching hers, his hands at her blouse and her first thought, *DON'T TEAR MY WORK SHIRT!* But he did tear. Two buttons popped off as yanked up her bra. He nuzzled her breasts, opened his pants and drew her face to his hips.

STRONGER THAN HE LOOKS!

She gagged on his hardness.

NOT EXACTLY WHAT I WANTED.

HOW FAR CAN MY JAWS OPEN?
MY JAWS ARE NOT A SNAKE'S!

Then it was over. He zipped up and stared through the bug-spattered windshield as Becky investigated the damage to her blouse, then bent and peered into the stale-beer darkness below. She found one button atop a damp girlie magazine and the other tangled in a pair of panties.

Two-Tone gestured with the silver flask. "Cool sunset."

"Yeah."

"You from round here?"

"Yeah. You?"

"Nope. From over there." He pointed east and offered Becky a pull. She took a slug and coughed.

After darkness fell, he dropped her off back at Dinah's.

As she pedaled home and as she brushed her teeth and as she sat on her bed sewing the buttons back on, she swore, *I'll never wait on that EFFIN' Two-Tone again, an' never get in that EFFIN OPAL AGAIN an' never look in those effin' EYES AGAIN!!!*

Smiling Man fisted one hand towards his mouth, anticipating a corrosive burp as he sat in his booth at Dinah's Diner.

This was bad news. Bad after bad.

His mother had fallen down the stairs again. He hadn't been home this time, but he could imagine her hands reaching out, fingers closing round nothing, compact body tumbling, towels flying, and wondered what to tell the regulars at Dinah's Diner.

Mother has broken her hip again. With bones like hers, fine as lace, all it takes is one misstep.

It broke his heart to see his mother bed-bound once more in Brownmound Mercy. Worse was what happened back home. No meals prepared, unless he or his dad prepared them. That was amusing at first, sausage and eggs for every meal, but quickly turned into stacks of dirty dishes and layers of grease, unless they nagged each other to keep on top of it.

NAG! NAG!

When she came home she'd have to be fed and cared for. *And who was going to do that?* Not he! He had guns to clean, places to go and people to meet. His dad could do it. The old man still had his health. He could climb the stairs, carry the soup, help her sit up and bring the spoon to her lips.

Well hell, she could feed herself!

The bathroom business, now that would be hard for a while. They'd been through this before. But she wasn't getting any younger.

He'd brought flowers to the hospital, a purple and pink bouquet from the Getwell Shop with a card covered in violets, Beloved Mother, and set the vase on the table next to her bed, but his dad had moved the vase, saying, she can't- there's not room there- put them on the window ledge. Well she can't smell them from there, he'd replied, and not in an angry tone, but his dad had snapped back, who needs to smell them, she can see them, and where do you think she will set her tissues and water glass and pills if you put them there? They'll get knocked over. Well what the hell do you want me to do with them? I said put them on the window ledge! Well if I put them on the window-ledge, then when the nurse comes to lift the shade, she'll knock them over! Well put them on the TV then! Well what if they get tipped over and spill into the set? Well put them wherever the heck you want, but don't put them there! He and his dad fought endlessly.

Mother's broken her hip again, he'd say to his friends in Dinah's Diner, and they'd send their get-well-soons, and she'd heal again, but until then, it was dangerous to be in the house with just his dad. Try as he might to hold his temper, there was just so much he could take. JUST SO MUCH. Some days he'd like to kill the old man, put his hands round his neck and be done with it.

One day the red-headed girl in the corner of Jimmy's room

made herself visible. She stepped from the wall, held out her hand and smiled at Jimmy. Jimmy wondered what *a girl* was doing in his room. As far as Jimmy knew, no girl had ever stepped into his majestic abode with the purple-painted walls and the accurately depicted solar system, but he took her hand, and of course could not take it. His hand slipped through hers and they were face-to-face. The girl gave off the scent of mock-orange blossoms and licorice. Jimmy hadn't smelled anything in ages. *Not since the pain back at Bluewinds, the smoke and the cinnamon.*

The redhead danced around Jimmy, smiling, a soft rise in her lips. As she circled, she gestured without words. Jimmy watched her hands move up, down, one across the other, circling, forming triangles, right-angles, half-circles, her fingers crossing and uncrossing, her hands bending and unbending in some finger-play, and Jimmy began to understand; the girl was telling him that not only could they play many interesting games together, board games, or card games, or any other form of amusement, but that these games would be unlike any Jimmy had ever played.

This turned out to be true. In the endless days that followed, Jimmy and the redhead sat on his bed with an imaginary gameboard between them. On Jimmy's move, the game, bed, girl, and Jimmy were suddenly on an African plain as a herd of elephants approached. Before the flapping ears of the bull shaded them, the girl moved her piece and they'd shift to a Siberian snowstorm, their pieces blown to whiteness, then they were under the blue glow of a snow-dome, then on Mars as the stars spun them into thin comet-lines, then back to Jimmy's bed with a plateful of cookies.

With each game there was a lesson. Whether cards, finger-games or rolls of the dice, Jimmy and the redhead taught each other tricks and factoids from their fields of expertise. Jimmy taught the girl how the angle of a dragonfly wing allowed it to hover and dip. The girl taught Jimmy how to ball your anger up into a hard black-nothing hot enough to melt through the center of planet Earth. Then the two shrunk down into seahorses and swam in a coral sea.

THE SAD PLACE

Two-Tone was in the parking lot again. Becky had heard through the grapevine that he was newly released from Blue Winds Workhouse for petty theft. *HOW COOL WAS THAT? A convict for a boyfriend! That was the coolest!*

But no matter how cool the guy, or how cool his car, or how much fire-water she drank, her brother still haunted her dreams. In some, Billy was tall, sober-faced, about to turn fourteen. In others he was a bunny in her hand, and she could feel the walnut-sized thrum of his heart, or he was a freak and made faces at her with engorged lips as he squatted on a midnight fence behind the Midway trailers, his teeth fangs, his mouth slobbering, one of the undead.

Dear Diary, hello! Two-Tone REALLY LUVS ME!!! He burned my name on his arm with a hot pin, yeah.

Dear Diary, Two-Tone is a nose drippin freak if you know what I mean.

Dear Diary, Me an Two-Tone gonna rob that Tom Thumb on 119. Like Bonny an Clyde. Yeah. Just need inconspickyuous getaway car. His Opal Cadet is way too conspickyous.

Dear Diary plus he has a WEAPON so yeah!!! Mark yer calander...

His mother did not come home. While at Brownmound Mercy she'd had one stroke after another, and was paralyzed, and could not feed herself. They fed her through a blue tube taped to her arm but she tore the tube out. They put the tube back in. She tore the tube out. The put it back in, again and again. Finally they left the tube out.

There was that science fiction horror film he'd taken his nieces and nephews to years before, THE THING FROM BEYOND MARS, about a flying saucer in a cornfield. Though the movie was terrifying, the girls held in their screams, bit their lips and squeezed each other's arms, and the boys set their teeth when the monster from outer space, with a suction tube for a mouth, sucked the life from its innocent victims and left shriveled shells for their loved ones to discover. That was his mother, a shriveled shell. At each hospital visit she was smaller in her bed. The woman who'd sat at her vanity each morning and did facial exercises, powdered her cheeks, dressed in fresh-pressed suit-dresses and ruled the house with finesse, was gone. That thing in her place, with the straggling hair, gray skin and round, frightened eyes-

That THING was not his mother!

Then the thing was gone. His nieces and nephews came for the funeral, and his sister and cousins, the whole town came. The church filled up. He sat, close-mouthed, by his father. Just a half hour before, they'd argued over his shirt and his tie and the breakfast dishes, but during the service he sat quietly.

And as the pastor spoke, and as the hymns were sung, *Blanket Me in Your Love Everlasting, Lord of All Above & Below, May We Rest in Your Arms Eternal,* and as the memories were shared at the luncheon after, he felt as if he were in a dream. The people he'd known all his life surrounded him. They gave him their hands and their smiles, their wrinkles lifted, their eyes watered, they patted his back, touched his arm, cuffed his chin. Everywhere he turned there was a cup, plate of food and a word of comfort. The voices filled the church basement with CHATTER! CHATTER! CHATTER!

They might as well be a garden full of songbirds!

And no one was throwing him a life line. He would have to find that for himself. He used a napkin to wipe his mouth as he imagined what adventures he'd have, what protracted privacy, when he finally purchased the camper-trailer of his dreams...

Then his father became sick. There was hardly time to get the relatives out of the house. The funeral casseroles, jellos and chicken salads still filled the Frigidaire when his father came down with a disease of the blood. A painful one, the cousin's wife said. It'll torture his sleep, wait and see, this will be slow hell every step of the way, and he's going to end up on the morphine.

Well *HE* was not going to take care of him! His father could take care of himself! He was not going to listen to him whining in his sleep. The babbling, the wasted tears! He would be out in his trailer, getting some peace and quiet! And planning his upcoming road trips.

Billy had been working on his gymnastics. There was the gymnastics of moving and the gymnastics of holding still. Moving was easy; holding still was not. Billy worked on hovering in one place, but instead he jerked right, left, spun a circle and ended up in the closet again, in his mother's congested chest, or next to Becky's salivary gland, or by his cheating dad's ear.

Billy didn't stick just to family. He also hovered, a ball of energy, beside a stranger's cheeks, then zipped away inadvertently, as if flipped by a magnet, attracted, repelled.

The way to hold still, Billy found, was to get in some sad person's chest. All he had to do was tuck his so-to-speak chin and think, *I'M LOST! CAN'T GET BACK TO MY MOM! SHE THINKS I'M DEAD!*

Then he was sucked into a sad person's chest. They were all over the place, THE SAD FOLKS. Billy loved the black-pudding of their hearts, and the heavier feeling when they drank to the bottom of the bottle, or ate through a package of Oreos, or put a needle in their vein and spun backwards.

The sad people were a long slow delight. Billy found he could float at heart level and fly through shopping centers, ball games and church services and get tugged into a sad chest. Then he'd worm in, like the fat, maggot-colored caterpillars he'd dug up from Turd's garden. Once in, Billy didn't try to make the sad people happier. *No reason for that! You can't hold still inside a happy person! You just get bounced out!*

He burrowed into sadness, stretched out, made himself at home. Billy found if he punched against the edges, the people sobbed! Sob! Sob!

HA! HA!

With each of his punches from within came that wondrous, uncontrollable sobbing! Or he'd lean back and kick, both feet at once, or alternate, kick, kick, and they'd sob harder, fall to their knees at the edge of a bed, couch or pew, put their heads down, close their eyes and pass out with grief.

There was low music at the bottom of their sobs, like the slow speed for the record player. *Oooh Myyy Goddd Whyyy? Why take my only son? Only son, only daughter, only chance at blah-blah-blah.*

Sadness was everywhere. It snagged Billy even when he wasn't looking. He could be sailing through a crowd at the state fair, those crowds never changed, the years packed them in thick, the same kaleidoscope of fools, and before Billy knew it, he'd be tugged back and nested in some poor sucker's broken heart.

"Oh, I lost my gal! Oh, I lost my keys! Oh, I lost my only chance at happiness!"

Smiling Man sat in his trailer smoking. He didn't see the yard beyond the window. His eyes were on the plaid drapes. He didn't smile much anymore, just when the waitress took his order, or on visits to his nieces and nephews. Just a quick grin, then his lips fell back over his teeth and his face fell back into sourness, as if whatever was in front of him, coffee cup, fried egg or newspaper, elicited repulsion.

Billy could feel the thickening inside Smiling Man's chest, the crusting-over, sadness into grief, grief into bitterness, bitterness into whatever the word was for a river stopped running.

Sludge. A river of sludge.

The Man kept distracted with his river of guns, river of books, river of greasy meals and pleasures-of-the-moment, but there was an dissolvable muck-bed in his ribs, and that was where Billy chose to sit.

LIVING DANGEROUSLY

Becky heard her mother fall. At the sound she dropped the tip jar.

BLASH!

The coins cascaded to her bedroom floor and the jar cracked into lethal pieces. There among the coins was that half-dollar bill from that night so long ago. Becky reached for the half-bill and cut her palm on a jagged spear. She pulled the shard out, ran to the bathroom, grabbed a cloth from the rag drawer and wrapped her hand.

The pink seersucker quickly reddened as Becky hurried to the front hall closet. Her mother lay in a pool of vomit. Becky spoke her name, tapped her cheek and nudged her leg. "Mom? Mom!"

Mrs. Bell did not wake.

Dammit! This is it!

Becky ran to the bathroom and returned with a wet washcloth. The front hall closet stank of farts, Kools and beer.

An' now vomit. Mom! I'm not gonna clean up after you anymore, Mom, Becky thought as she washed up her mother, sponged the vomit and held her head in her lap. When Mrs. Bell woke moaning for beer, Becky gave her sips of water instead, then spoonfuls of chicken broth, then dragged her into the master bed that Mrs. Bell hadn't slept in since Billy disappeared.

While her mother moaned, Becky ran a hot bath. As the tub filled, she went to her room, carefully plucked up the old half-bill, now stained with her blood, and fingered the torn edge.

Some things you don't forget: her sore throat from calling for Billy, the feel of his fingers breaking her grip, the colored lights, the screaming crowd...

She shook the dollar.

Well dammit, I still have this! An' where are you, Butt-face? Oh I know right where you are. You're in my dreams every night, Butt-face Billy.

At the wedding reception of her dreams, Billy stood off to the side in a powder-blue tux, hands in pockets, tall and smiling. She lost sight of him as she was carried off in the drunken circle of dancing. Then he was sneering over her as she lay in the cornfield in a shallow pool of muddy water, then stood amidst wafting butterflies in the shade of a dappling maple. Then he was grown up.

An' how old would he be?

Every year the same question. Now Billy would be *how old? Now fourteen, now fifteen, now sixteen with hairs poppin' out, an' his voice crackin', an' girls hangin' on him. An drivin'! Billy drivin'! That's a laugh! An' now eighteen...*

Then the grown-up Billy in the powder blue tux at the wedding reception of her dreams would bow, and when he stood up his skin would split starting at the boat-shaped scar on his cheek and ripping down to his feet, then the skinny kid with the mustard smear on his chin would step from the skin, kick it behind, put his hands on his hips and sneer, "Hey Bitchster, what the hell you been up to?"

What the hell I been up to!? How the hell do you shape the memory of a person who isn't there to fill up the hole he left? You can't go back an' find your missing brother. Or unhit him.

Booze helped. Pills helped. Living dangerously helped. Two-Tone was serving time for waving a gun around at that Tom Thumb. He'd be out soon with good behavior...*an' then what?*

Becky remembered that moment in the getaway car, as she'd sat staring at the dash as Two-Tone stood waving the gun at the cashier. She could see him through the plate glass, jerkily waving, his face scared, mouth drawn. She could read his lips: THIS IS A STICK UP!

Then she heard the unmistakable voice of her baby brother. *BITCHSTER! TURN THE KEY. START THE CAR. DRIVE*

THE HELL AWAY!

She'd listened to the Billy-voice, turned the key and drove the hell away. She'd left Two-Tone with no getaway car and the cops had shackled his hands and now he was incarcerated in Redtail County Workhouse.

But Two-Tone's death threats got out somehow, the crumpled yellow papers in the mailbox:

FICKIN BITCH!
YOU SINT ME DOWN THE RIVER!
I'LL KILL YOU GOOD WHEN I GIT OUT!

THE STONE PRINCE

The Shopping Boy leaned against the brick wall by Montgomery Wards. On his lean legs were tight jeans, on his slim torso a white sweater, and underneath, a shirt of pure crimson.

Billy saw the red triangles against the snowy white, and saw that Shopping Boy was older, and one of those boys who liked boys.

Smiling Man stood near Hank's Hardware. He was very sick by this time, not only spitting gobs of blood into the toilet back home, but also filling the bowl with shiny red pools. But his sickness didn't stop him from shopping. He still had the strength to drive into West Brownmound with a walletfull of bills and that hunger.

Billy felt the Man harden as he honed in on the boy, his skin tightening, chin dropping. Smiling Man rubbed his hand over the back of his head, cleared his throat and stepped forward. There were fifty paces between him and the Shopping Boy.

In those fifty paces Billy could read the whole story.

Smiling Man will say HEY YOU. Shopping Boy will ignore him. Smiling Man will ask, WHAT'S YOUR NAME, then give a deeper grin, a nod of the chin. This boy was hungry. He might take money. He might be good for a quick spin then goodbye. Or he might go under.

Smiling Man was thirty paces away. Shopping Boy bent forward. Billy saw what was coming next, the man-sweat, the tidal wave of rage that always came when Smiling Man got too close to a boy's fresh pain.

Twenty paces...

Billy knew what the soul would feel like slipping from the body, then the drag as the body tugged back and the burst through chiming layers. This boy's life would end, Billy guessed, before sunset.

Ten an' closing...

But there was a girl in the way. A redhead. From the sheen of Brownmound Mall she stepped forward.

In a dumb plaid dress. An' kitty-cat glasses. An' pushin' a stroller.

On the handle of the stroller were little colored wooden balls for a baby to play with. Only there was no baby in that stroller.

An' no kid. Not even a dumb doll.

The redhead pushed the stroller straight toward Billy.

She sees me! She must be in the Triple X Dimension!

She gestured: *get in!*

Me? In that stroller? No way!

Billy would never get in a stroller! And never do what a girl ordered! But this girl wavered close with her kitty-cat glasses and pale face, then formed her lips in a soft grin, and began to move her hands in hypnotizing shapes.

Beyond her wavering hands, Billy spotted the Jimmy by Blackthorn Bookstore.

What's the Egghead doin' here?

Jimmy made a brain hiss at Billy: *Do what she says!*

Billy hissed back: *No way!*

Jimmy: *She knows what she's doing!*

Billy: *No way in a rat's ass!*

But he felt his resistance slip as the girl's hands wavered into shapes, birds, dinosaurs, flying bats-

An' that smile! It could charm a snake from its venom!

Billy got in.

His ghost hands went for the stroller's hand-hold, but his hands went right through, of course. Then the redhead put her face close to him and whispered. And what she whispered was *a million times worse* than getting in a stroller.

Call me Mom, she said. *Call me Mom.*

That went against everything Billy believed in!

But the Jimmy nodded: *She knows what she's doing.*

In spite of himself Billy opened his mouth and said *Mom-*

Smiling Man closed in, four paces from Shopping Boy-

Mom, Mom-

The girl slowed time as she replied. *Yes, I am your pretend mom! And I'm Queen of this Shopping Senter! And you are my own baby Prince. You are my baby Prince made of stone. Your legs are stone, your arms are stone, your whole body is stone. You are SOLID STONE! And here we go!* The girl ran head-on towards the Smiling Man.

Now KICK, Stone Prince, KICK! Hard as you can!

Billy was happy to kick, though he knew his foot would go nowhere, it never did in that Triple-X Dimension. Billy shot his legs out anyway, both feet aimed at Smiling Man. As the Man opened his mouth, nodded at Shopping Boy and said, "HEY YOU," Billy's feet connected with that belly.

HOUSTON WE HAVE CONTACT!

A gob of blood flew from Smiling Man's mouth and landed at the feet of Shopping Boy.

Splat.

Shopping Boy looked down at the shimmering, shivering garnet-red blob, then up at Smiling Man. Then turned and ran. Shopping Boy ran past the Dress Barn, the Red Owl, Sears & Roebuck, Sleep-Land and Young Quinlan's and Ken's Keys, all the way to the exit and out into the bright autumn afternoon.

SAFE!

Part Three

MY ROAD TRIP

SOMETHING SOFT AND SQUISHY

Now back to me, Cat, with the black mark on my soul and my puny life in White Rock and my unkissed lips. Most mornings I woke up in my flowered sheets with Marshmallow purring on me and my Edgar Allen Poe paperback facedown by the empty bowl with the sticky glaze of last night's vanilla ice cream. But one morning after Dad and Uncle Ned got tangled up like plastic monsters, I woke up down by the lake in the gray before sunrise. No birds sang, no fish leapt, the mist rose like ghosts over the water and *something* was touching my back.

Or *someone*.

I reached back to feel, felt cloth over flesh and rolled over to look. It was a man lying face-away and he was cool to the touch. I couldn't see any hole on him, no gaping wound or gushing blood, but I knew he was dead, and I killed him. I couldn't see his face, *didn't want to*, he was just some stranger I killed in my sleep, and I had to get rid of his body before the sun rose and threw diamonds on the water and the Andersons came out for their morning coffee.

How do you get rid of a body? Chop it up? Burn it? Bury it? I was in a suburb full of sleeping people. The burning smell would wake them. I'd need a large amount of flammable liquid, lighter fluid or kerosene. There was the lake. I could weigh the body down and sink it deep. But we swam every day. I didn't want some corpse rotting in the muck and pieces popping up.

The Johnsons were away on vacation. *I could cut the body up and stuff it in the Johnson's trash.* Up the hill I went, making footprints in the dew. I opened the sliding glass door. *Shh! Mom would be up soon to turn on the percolator, Dad up soon to shave.* I crept to the backdoor closet, found the trash bags by the Cream of Mushroom Soup and Kosher Dill Pickles, slid a bag out, stepped into the garage, the cement floor cool on my feet, and felt atop the greasy tool cabinet for Dad's old saw. *There it was, rusty and dull, but it would have to do.*

Down the hill I went in my own footprints, grabbed a wrist and started slicing away. It's hard to cut up a body. I struggled through skin, muscle, bone. The body heaved. My shoulder ached. Finally I got an arm off. The inner cartilage of the joint was untouched, perfectly smooth, like inside Gram's conch shell on the glass shelf in the yellow house.

I started on the other shoulder. Sweat dripped in my eyes. A mosquito landed on my cheek. Another on my neck. *Shoo!* One bit me. I dropped the arm.

Shit! I saw his face!

This guy was no stranger. There was something familiar about him. *Was he a neighbor? A relative? A teacher? No, just some blank-face I killed in my sleep.* And touching him felt like touching yourself when you're dead or touching someone else who didn't feel dead yet, like Dad didn't feel dead in his hospital bed.

And some things are hard to kill, like when Jill and I smeared dirt on our faces, took Dad's razor blade and went into Dead End Woods with a mission: KILL A WILD ANIMAL, COOK IT OVER A FIRE AND RIP IT APART WITH OUR BARE TEETH LIKE NEANDERTHALS!

Jill was off getting firewood when I quick-pinned a garter snake, touched the blade to its back then screamed and flung the snake into a dead tree. That snake hung up there like a lost sock, too high to reach. I screamed the instant my blade touched the snake's skin, it was my own skin I was cutting into. The snake and I were one, and I couldn't kill my own self.

But in the dream I do kill. If you have, you know the feeling, the boulder in your gut, the copper taste at the back of your throat, the guilt that won't go away. So I hid the corpse.

Sometimes in Mom's tulip bed, sometimes down by the lake, sometimes in the Johnson's trash, then hoped that no one noticed, hoped the garbage men came before the head started to stink, hoped the Anderson's dog didn't dig up a foot, hoped Mom didn't find a hand in her tulip bulbs.

But I knew I'd be found out. Someday. Someday other people would live in our house, and new kids would play down at the lake, find a toe bone, and run up the hill screaming, "Mom look what we found!" And the mom would wash the bone and leave it on the windowsill over the sink, and years later they'd have the police chief over for dinner, and he'd dump his martini ice in the kitchen sink, see the bone and say, "Where'd you get this?" And the mom would say, "Oh, that's just a turtle bone the kids found down at the lake," and he'd say, "No ma'am, this is HUMAN!" And they'd trace the bone back to me, find me GUILTY and throw me in prison FOR LIFE. The question was, when caught, would I come clean and confess, or lie, to save my own skin?

Then I'd wake up in my flowered sheets with Marshmallow purring on me, *so relieved! It was just a dream!*

But I did kill. Somewhere. Somehow. I just didn't know who, how or when. And the morning after my seventeenth birthday, it was not a dream. That morning I woke up down by the lake with the mist rising, covered in mosquito bites. And a black plastic trash bag beside me filled with something soft and squishy.

So I hit the road for Iowa, headed for the yellow house.

I love road trips. I love how the corn flies by and how the wind tears through the wing vents, tearing the thoughts from your head so you get one last look at your thoughts before they go sailing over the cornfields. *BYE-BYE THOUGHTS!*

And I loved how my hands felt on the wheel and my eyes

flicked between the road ahead lined with thrashing foxtail and red clover back to the purple-black storm clouds in the rear view mirror then to the passenger seat where my dead sister sat all dolled up like she was for her funeral.

I loved how the sun shimmered off Rosy Sue's gold mini dress like sunrise off the lake and how her arm disappeared in the light then reappeared in the shadow, and how her ghost-smoke curled up then, snapped out the wing vent, *whoosh*, and when the clouds blew across, I got glimpses of her eyelashes and penciled-in mole, and when the clouds cleared I could see my Tareytons, black licorice and the Iowa map on the passenger seat. Then I thought, *Rosy Sue's not here! She's buried back in White Rock! I drew eyelashes on her sewed-shut lids!* But I felt the excitement like when she was around, that scared feeling in my gut, wondering, *what crazy secret will Rosy Sue tell next? What crazy tale will she tell next? What trouble will she get us in next?*

I didn't invite her on that trip. She just showed up in the bathroom mirror that morning. I took the washcloth from my eyes and there she was, whispering, *there's nothing left for you to do Cat, but kill yourself.*

Yeah right. Ghosts aren't real. They're make-believe, like sparkly shoeboxes, Frankenstein monsters and UFOs. I threw my washcloth at the mirror. But she followed me down to the lake, hissing *don't look in that garbage bag. Might be body parts in that.*

I ran up to the house. No one was home. Mom was at some Quilting thing, Holly was moved out and Dad dead, and the whole house so quiet I could hear all my self-hate whispering, *STUPID CAT! UGLY CAT! YOU ARE A DOG WITH NO ONE TO LOVE YOU!*

So I took Mom's tomato knife and raked my wrist. Then swallowed a handful of Dad's Tums. Then rubber-banded a bread bag over my head, then tried to drown myself. But the knife was too dull and I coughed up the pills and something would not let me die, so I weighted the trash bag with a cement block without looking in first to see who I killed in my sleep, sunk it deep, stuffed my army surplus backpack with travel stuff, grabbed my sleeping bag, swept Dad's silver Liberty dollars from his dresser, found the Iowa roadmap and out the door I went.

The Dodge was parked in the garage and Rosy Sue was in it. As I pulled out she whispered, *don't* and a spider on the rear view of Ned's old Blazer curled up and died, and when I drove past the Anderson's mailbox, she whispered *stop* and a moth by Mrs. Anderson's petunias curled up and died, and after my Mini-Mart stop for cigarettes which the pimple kid did sell me, she hissed *you'll regret this* and a sparrow dropped to the parking lot.

My friend Jill told me once down in our rec room with the lights off and a flashlight on her face all her fake-facts about ghosts. Jill said ghosts can only move stuff that once belonged to them, like old jewelry boxes, dolls or scarves, and that when a dog or cat gets hit by a car their ghost just keeps running, because they don't know they're dead, and when a ghost shows up in your house, you feel the hairs go up on your neck or get a ringing in your ear. And Jill told me what it takes for a ghost to speak. She said it takes the energy of small living things. That every time a ghost speaks something somewhere falls down dead. *Yeah right.*

As we neared the Iowa border my dead sister wasn't talking, but I could tell what she was thinking, because she taught me everything I know, how to soft boil an egg so the yolk is creamy and the white rubbery, how to sweep a floor in small strokes, how to walk and talk like a lady, *well she tried,* how to read a poem out loud in a rhythm that gets in your belly so you can return to the rhythm every time you read the poem or say the poem or think the poem, so the same rhythm carries you through like a ballroom dance, and how to read between the lines to get at the story behind the story, what's buried between what a person says and doesn't say, how they cross their legs, press their lips, tilt their chins, even old photos, who's smiling, who's not, like Mom and Uncle Ned as kids in Gram's garden, Ned smiling in a sailor shirt and wool britches, Mom standing behind with stormclouds in her eyes and a string of pearls round her turkey neck. Like Rosy Sue said, you have to read between the lines especially when your Dad has a temper like lightening that could strike any moment and crack your world apart.

So I knew what Rosy Sue was thinking by how she tilted her chin, blew smoke through her nose, snuck a peek at me then turned back to the corn as if she'd never speak to me again. Body language. She was thinking *Cat you stole this car! Cat you stole Dad's silver dollars! And you're driving illegally! Dad would be so upset! And you're about to BRING SHAME ON THE FAMILY!*

I didn't steal that car. I borrowed it. And I wasn't driving illegally. I had my Learner's Permit. And Rosy Sue was my ghost chaperone. And I wasn't trying to BRING SHAME on the family. I was going to RULE OUT the possibility of Uncle Ned being a kid-killer.

And I wasn't trying to upset Dad. I loved Dad, even if he was dead. I didn't want to squeeze Dad's throat as he sat at the head of the dining room table and I didn't want to squish Dad's face till his eyes popped out and I didn't want to shake Dad till his guts shook out and break his jaw like mine needed to be broken if I was ever going to open my mouth and speak. And I knew he would want me to have those silver Liberty dollars. For gas money.

The storm was catching up. The clouds in the rear view were packed thick like the blood in the woodticks I pulled from Rosy Sue's boyfriend's dogs up in Black Oak, ticks stretched pearly gray, and so hard-shelled, I had to use a utility knife to cut them open, and out came this thick paste, blood condensed into a black pudding.

We'd just crossed the border.

WELCOME TO IOWA!
HOME OF THE JUMBO CORN!

I pulled off at the IOWA WELCOME CENTER. Three big rigs were parked with their engines running. A jumbo family piled out of a station wagon ahead of me, plucking their jumbo shorts from their jumbo buns and tugging their jumbo tees over their jumbo bellies. I let them get ahead of me and looked up at the jumbo clouds about to burst. Rumble-rumble.

As I washed my hands in the Ladies' Room, I glanced up at the girl in the mirror. Strawberry shag, green eyes and a lime-green gingham-check blouse with white collar and cuffs.

Me, me.

After the Ladies' Room, I sat atop a picnic table and lit a cig. Sparrows chattered. Three layers of bruise-blue clouds bulged in. Daylight dimmed. Gnats bit my ankles. The sparrows stopped chattering. The sun peeked through a crack. There was one woodle-woo of a redwing blackbird. The temperature dropped. The wind rose. A Burger Chef wrapper lifted. A Three Musketeers wrapper cartwheeled. The trees showed their silver undersides. The sky rumbled. Rain poured! The Jumbo family ran from the Welcome Center with free magazines held like tents over their heads. The big rigs rolled back on the freeway.

Better hit the road too.

But I didn't move. This wasn't the big storm. The big storm hadn't come yet. This was just a little rain and thunder. Rain sizzled my cigarette, rain pelted my face, rain hid the Welcome Center behind sheets of gray and secrets grew on secrets, one inside the other, with no way to tear one from the other without tearing the whole thing apart.

I should have just killed myself back in White Rock, I thought, because there was no hope for me and David White. *David White!* I'd given up hope on Kirk King in my Social Studies Class, but, oh, *David White! David White in my Summer School Chemistry Class! David White with his gray eyes, dark hair and pale, bulging forehead like Edgar Allen Poe's. David White's jeans sagging from his butt as he walked to the backboard for a chemistry equation!* That summer I thought David White could be mine. I thought I could get a date with David White. Ha. Right. A DATE WITH DAVID WHITE.

Why do they call it a date? *We dated. She dated. They dated. Who's dating who?* I get it. They call it a date because it's a plan on your calendar on a specific DATE. On this day, in the near future, I am spending this time with YOU, because you are special enough for a marked-off calendar date. Guess a black-marked freak like me was not special enough for a mark on anyone's calendar.

And the day before NO ONE said HAPPY BIRTHDAY. Yes, Cat we love you and yes Cat we need you and will throw you a big surprise party with all the coolest kids from White Rock, and yes even the new boy with the Edgar Allen Poe forehead and your best friend Jill and all your fantasies of David White reaching out and touching your nipple with his fingertips and heating up your magical place with pleasures-to-be will come true. But NO he did not come and NO she did not come and NO they did not come. Who came? No one. Not even a card to say HAPPY BIRTHDAY.

I did not effing care. Alone or not, forgotten or not, kissed or not, that night before my road trip, I threw myself one HELL of a party. I found a half-smoked roach in my closet, a half bottle of Boone's Farm Green Apple wine below Dad's liquor cabinet and three dollars and fifty-two cents of babysitting money in my third drawer down, then walked to the Mini-Mart and bought Pizza-Spins, Cheez Whiz and Black Twisters, set the snacks in front of the TV in a sunburst and watched Johnny Carson.

After the Tonight Show I went into the dining room, turned off the lights, parted the curtains and looked across to where David White's car was parked to see if I could see the Jill-and-David-White-French-Kissing Silhouettes. They were in there somewhere, tongue-kissing like maniacs, his hand on her dumb breast. Not my breast.

Then I looked at the blank spots in our house, the empty hangers in the front hall closet where Holly's coats used to hang, the empty chair in the living room where Dad used to sit, the blank spots on the walls where Rosy Sue's glittery shoeboxes had hung. Then I went down to the basement. Alone. Down, down.

I was NOT afraid of sleeping monsters in the laundry room skirt-box and NOT afraid of long-armed hairies behind the furnace and NOT afraid of the old lady in the mirror. I stared into Holly's old room. Empty. Her bed, dresser, desk, gone. One balled-up tissue on the floor. I imagined all my sisters sleeping down there, and heard the whispers from all those years of giggling, secrets and dressing up, and smelled the period blood, lipstick and Final Net Hairspray. Then I turned on the light and wondered, *what am I going to do with this room? Paint it?*

But I wasn't scared. And wasn't afraid to go back up and touch the back of Dad's chair and say, hi Dad, I know you're not there. Maybe there are lingering wisps like nylons draped over a chair or feelings stuck in an undusted corner, but not REAL DEAD PEOPLE staring at you. Not solids with the power to move objects or do harm. Ghosts aren't scientifically possible.

And I wasn't scared of Dad's shadow and wasn't scared of Dad's cough and wasn't scared of his avocado-green easy chair creaking back as he stretched out his legs because *dead is dead*. But I wasn't ready for sleeping in the basement yet. So I slept in my own room with my ice cream and Edgar Allen Poe and Marshmallow purring on me.

Then I woke up down at the lake in my underwear and t-shirt, in the gray before sunrise, with the mist rising like ghosts over the water and my arms and legs covered in mosquito bites, right beside that black plastic trashbag. I was wide awake. And not stupid. I'd read books. Freud and Jung. I knew about GUILT. I knew where GUILT came from. GUILT came from WRONGDOING. And I knew where guilt went when someone did WRONG but feels no remorse. Guilt doesn't just disappear. Guilt doesn't dissolve like the morning mist. Guilt is heavy. It stays around the house and seeps down through the family.

I was the baby. The last in line. There was nowhere for the guilt to go but me. That's why I couldn't get kissed. I was stuck with guilt that wasn't mine. So I MADE UP MY MIND.

Because if a person could sleep-walk down to the lake, stuff something into a Hefty bag and sleep on the sand all night covered in mosquito bites, then a person could sleep-kill the whole neighborhood. I could wake up beside ten Hefty bags of body parts. *Was this foot Mrs. Johnson's? Was that hand Mr. Anderson's? Was that part of Jill's bratty brothers'?*

I thought before I sacked all of White Rock, I'd better pull my head out of my ass and head to the yellow house to see if what Rosy Sue said about Ned was true.

TURN BACK, LAST CHANCE!

The downpour outside the Welcome Center had stopped. It was just drizzling. Everything was shiny, cars, asphalt, trees. I climbed down from the picnic table, tossed my cig in the *DON'T BE A LITTERBUG* trashcan and headed back in. A skinny girl skipped out followed by her older sister. They lifted their palms to the sky, opened their mouths and stuck out their tongues.

In the Ladies' Room I checked under the stalls, peeled off my cut-offs and checkered blouse, pressed all the fans on and felt the hot air on me like Rosy Sue's belly on mine that night she told me her secret.

When I returned to the Dodge Dart, Rosy Sue was still there, along with a trapped fly buzzing at the windshield.

Bzzt.

I rolled down the windows and hit the road. Back on the interstate, Rosy Sue wiggled her fingers and said *so you really want to know Cat? How it felt? When I got my cherry popped?* The fly dropped dead to the dash. I didn't answer her, because she was just a fake ghost, but yes I wanted to know. Ever since I learned Rosy Sue's boldface lie was true, I'd wanted to crawl into the head of that little girl in her plaid hand-me-down and kitty-cat glasses who said *call me mom* as she pushed me to Sunnyvale. *How did she feel after Mark broke her open? How did that turn her world upside down?* Her hands at the supper table, her laughing with visiting relatives...

The fields glistened, the wing vents sang and the windshield wipers hummed along with Rosy Sue as she said *what do you want me to say about it Cat? Do you want me to say that it felt great when I got my cherry popped? Do you want me to say it felt groovy? Do you want me to say it felt like I was finally noticed, finally seen, finally crowned Queen of the Universe? Is that what you want me to say?*

She took a long drag, looked out at the corn and back at me, saying *or do you want me to say that it hurt? And I cried? And was scared? And had no idea what was happening to me! And I ached from our damned brother. And his damned prick made me bleed. And it stank sliding out of me and I couldn't get my breath, and they told me lie still and never tell OR ELSE. Is that what you want me to say?*

And do you want me to say it changed my life forever? That from that moment on nothing was ever the same? Never the same at the supper table, never the same folding my hands, never the same laughing with relatives?

Or do you want me to say that when I became a teenager I had to erase it with boy after boy, fuck after fuck and date after date of maniac fucking like trick birthday candles that never blow out because every time I parted my legs it reminded me of my damn brother?

Well I'm not going to say any of that. Because you can't know how I felt. You can never know. No one can. Only I know. And it's none of your business. Not yours or any of the other sisters! IT'S MINE! It happened to me, not you. It's nothing to do with you! Or with Uncle Ned.

So listen up. Before it's too late. Stop while you still can. Go home. Dead is dead. Past is past. Done is done. Don't open a can of worms. Don't air our dirty laundry. Let sleeping dogs lie. Turn back Cat! Right now! Last chance!

Then schwoook!

Rosy Sue got sucked out the wing vent.

FRUITS OF THE LOOM

Bye-bye, Rosy Sue!

She wasn't real anyway. A real ghost wouldn't come back from the grave to shut you up. A real ghost would come back for the truth to be told. A real ghost would come back for the culprit to be found. A real ghost would come dragging their bones or pressing their face in the window or crawling up over the foot of your bed covered in pond-muck, ashes and dissolving flesh to tell you WHAT REALLY HAPPENED.

Then CLACK the glove-box fell open. I leaned over and pushed the box shut. CLACK it fell open. I pushed it shut. Clack it fell open and my list fell out. Oh yes I had a list. Of the where, when and who. I couldn't grab it then without taking my hands from the wheel, but I had that list memorized.

1. October 31 1974, Jack is taken by masked man.

2. Thanksgiving 1974 Rosy Sue says Ned took Jack.

3. One hour later she says it was Jack's fault.

4. The Wanted Poster looks just like Ned.

5. Rosy Sue says drop it.

6. Next summer she dies.

7. After her funeral I learn her cherry secret is true.

8. After Ned dies, we find his nasty stuff.

We sisters all rode together to Ned's funeral. The brothers didn't come. It was just us girls, Little Mary and Mom packed in Anne's van. We sang songs off-key, pulled red licorice through our teeth, mooned the cars behind us and got to Pearl Pond Methodist just in time.

The crowd was already gathered, the relatives and townfolk, and after the Hymn of Forgiveness, people shifted in their seats, opened their programs and looked up. Mom was first to speak.

I wasn't really listening when she adjusted her glasses and said, "We were very young, and I'd never seen a real balloon before, just a picture of a balloon in a book, then the fair came to town and Ned and I each got a balloon on a stick. Mine was pink, his was blue. My balloon bobbed along like a new friend. Then it caught on a shrub and burst. I didn't know a balloon could pop. I thought it had died, and I cried and cried. Ned said, 'don't cry sister, you can have my balloon.' And he gave me his balloon. He was the little brother. I was the big sister. He didn't have to do that."

Mom adjusted her glasses and returned to her seat dry-eyed.

There were sniffles from the pews. I wasn't crying. I was remembering the other yellow house funerals. During Gramp's funeral, this picture of Gramps came into my head, not of Gramp's nut-brown hands that could fix any broken thing, or his chuckling mouth that calmed us girls when we cried, or his lap where he nibbled our earlobes and made us giggle. Instead I got a picture of this dark pink sac, this fleshy sac, this old-man sac shifting in my hands, but there was no way I could remember that, because it never happened.

Next up was my second cousin Little Arnie who lived across the road from the yellow house. Arnie stepped up to the pulpit and disappeared except for the top of his white-blonde head. Then started to talk, but so quietly we couldn't hear. There were giggles from the pews. His mom Beth whispered, "Arnie peek around." His sister Trisha whispered, "Arnie peek around." Somebody said get him a chair. Finally Trisha got him a chair. When Little Arnie stood on it, we could see his face, but he was still too quiet. Finally Trisha shouted, "LOUDER ARNIE!"

Then Arnie shouted. "NED WAS A GOOD HUNTER! NED WAS A GOOD MARKSMAN! NED WAS A GOOD UNCLE! NED TAUGHT ME HOW TO SHOOT! NED TAUGHT ME HOW TO HUNT! AND UNCLE NED! WAS MY! BEST! FRIEND!"

As Arnie went back to his seat everyone was crying. Except me. I was thinking *what a monster I was to think Ned could hurt a kid.*

I was also remembering Gram's funeral. At Gram's funeral the pastor's voice faded off and this vision appeared to me, of Gram rising above the altar and twirling before us. Not the old little lady in the sunhat, or the refined lady in the gray-blue curls, but this big flowering blue, lavender, fuchsia, green, a translucent, shimmering amorphous beauty of shifting petals, silks and feathers twirling round a center of light and rising up through the ceiling. *Bye-bye Gram!*

But at Ned's funeral I didn't see anything. After the usual church basement lunch of coffee, pastel mints and ham sandwiches, we sisters eyed each other: *let's get out of here!* We rushed from the church and headed for the yellow house like crows on roadkill. Past the grain elevators, over the railroad tracks, down the gravel drive. There was the butter-yellow house with dark green shutters, the corn crib and silo, the blank space where the barn used to be and a big brown dumpster out front.

We piled out of the van and went in through the sitting room door. I was first in. Everybody followed with their arms full of groceries. I stopped just inside. There was something on the floor. Tammy bumped into me, Holly bumped into Tammy, Molly bumped into Holly, Polly bumped into Molly, Anne bumped into Polly, Mom bumped into Anne and Little Mary bumped into Mom as I stood staring down at a big stain on the carpet, thinking *what is that? Is that blood? It looks like blood. Bet it is blood. Bet that blood is human. Bet Ned did take Jack. Bet he took Jack right here, and right here Jack struggled for his life, and right here the knife slipped and right here Ned slit Jack Jackoway's throat.*

"What's the hold-up, Cat?"

I stepped aside to let Tammy pass, thinking there must be another explanation. Because in real life it's never a murder victim's blood you see. It's always ketchup or a cat fight and the blood's not blood.

"Tammy, what is that?"

"That's blood."

"Who's blood?"

"Ned's. He vomited that up. That's what killed him, Cat. Cirrhosis of the Liver. He was throwing up his insides. Didn't you know that?"

What did I know? Nobody told me anything. Poor guy, all alone in the yellow house, throwing up his insides.

"Did he die right here? On this spot?"

"No. He called an ambulance and died in the hospital. From alcoholism. The drinking ate up his liver."

"I thought he stopped drinking."

"He did stop. He drank mouthwash instead. When Holly and I were here earlier to clean out his trailer, we found over one hundred empty Red Lavoris bottles."

"Yeah," Holly said. "That dumpster is full of empties."

"And we tried to wash that stain out. We got down on our hands and knees and scrubbed."

"Yeah, we tried cleanser, baking soda, bleach-"

"But we couldn't."

"Trisha tried too."

"But she couldn't either."

I imagined second cousin Trisha on her hands and knees scrubbing, as my sisters went on about how hard it is to get blood out. Then we stopped talking about bloodstains and started making supper. We found the spaghetti pot and the colander, and found and mouse droppings in the cupboards, and stinking meat in the fridge and mysterious blobs in the Tupperware. We threw out the Tupperware and wiped out the cupboards and made supper.

After spaghetti, salad and garlic bread we started to touch the stuff. Anne picked up a vase, dusted it off and held it up. "Mom do you want this? Tammy do you? Molly do you?" Tammy picked up a carved cardinal. "Mom do you want this? Anne do you? Holly do you?" Mom picked up the blue teapot. "I want this." Holly picked up a cream pitcher. Anne touched the virgin in the stairway niche. Polly touched the mirror at the foot of the stairs. Tammy held up the painting from Mom's old room, the white lilies surrounded by green leaves. Each thing had sat in its own spot for decades, and as we moved each, a small spirit escaped.

Whee!

That's how it felt to Little Mary anyway, like little spirits zipping free, zooming every-which-way. By midnight, she said, the house felt packed with zipping spirits.

"Can you feel them, Auntie Cat?"

"Feel what, Little Mary?"

"Those little things zooming through?"

"What little things?"

"Just…little things. Flying around. There's hundreds in here!" She raised her arms and spun as we kept picking stuff up, roll-top to Tammy, teacart to Holly, lemonade pitcher to me. I put my pile on the sewing room bed. There were piles all over the house, and all night our piles grew…

After midnight Tammy and Holly brought Gram's hat collection down from her dressing room. We each chose a hat from their nests of striped and checkered boxes and posed for a mock-serious photo on the stairway. Then Tammy and Holly went back upstairs, Molly and Polly went to the kitchen and

Mom went for a moonlit walk. Little Mary, Anne and I headed down to Gramp's woodshop. We were just putting our hands into the dusty nooks where Gram kept his carvings when Tammy called out.

"Cat, come up here."

Her voice cold and flat.

A stone dropped in my gut.

Bad thing coming.

"What, Tammy?"

"Just come up here."

"What for?"

"Just come."

"Why?"

"Holly and I want to show you something."

I started up the stairs. Little Mary followed. Tammy stopped us halfway. "Not Mary. Just you."

"Why?"

"Not Little Mary."

"Okay. Go back down. Go find more treasures."

Little Mary descended reluctantly as I followed Tammy up. Tammy stopped at the linen cupboard outside Ned's room. Holly knelt there cradling a stack of white cloth.

"What do you have to show me?"

Holly lifted the stack of cloth. "Tammy and I were just going to throw these out."

Throw what out?

I peered into Ned's room. I'd never been in there before. Not one toe in. I'd only peeked in. Ned's room was off-limits. Nothing had changed in all those years. There was the same redwood single bed, redwood desk and dresser edged in cigarette burns and the same old tobacco scent. I stepped in. Holly and Tammy followed. Holly fingered a burn on the dresser. Tammy touched the bare mattress. They room was empty except for something folded on the bed.

They'd been in there already, clearing stuff out.

Tammy picked up the things from the bed. Ned's cardinal-red work-jacket and cap. "You want these? No one else wants them."

"Okay."

I put on the cap and zipped up the jacket.

"Ha! Look at you!"

"Ha! Look at Cat!"

Holly stepped to Ned's open closet. "Check this out."

On the wallpaper outside the closet at shoulder height was a brown smudge. Holly put one hand on the smudge and reached into the closet with her other hand. "Ned must have rested his hand here every day, over all those years, to make this smudge."

I put my hand on the smudge then walked into the closet and pushed my face into Ned's clothes, his khakis, flannels, plaids. Surrounded by the heat of him, his scents, of soap, booze, smokes and aftershave, I inhaled Ned, and stepped from the closet as him. I opened my mouth. Ned's voice came out.

"HEY YOU!"

Tammy and Holly startled.

Holly dropped the shirt she'd been folding.

"Ha! Cat! You sound just like him!"

"Yeah! Do it again!"

"HEY, YOU!"

"She's him. You're him. How'd you do that, Cat?"

"Do it again."

A column of heat rose in my gut.

"HEY YOU. COME HERE."

"Cat you're spooking us!" Holly hugged herself.

Tammy covered her ears. "Yeah, Cat, you're spooking us!"

I kept taunting them. "HEY YOU! COME HERE!"

"Stop!"

"I SAID COME HERE!"

"Please stop!" Holly pleaded.

"HEY YOU. CAT GOT YOUR TONGUE?"

"Cat please STOP!"

I closed my mouth and shook my head to shake Ned out.

"Oh my god Cat."

"Yeah, Cat. You scared us."

"Yeah."

I scared myself.

I took off the hat and unzipped the jacket.

Tammy and Holly shared a look.

"Do you want to see what we found, Cat?"

I touched the wall-smudge.

"Not that," said Tammy, "something else. But we're only going to show you on one condition. And you have to agree. Okay?"

Secrets on secrets...

They led me out of Ned's room and back to the linen cupboard. Tammy squared herself in front of me, her face close to mine. "The condition is this, Cat. That right after we show you these things, they're going right in the dumpster. When we found them, we weren't going to show anyone. We were going to throw them right away. Holly and I agreed that was best, but with the questions you asked about family, we thought you should see, because, you know, maybe someday you'll be a writer. And make up stories. But not true ones, right?"

Tammy was so close, our noses almost touched. "Now they're going right in the dumpster. Right after we show you. Agreed?"

Tammy and Holly stared at me like stone guard dogs.

I get it. Stone guard dogs protecting the castle.

I nodded. Holly knelt by the stack of white cloth and gingerly lifted. The stack fell open. She pulled out one cloth and shook it tenderly. It was a small pair of boys' underwear. Clean white jockeys.

I thought, *little seconds, little presents, little nephews-*

"Look."

Holly turned the briefs around. On the back was a small hole, cut just where a boy's bottom-hole would be.

Questions flashed through my mind: *Why? What? Who?*

Holly tenderly shuffled the stack. There were many pairs, all white. "They're all like that Cat."

"Each with a hole cut? In that place?" I asked.

Holly and Tammy nodded soberly.

"But look, Cat, they look new."

"Yes, Tammy and I agreed, these are all new."

"Don't they look new to you, Cat?"

"We don't think these were ever used."

"We mean, ever worn, by a boy."

"Not ever."

"One more thing."

Holly picked up a coverless paperback. I reached for it. She closed her arms round it.

"You don't want to see this, Cat. I looked inside. It's very bad. I'm throwing this right away."

Holly had the saddest look I'd ever seen on her face.

"What is it?"

"You know," Tammy said, "What sick people read. What's the word? ...It's nasty."

I wanted to hold the book, open it in private and read the words. Holly's arms stayed tight around it, but I could imagine what was in there. A few years before I'd found a yellowed paperback under the sofa in our rec room and read a little before I slammed it shut and stuffed it in the trash. *Good riddance!* The book was about a little girl on her way home from school, pushed up against a chain link fence by a stranger. *Nasty.*

"Auntie Cat!" Little Mary called up from the basement.

"Just a minute, Little Mary!" I called down.

Tammy and Holly stood at the head of the stairs, blocking my way. Tammy said, "Now they're going right in the dumpster, Cat, alright?"

"Auntie Cat! Come down!"

I hesitated, staring at Holly and Tammy.

Tammy nodded. "Right in the dumpster."

Holly whispered, "He's dead now. What harm can he do?"

"Auntie Cat, come see!"

I yelled down, "Coming, Mary!"

"Wait." Tammy stopped me. "We found something else that you can have. From Ned's desk."

Holly handed me a small red book, the pages gilt-edged. The cover read, *Five Year Diary*, and written inside, in a scrawly blue fountain pen, was a name. *Ned Robert Downs.*

I put Ned's diary with my treasure-pile on the sewing room bed and headed down to the basement.

The stairwell walls were sided with pegboard. Tools hung within easy reach, a whisk broom, a dust pan, a gardening hat. The stairs to the basement were slats with no backs. My first time down those stair, as a kid, I froze. I'd never seen stairs with no backs. Our stairs back home were solid. Those slots in the yellow house stairs- *you could fall through!* My little legs couldn't move. I was afraid to go back up to my family, afraid to go down and afraid to catch a glimpse beyond the gaps. Finally Rosy Sue got me and took me out to lie down in the road.

On the night after Ned's funeral, I went down, inhaling the scent of the deep-dug basement. I joined Anne and Little Mary in Gramp's workroom where the wood-carving tools were kept, knives to scoop, knives to gouge, knives to slice. Below the knives was a row of cubbies. Anne reached in and dragged out a dust-covered wooden bird. She cradled it towards Little Mary.

"Don't be scared. It's just a little dust."

Little Mary cupped her hands. A voice said, "Careful." We startled. The half-carved wooden bird dropped to the floor. Tammy and Holly stood in the doorway.

"It's falling apart," Tammy said.

"Yeah, it's falling apart," said Holly.

"What is?"

"This house."

"Yeah, it's falling to pieces."

"Come see."

Tammy and Holly led us into the canning room. Holly opened a cupboard. It was dotted with dark specks.

"See? Black mold."

"And see?" Tammy pointed up to water stains on the ceiling.

"And this." Holly touched a crack in the wall.

As Holly fingered the crack I imagined the hairline widening under her touch like Edgar Alan Poe's *Fall of the House of Usher*, and the whole house cracking open and crumbling apart. *Hush! Everyone is dead! Gram is dead, Gramps is dead, Ned is dead! There's no one left alive here! Just mold and mildew! Hush! Speak too loud and the whole thing will fall to pieces!*

"But come see this." Holly headed towards the dark coal room. We followed.

"Wait." She stopped us with her hand. "Before you go in, I have to tell the story. I gave Gram a birdfeeder a few Christmases ago, filled with sunflower seeds. Then she got sick, and never had a chance to put that feeder up. Then Gramps got sick too, and Ned must have thrown that feeder down in the coal room with some other trash, because I saw it tipped over in there after Gramp's funeral-"

I tried to peek in. Tammy blocked my way.

Holly went on, "When Tammy and I were down here earlier to clean up after Gramps died, we found this small pile of trash in the middle of the coal room. Just dust and stuff. It's still there. That pile must have sat for years, undisturbed, and when the floods came earlier this summer, some water must have gotten in. And look."

Tammy and Holly stepped aside. We all tiptoed into the dim coal room with its gray-stone walls and gray cement floor. Gray light from one dust-opaqued window lit a small dirt-pile in the center. Holly gestured to the pile as she whispered.

"And some crack of light must have gotten in, too, with the one bit of moisture, because look."

I couldn't see, till Tammy pulled the light chain and the pile was illuminated. From the dust heap rose one long, lean, white, leggy stem. *Up, up, up.* The ghostly stem ended in two albino leaves, one leaf gently capped by an opened sunflower seed.

That night we fell asleep all over the yellow house, Mom and Anne in Mom's girlhood room, Tammy and Holly on the living room floor, Molly and Polly in Gram and Gramp's bedroom and I in the sewing room.

But I couldn't sleep. I lay awake with the sound of the crickets, the house-creaks and the copper taste in my mouth. *What was that?*

I sat up and listened. *Nothing.* All the little spirits I didn't believe in had stopped zipping. I went to the bathroom, glanced at my silhouette, snuck down past Tammy and Holly snoring in the living room, past the mirror at the foot of the stairs, through the kitchen, down the back hall and into gray dawn.

Gram would never have allowed that ugly brown dumpster in her yard. I dragged an old wooden chair over and climbed in. With all the junk in there, and the dim light, it was hard to keep my balance. I couldn't distinguish much. But as the light grew, the contents revealed themselves, broken jars, mildewy National Geographics, planks of rotted wood, an old milk jug, moth-eaten drapes. But no nasty paperbacks or small pairs of underwear.

I smelled something burning. As I climbed from the dumpster I spotted a wavering wisp of smoke where the barn used to be. I walked to the rising smoke. Someone had started a small fire. At first I saw nothing but chalky lumps. As morning light gilded the corn, I found a fallen stick, prodded the smoking lumps and uncovered an accordion of blackened paperback. I barely touched the book with the stick. The accordion disintegrated.

Poosh.

Under those whispery ashes was a mound of gray. I pried the gray apart with my stick. It was a congealed mass, burnt to ash, of what was, once upon a time, a stack of white cotton knits, many little Fruits of the Loom.

THE ELEPHANT'S BELLY

On the ride home, I felt the copper penny rise in my throat like the sunflower in the coal room, up, up. I swallowed it down, and it came back up, I swallowed it down, it came back up, the whole ride home.

When I got home I sorted my treasures. I put the Ned's diary on my dresser by the glass pitcher, surrounded by the wooden birds, and imagined where I would put that lemonade pitcher in my future home.

On summer days, I thought, I'd have it full of lemon slices and spinning ice cubes. And in the winter it would sit on the hearth in a big sunken living room next to my indoor pool, and I'd stand in a new swimsuit. Or naked. Yes I'd stand naked and dive into the pool and dry off with a big fluffy towel and sit on the modern hearth while David White sat in his easy chair smoking a pipe. David White would take the pipe out of his mouth and give me a knowing wink. I'd give David White a knowing wink, and together we'd stand. Then I'd let my towel fall from my body, and I and my naked self would follow David to the master bedroom, where on the king-size waterbed we'd entangle ourselves in unspoken agreement.

I imagined all the pinching, stroking and poking David White would do to me, then washed and dried my hands and carefully picked up Ned's diary.

January 1, 1937. Folks went to Town. I stayed home. Did Chores.

January 3, Cousin Ben came over. Played Chinese Checkers. Ate ice cream & talked. Had a lot of Fun.

January 5. Went back to School. Studied for Semester Tests. Brought in a Load of Beans.

Tomorrow is Ground Hog Day. Hope it is cloudy.

Ground Hog saw his Shadow so 6 wks. to Spring.

Went to School. Discovered book written by Hitler. Today is sixth anniversary of his Rule in Germany.

Went to School. Read My Battle by Hitler a story of his Life and how he came to Rule.

Today Hitler's birthday, big celebration in Germany.

Went to School. Got in a load of Beans.

Cousin Ben came over. Stayed till his folks came. Swell Sunset.

Ben and I went down to creek. Went wading. Got wet.

Mom and Dad went to town. Stayed home alone. Ben came over. Had a bit of fun in basement.

Got in a load of Beans. Went to School. War in Europe getting worse. Rushia entered war against Poland today.

Poland almost smashed by Germany and Rushia. Shoveled load of Coal. Rained today. Froze. Ground all icy.

Hitler made a speech on Germany's condition in the World. I cut up some wood.

Went to School prepared for a fight.

This morning Germany took Denmark. War in Europe getting worce.

This morning Germany attacted Norway. War expected to spread to Sweden.

Had assembly program. Puppies born.

Puppy ran over today. Died. Went to Father-Son banquet at Church.

Went to School. Took in a load of Beans...

It went on like that. *Went to school, took in a load of beans.* I'd been looking for a glint of evil, a dab of blood, a glimpse of the monster-to-be. But this was just a farm kid's diary, a good kid going to school and taking in loads of beans. And back then, who knew what a monster Hitler would be? And like Holly said, *Ned was dead.*

But my subconscious would not let me forget. Every night after returning home from Ned's funeral, I dreamed of us girls going through the yellow house, picking things up, turning things over and deciding what to keep, what to throw and what to pass on. As we sorted, the house grew rooms, stories and wings. The sitting room expanded into a huge conservatory filled with big ferns and white wicker furniture, the master bedroom swelled to the whole second floor and the basement bulged into an ancient underground city with huge columns, cavernous arched ceilings and table after table of stuff, stuff, like an endless church sale. Anne picked up a lock of hair, Rosy Sue picked up a golden blade, Tammy a shield and so on. One night during our endless sorting Mom picked up a silver elephant, dusted its belly and handed it to me, saying, "You better take a look at this, Cat." I took the elephant and turned it over. It had numbers etched on its belly. When I woke, I wrote down the numbers in my journal like I write down all the flowers of my swampy subconscious.

Six-four-seven-seven-six-four-four.

Then I had another dream. It was Thanksgiving. We were about to eat. In the center of the table was the bird. I stepped closer for a better look. I saw that the bird was not a bird. The bird was a kid. The bird was a pale naked kid crouching facedown, surrounded by onions, carrots and potatoes. I put my hand on the kid's back and reached in. From the kid's back I pulled out a long white root. Then stepped into the kitchen, held the root up and said to my whole family, "We have to take a look at this." Then Uncle Ned opened his mouth and a river of blood flowed out.

Dreams like that. Every night. And one day when I was wide awake and walking to the Mini-Mart I saw another MISSING poster. Of a girl. Heart-shaped face, red hair and the words, HAVE YOU SEEN ME? IF YOU HAVE ANY INFORMATION CALL 1-800-647-7464.

I never saw that girl before, but as I walked home something felt funny. Not the girl's face or her name, but something else. Later that day I realized what was funny. The 1-800-number. It reminded me of some other number. Some numbers you never forget, like your best friend's number. I could be an old lady all gray and withery and still spit out Jill's number. But these numbers kept dancing in my head, then sprouted legs with go-go boots and can-canned in my brain till I walked back to the Mini-Mart and looked under that redhead's chin. 1-800-647-7464. Same numbers as on the elephant's belly that Tammy nodded. "Right in the dumpster."

Mom dusted off in her dream. I mean my dream.

You better take a look at this, Cat...

I picked a day when everyone was away, Holly at work, Mom at a quilting thing and Dad dead. I went into the kitchen, picked up the phone, stretched the cord and sat on the living room carpet with my heart knocking my ribcage, BOOM, BOOM, BOOM.

You're putting together a puzzle. You pick up a piece. You think *why is this red? Why is this white? Why is that striped?* I sure as hell did not want to make that call but the voice on the other end kept saying, "If you'd like to make a call please hang up and dial again, if you'd like to make a call please hang up and dial again, if you'd like to make a call please hang up and dial again."

So I hung up and dialed again.

RING! RING!

"Institute for Missing Children. This is Debbie speaking. How may I help you?"

"Um, I'm calling about the Jack Jackoway case?"

"Yes?"

"Um."

"How may I help you?"

"Um, I have a suspicion? About a family member?"

"Yes?"

"I feel, um, we need to rule my uncle out."

"Your uncle?"

"Yes. We found some. Um. Pedophilia? In his house-"

"This is your uncle?"

"Yes. He lived in another state, but-"

"At the time of the abduction?"

"Yes but-"

"And where is he now?"

"Um, he's dead-"

"Your uncle is dead?"

"Yes."

"And what did you find in his home?"

"Um."

"Did you find any clippings from the Jackoway case? Or any news articles about the missing-?"

"No, but-"

"Do you have these objects? That you did find?"

"No, but-"

"What kind of vehicle did your uncle drive?

"Um, I'm not sure. Chevy, maybe? A Blazer? No. I'm not sure."

"What color was the vehicle?"

"I'm not sure, because, um, well, first he drove uh, then he drove the, uh, blue, maybe? Maybe light blue?"

"How old was your uncle at the time of the abduction?"

"Um. Not sure. Let me do the math...you still there?"

"Yes."

"I think he was about fifty-five?"

"And now he is dead?"

"Right."

"How did he die?"

"Cirrhosis of the liver."

"And when did he die?"

"This summer."

Debbie took my number and said, "Someone will call you back."

Dial tone.

Stupid me! I was the Quiz Show contestant with all the wrong answers. *Wrong car. Wrong state. Dead wrong.*

1-800-MISSING never called me back.

I found the number twenty-nine bus schedule under old notebooks in my third drawer down and went to the downtown library to see if I could find out anything more about Jack's disappearance. As I rolled through the purple microfiche I found an article that raised the hairs on the back of my neck.

MINNESOTA MONITOR

November 29, 1974

COME BACK JACK

Greendale, Midland. The crime scene ribbons are gone and snow hides the weedy spot where 11 year old Jack Jackoway was last seen on Halloween night. One month has passed, and everyone in America is wondering what happened to Jack. The townfolk hold nightly watches with candles, yellow ribbons and growing piles of teddy bears.

Federal, state and local investigators have been working 24/7, ever since that unseasonably warm evening Jack walked home after trick-or-treating with his two friends and was abducted by an armed masked man.

Investigators have no prime suspect. They are focusing on known offenders. They have compiled over 30,000 bits of data. The MISSING hotline receives more than 5,000 tips daily and 3 psychics enlisted by the investigators all envisioned Jack standing by an abandoned barn.

"We have to look at every bit of evidence," an FBI investigator said. "Any tip could break the case."

Tips have combined to create a composite suspect. Investigators hope the sketch of a man in his 50's, seen at the Mini-Mart in Greenwood, along with the description of a man seen at Seven-Eleven near Maple Hill, and a man at the Mini-Mart in White Rock will elicit a solution. The Maple Hill man reportedly followed a boy into the parking lot and a similar man tried to abduct a boy at the Mini-Mart in White Rock.

"The task is daunting but in this abduction we have more to work with than investigators had in the cases of three

boys who disappeared in West Brownmound Iowa. They had nothing, no suspect, no witnesses. Those West Brownmound boys just vanished. Poof. Gone. We have a masked man with a gun."

I rolled the microfiche back.

Three missing from Iowa. Ned's state. Not just Iowa, but West Brownmound. Pearl Pond was the small town near the yellow house. West Brownmound was the nearest city to Pearl Pond. and I had no idea how close West Brownmound was. *Twenty miles? Ten?* And the words: *a similar man tried to abduct a boy at the Mini-Mart in White Rock.* That White Rock Mini Mart was five blocks from our house. That's where Ned went on his visits for cigarettes or candy or just to get out of the house. That's where we were going to go on his birthday visit. We were going to stand in the parking lot and lean on Ned's car and feel the heat through our shirts and watch the boys do wheelies as we licked our cones but then there was that incident, so we didn't go. But those words: *'a similar man tried to abduct a boy at the Mini-Mart in White Rock.'* I wondered *what man? What boy? When?*

My friend Jill across the street was an In-Between, so she could talk to the Burnouts, the Born-Agains and the Eggheads. Plus being Catholic she had umpteen sources, so I asked her to find out who that boy was in the Mini-Mart. In under one week. Jill's bratty little brothers came up with a name: Halbert Evans. Halbert was a sixth grader in Little Rose Lake Elementary at the time of the attempted abduction. Jill's brothers told Halbert I was a Secret Investigative Reporter for Seventeen Magazine and that my expense account would cover a Big Barney's Pizza of his choice. Halbert agreed to meet me for an Extra-Large Bacon and Pineapple Pizza. That would use up all my babysitting money but I wanted to show Halbert a picture of Uncle Ned and watch his reaction.

That photo wasn't easy to find. In our shoeboxes I found just one of Ned, sober-faced on a fishing trip. On my way to Big Barney's I was running late, and my bike tires were flat, so I tried to pump them, then figured by the time I got them filled up, I could have run there, so I ran against the wind, and the wind ripped the folder from my hands and all the articles about Jack went flying across the sloping vacant lot. By the time I gathered them I was late.

Halbert was sitting in the air-conditioned dark of Big Barney's slurping large chocolate malt. "I've already placed the order. I trust you will pick up the tab."

Then Halbert told me all about that day, the weather, his touchdown pass, and how his mom had to sew his Batman costume before he went out trick-or-treating.

"Wait," I asked, "What day was this?"

"You know, Halloween. Before trick-or-treatin', I biked to the Mini-Mart for a snack, you know? An' that guy in the Mini-Mart was starin' right at me. He looked about to pop a gasket. He was eyeballin' me the whole time I was decidin' between a Dreamsicle or a Drumstick. He went 'HEY,' an' I turned away, like I didn't hear. But he kept goin' 'HEY YOU.' An' I kept ignorin' him. Finally he left an' I looked up at the checkout guy like, *that guy was weird, yeah.* Not just 'cause he was goin' 'HEY' but because he had this smile on his face, not a smile but a *what-do-you-call-it.*

"A sneer?"

"Nah."

"A leer?"

"Naah."

"A grimace?"

"Yeah! Like he was a grinnin' jack-o-lantern! An' after he left I picked out a Drumstick, then kinda stuck around. 'Cause I didn't want to bump into him in the parkin' lot. Then my Drumstick was meltin' so I went out to my bike. An' the guy was still out there in the parkin' lot, an' he goes, 'HEY, COME SEE THIS.' Whatever it was, I didn't wanna see it. An' he comes closer an' goes, 'COME HERE' like an order, you know? Then he reaches for me. That's when I threw my Drumstick at him. Yeah. I took off on my bike an' peeled out."

Halbert slid a pizza slice into his mouth. That was when I'd planned to show Halbert the photo of Uncle Ned and ask, 'is this the man?'

I opened my folder. The snapshot was gone.

"Excuse me a minute."

I ran out of Big Barney's and down the sloping vacant lot, searching between the weeds and wagging candy wrappers. I was about to give up when I saw the photo of Ned wavering in the fork of a dead weed.

When I got back in Big Barney's, Halbert was gone. The waitress nodded toward the Men's Room. I set the snapshot face down on the table and waited, wondering what I would do if Halbert recognized Uncle Ned...

Halbert finally came out of the Men's, scooted into the booth, laced his fingers and leaned forward, "So, then I hear about that Jackoway kid. An' they say maybe the same guy took Jack. As bugged me. The same guy. Weird, huh? Yeah. What a freak-out. I almost pissed my pants when I heard that. Just kiddin'. I didn't really piss my pants. Don't put that in the Seventeen Magazine."

He glanced at the facedown photo. "What's this?"

He picked up the photo, turned it over and turned white.

"Hey! Who? What the-? 'Cause man! Whoa! Feel like chucking my cherries! 'Cause that dude's some dead ringer. Of the guy! In the Mini Mart!"

Then Halbert Evans projectile vomited on my snapshot of Uncle Ned.

I wiped off the snapshot, ran home, filled my tires and biked to the White Rock Police Station. Officer Blockhead shook my hand.

"Hello Miss McCloud. Course I knew your dad. Helluva man.

What's this about?"

I took a breath and told him about the underwear in the linen cupboard and Halbert throwing up on Ned's photo and my dream about the Missing Kids phone number.

Officer Blockhead wrinkled his forehead.

"Miss McCloud, first of all, you do not carry on an investigation. This is an Official Police Matter. And you do not corner a witness, show him a photograph and ask, 'is this the man?' That is called LEADING THE WITNESS."

He scratched his neck.

"And even if your uncle did have questionable objects in his possession, that is not proof of anything. Even if your uncle accosted Halbert Evans in the Mini-Mart, there are certain things I'm not at liberty to say. For example, the Jackoway investigation may no longer link *this* with *that*, get my meaning? And your uncle is deceased, correct? Well, there's not much we can do with a dead man. If you want to tell your story to the Greendale County Sheriff, about numbers on an elephant's belly, be my guest. But do you know how many leads get called in in cases like this? Thousands get called in. In the first week."

He squinted at the snapshot of Ned.

"And does your mother know what you're up to? This is serious business, Miss McCloud. You could ruin a man's life with your elephant."

He removed a speck of something from his eye.

"And a nice young lady like you has no idea how many nuts are out there. There's probably one living right on your street. These guys, they hide in their dirty little houses with their dirty little pictures and their dirty little minds, but guess what? They're cowards. Most of these guys hardly have the courage to open their door and walk to the store for a carton of milk. Why do you think they pick kids? Because they're scared of adult relationships. Ninety-nine percent of these guys never take it outside. Chances are, your uncle was in that ninety-nine. My advice to you, Miss McCloud? Let it be."

TOO MANY MISSING

Let it be...

It was a full-time job being a sixteen year old outcast with a black mark on her soul. So I let it be. Then Holly moved out and my seventeenth birthday came with no good wishes and I woke up down at the lake with the trash bag beside and Rosy Sue whispering, *kill yourself*, but some life-force would not let me die and I had to get rid of the GUILT and find out the truth about Ned and stop sleepwalking and start living and GET KISSED. So I dragged the trash bag into the lake, sank it deep, threw some stuff in my backpack and grabbed the Iowa map.

And off in the Dodge Dart Swinger.

And there I was on the road to the yellow house...

The corn got parted by lawns and houses, then more houses, then billboards, gas stations and BIG BURGERS, and CHEESY BURGERS and CHEESY TRIPLE BURGERS and freeway signs.

BROWNMOUND EXITS 1 MILE.

WEST BROWNMOUND ½ MILE.

EAST BROWNMOUND ¼ MILE.

Which exit to take? I remembered Anne's lips on our trip to Ned's funeral as she pulled red licorice through her teeth: *Take the West exit!* But I couldn't get over. I missed it. *I'd take the next,* I thought, *before I pee my pants.* I took the East Brownmound exit into the poor side of town. Street after street of houses no bigger than the living rooms back home. Bluebird, Fifth, Cardinal. Crumbling steps, tipped barbeques, old motorcycles, dangling shutters, a dingy kid on a trike clutching a stuffed tiger and fiercely pedaling down an uneven sidewalk past boarded-over businesses. *Where was a gas station? Or someone to ask?*

Outside one house a draggle-haired lady in a housedress stood watering the grass. The spray from her hose caught a rainbow.

"Hi. How do I get back on the Interstate?"

She was glazed in sweat. "Two blocks to the stop then a right, go two blocks, you can't miss it."

"Thanks."

Two blocks to the stop then a right you can't miss it. Two blocks and a stop you can't miss it. Two rights you can't miss it.

I missed it. The road dead-ended at a wooden fence and a big brown sign with yellow lettering.

IOWA STATE FAIR.

The gate was open but the place deserted. I drove in past plywooded-over concessions, the Sweet-Swirl, Tilt-a-Whirl and Wall of Death, parked between Pete's Pronto Pups and Froggy's Frosty Lemonade and squatted in the dust. Just in time.

Ah! Sweet relief.

Above me Froggy's painted Lemon Frog danced a jig under a giant orange slice dripping juice into an open-mouthed clown who was looking up the skirt of a forward-bending girl with her nose in a red tulip under a burger grinning EAT ME.

Then came a *ringing in my ear.* I shook off my drip, pulled up my shorts and worked my fingers in my ears, trying to work out the ringing as I scuffed through the smashed cigs and dead balloons and imagined girls pressed close to their dates before the Death-Drop plummeted and kids pointing at stuffed animals and whining, *I want that*, as barkers called *Step Right Up!*

He was there, I learned later, little Billy Bell, trying to get my attention, bouncing around in the air, trying to lead me to where Smiling Man took him, but in that moment, I didn't see Billy Bell running ahead of me, his bare feet, flapping overalls and closed little fists.

Back on the freeway I worked on my plan. *What was I doing in Iowa?* I was being a detective. I was going to use reasoning. I was going to rule Uncle Ned out. *How was I going to do that?* I was going to find out the dates those three West Brownmound kids were taken. I knew Ned had driving license suspensions from driving drunk. *If Ned had a suspended license when those kids went missing, then he couldn't have nabbed them...*

And the yellow house. *Maybe some clues were left there. But how would I get in?* It had gone up for sale after Ned died. I'd heard Tammy say it hadn't sold yet, something about the damp basement. I wondered *how could I get in to search the place? I couldn't just walk in. The cousins across the road would see the Dodge and come running.*

And what would I say to Beth and Ben? 'Hi! I think maybe Ned took a kid or three and maybe there's a clue left in the yellow house.' No. I could knock on their door like a good relative and say hello. But I wasn't a good relative. I was a bad relative with bad questions, cold, hard, detective questions. To be a good relative you have to NOT ask hard questions. To be a good detective you have to ask and ask, slouch down in your car and wait...

I could park in Pearl Pond till sunset and walk to the house in the dark, or find the back way, the dirt road that led to the pond and sneak in. Maybe there was an open window and a ladder in the barn. No, the barn had burned down. Maybe there was a chair in the shed, or a what-do-you-call it...

I drove past strip malls, Frank's Fish House, Karpet King, Kentucky Fried, Taco Bobby's. I'd reached busy West Brownmound. There was the sign:

SAVAGE ROAD EXIT.

PEARL POND 5 MILES.

Wait, I thought, *that can't be. Pearl Pond is twenty miles from West Brownmound, not five. Or so I thought. And where'd the country go? There used to be corn there on all sides, not big beige townhouses with shiny windows...*

There were more townhouses, then farmhouses, cornfields. Then the familiar silver grain elevators by the railroad tracks. A left over the tracks led to Pearl Pond. A right led to the yellow house. The Pearl Pond Library could tell me about the missing boys, and the Pearl Pond Police could reveal Ned's arrests.

I turned left.

There was a little carnival going on, with the scent of boiled hot dogs, families with sticky toddlers and bunches of floating balloons. And there the library with its old stone columns. I climbed the wide steps. The big doors were locked.

"You want the new library." A man on the sidewalk held the hand of a hot-pink toddler. He pointed. "That way, five blocks."

"Thanks."

I walked. It was hot. And not five blocks. More like ten. And I was thirsty. I picked up a sprinkler from one of the many neat flowerbeds with spinning whirligigs, plaster elves and blue yards signs with white eyeballs proclaiming, NEIGHBORHOOD SAFETY WATCH and drank and drank.

Ah! Sweet relief!

When I reached the new library it was locked. The sign said OPEN SATURDAYS NOON-5PM.

Fifteen minutes. I could wait. But I had to pee. Again. There was a big red brick schoolhouse across the street. And some vehicles in the lot. A schoolbus, station wagon, cop car. Maybe the school was open. I crossed and tugged one of the doors. It opened. A lady cop stood just inside.

"May I help you?"

"Restroom, please?"

She pointed down the shiny hall.

"Thanks!"

"Happy to help."

Whoo! Just in time! And what were the chances? A cop right out there. I thought *might as well ask her...*

She was still there when I got out of the restroom. "There is one thing you might be able to help me with."

"What might that be?"

"Who would I talk to about police records?"

"That would be me. I'm Officer Nancy. I'm in charge of the records. What might you be looking for?"

"Uh, some information on a relative. For a summer school class. On Family History."

Liar, liar.

"What time frame are you looking at?"

"About 1970 to 1974."

"I can help you with that. And you got to me just in time. We're about to switch over to computer files, and we're going to destroy all the old files first thing Monday morning. So your timing is perfect. Come Monday, those files will be up in smoke. Here's the deal-"

She adjusted her holster.

"I have to be here for the Safety Fair. But in about, say, a little over an hour, I have my lunch break. I could meet you at the station, for a little window, say of fifteen minutes. Unless you want to come back bright and early Monday morning before-"

I broke in, "No, I'm from out of town, so-"

"Well. You know where the Safety Station is? Just around this curve. Small white building. Head that way, round the curve, you can't miss it."

"Okay! Just round the curve?"

"Just round the curve."

I ran back to the Dodge thinking *what were the chances?* My tiny bladder led me to a friendly cop. A friendly lady cop. A friendly lady cop in charge of the files! A friendly lady cop in charge of the files who would see me in the fifteen minute window before the files went up in smoke! *Lucky me! You can't make this shit up.*

I got in the Dodge Dart dripping with sweat and drove towards the cop shop. I'd get there early, not to miss my golden opportunity.

But before I reached it I spied a little church with a graveyard. The white clapboard surrounded by cornfields reminded me of the boathouse at the pond, sweet, peaceful, protected.

I veered into the gravel lot. There was a picnic table shaded by an oak. I sat down, lit a cig and smoothed out the Wanted Poster. HEIGHT: 5' 8". WEIGHT: 185. HAIR COLOR: Brown/gray. EYE COLOR: Brown.

I chewed on a licorice twist, wishing I had time to smoke that joint rolled up in the toe of my sleeping bag so I could let my mind wander and be ready with all the right detective questions for Nice Officer Nancy.

Then the hairs on the back of my neck stood up.

I turned round. A cop car was parked right next to the Dodge Dart. *What was that doing there? Stay calm Cat. Just walk over.*

I folded the poster, walked to the cop car and put on my smiley-face. The window slid down. Inside a cop in dark shades toggled a toothpick.

"Hello Officer. How are you?"

Dark Shades didn't speak or move.

"Hi, I'm Cat." I put out my hand.

He stared at the windshield.

"I'm visiting. From out of town? I've got family here. The Downs? Ned Downs was my uncle."

He turned to me, took out his toothpick and smiled.

"Ned! Oh yeah! Ned was such a gun nut! What a gun-nut Ned was!"

Play dumb, Cat.

"Ned had guns?"

"Are you kidding me? What guns didn't Ned have?"

"Really? What kind of guns?"

"Oh! All kinds. Rifles, revolvers, handguns. Oh yeah, Ned was a real gun collector. You didn't know that?"

"But he didn't shoot his guns, right? He was just a collector?"

"Did you know your uncle or what? Target shooting, skeet shooting, deer hunting! What didn't he shoot? Oh yeah, Ned and me, we had some fun playing with guns."

"Yeah?"

"Oh yeah. After the barn-fire we-" He paused. "When did that barn burn down? Musta been... What did you say you were doing here?"

"Uh, just looking up a little family history. For summer school."

"That so?"

"Mm-hm."

"Huh. What did you say your name was?"

I squinted at my watch. "Excuse me. I have to-"

"I know. You have an appointment. With Officer Nancy. At thirteen hundred."

"Uh. Yeah. Nice talking to you."

Before he put his toothpick back in Dark Shades stopped me with his index finger.

"Wait. One thing."

He lifted his shades and locked me with glacier-blues.

"You be careful, Cat. You hear? Take care."

As I walked back to the shade of the picnic table his words rang in my ear.

Take care, Cat. Take care...

I got back in the Dodge and headed for the Cop Shop. It should have been just round the curve. But something took over my arms and drove onward. So I never saw the curve to the Cop Shop. There were cornfields, more cornfields, then an old barn leaned, then clapboards, then stuccos, then new brick-fronted split levels, then apartments. Then the road widened to a four-lane with traffic lights and cars, packed in car-to-car, past taller, bigger buildings with big panes reflecting other big panes.

Where was I? Stuck in the honk-honk beep-beep lunch-rush of West Brownmound. And what time was it? And where was the road back to Officer Nancy?

I turned left into a quiet neighborhood with manicured lawns, two-car garages, smooth black driveways, kids shooting baskets, splashing in kiddie pools and breezing by on ten-speeds. I checked my watch. *Twelve-fifty. Shit.* Just ten minutes to get back to Nice Officer Nancy.

I got out, stood on the sidewalk and unfolded the map.

Other side.

Sweat stung my eyes. I don't know how people read maps. Maps are colored lines, intertwining squiggles. I didn't see anything like those squiggles out in the real world. I looked up towards Savage Road. It was packed bumper-to-bumper with the lunch hour traffic. *No way was I getting back to Pearl Pond in time on that.*

"Rhuh! Rhuh!"

A golden retriever stood before me. An old female with gray round her muzzle. Her bark was urgent.

"Rhuh-rhuh!"

"Hey girl! I didn't see you!"

"Rhuh-rhuh!"

I backed up and almost tripped on a kid's red wagon.

Didn't see that either. Or the yellow newsbag on the pavement with Brownmound Bugle papers spilling out.

"Whoa girl, you're gonna knock me down."

I stumbled over the spilled bag and whirly-gigged for balance. Then the wagon was gone, newsbag gone and dog gone.

Where'd she go?

And where was I? I looked up at the street sign.

Corner of Maple and Seventh...

I got my bearings and picked up Savage Road further north after dead-ending at Orangevale Creek, where I parked and walked over a damp bridge of railroad ties and stood by the creek, smoking a cig and wondering how I was going to get back in time for Nice Officer Nancy. On the bridge was a kid with a fishing pole, standing silent and still like fishing kids do. I wanted to ask him for directions, but then came the ringing in my ear, and I was afraid, even if he could tell me the way, that I wouldn't be able to hear him over all that ringing.

I found my own way back. There was the Safety Station, past the school, just like Officer Nancy had said.

How'd I miss that?

I walked down the new cement path, past marigolds and

petunias in a bed of white rocks, and pushed through the glass doors. Inside was shiny-clean and air conditioned, with white-tiled walls and silver-framed safety tips. A calm-eyed man behind the counter looked up and spoke in a hush.

"Hello. How may I help you?"

"I'm here to meet Officer Nancy. To look at some files."

"Oh, Officer Nancy's gone now. I'm sorry. Perhaps I can help."

"Okay, I had some questions about-"

The phone rang. Officer Calm picked it up.

"Excuse me. Pearl Pond Safety Station. Just one moment." He covered the mouthpiece and handed me a notepad. "If you'd like to write your questions down here, I'll help as soon as I'm through with this call, if you don't mind waiting."

He pointed to a row of shiny new padded chairs. I sat and rewrote my questions neatly on the official paper, adding one question about guns to my list.

> *Ned's weight, height and eye color?*
> *Dates of his DWI's?*
> *Dates of his driving license suspensions?*
> *Any arrests?*
> *Car models and license numbers?*
> *Ned's guns, makes and registrations?*

I was biting the pen and wondering if there were more questions I hadn't thought of when Officer Calm spoke.

"Miss? I'm ready for you now, if you're ready for me."

I handed Officer Calm my list.

"Hmm. Let's see."

He touched his ear. "Unfortunately, I can't get into the files. The files are Nancy's territory. But I can try to answer your questions. How tall was your uncle?" He held his hand out palm-down near the top of his own head. "I remember he was about-"

"You knew my uncle?"

"Yes, I was the EMT on call when he phoned in."

"He- phoned in?"

"Yes, when he was dying. He called in, and we came in the

ambulance and brought him to the hospital."

"You were...there? At the house?"

"Yes...and there was...quite a bit of blood."

Officer Calm gave me a tender glance. I envisioned him holding my uncle in a blood-drenched pieta.

"So, height. Ned was about my height. Five eight, five nine. And weight? Well he'd lost quite a bit of weight near the end with his illness, so I'm thinking he was one-fifty-five, one-sixty then. Add twenty or so pounds. Say one-eighty, one-eighty-five. And eyes? Brown. And car models and plates? Hm. I can't help you with that. You could try the DMV."

"The DMV?"

"The Department of Motor Vehicles. I'm not sure they could give you anything. And the only way we'd have a model or plate here is if there was an arrest. And that would be in the files, which I don't have access to..."

"But his guns, I do remember. Oh yes, Ned had quite a few firearms, rifles, long guns, shot guns, handguns. But we'd have no record of those, unless, say, the firearm was involved in an arrest. But, if he bought the firearm from a dealer, or in another state, then we'd have no record of that."

"No record of any guns?"

"That's right. Now as far as arrests or DWI's, do you know for sure he had some?"

"Yes," I said, "I remember him not being able to drive because of a suspended license, but I'm not sure when. That's what I'm trying to find out."

"Well as I said, I can't get into those records, but you could check with the Redtail County Sheriff's. Sandy over there could tell you about any arrests. Let me get Sandy on the phone. Just one moment."

Officer Calm got Sandy on the line, explained to her what I wanted, and handed the receiver to me.

"Hi Sandy, I'm just asking about-"

Sandy shouted in my ear.

"Why would you want to know a THING LIKE THAT!?"

"Well, I want to ask about my uncle's-"

"Well why ask about a thing like THAT!?"

"To write a summer school family history report about-"
"Well, THAT'S nothing to write about!"
Slam. Click. Dial tone.

Officer Calm shrugged and traced his finger on my Iowa map. The Redtail County Sheriff's was past East Brownmound, in the small town of Prairieville, close to the big green splotch called Redtail Rise.

Heading east towards Prairieville, I got the bad-thing-coming feeling in my gut. I had to fist the wheel and force myself to breathe.

Five miles past East Brownmound I saw the exit. The town of Prairieville to the left, Redtail Rise Wildlife Preserve to the right. I turned left, then right onto Main Street, past the Post Office with its taped window, past Dave's Donut Hole with its pink confections, past the dress shop with its reaching mannequins in last decades' fashions.

The Redtail County Sheriff's Department was a low, dog-yellow brick building across the street from a white and robin's egg blue café called Dinah's Diner. I parked in front of the diner and stared at the yellow brick as sweat rolled down my cheek. I was thinking *maybe I should skip the Sheriff's and eat a big burger in that diner instead...*

I was imagining the big greasy burger popping as I bit in, and the ketchup oozing out, and the tang of the dill pickle slice...

But screw your courage to the sticking place, Cat. Sandy in there won't know you're driving without a license or that you buried a black plastic bag in the lake back home, or that there's a joint rolled in the toe of your sleeping bag.

I got out, pulled my shirt from my belly, tugged my cut-offs from my sweaty crack and turned to check my parallel parking.

Fine, since there were no other cars on this street.

I crossed, pulled open the heavy door with its small square of reinforced glass. The entry was tiled in chipped black-and-white hexagons. Past the tall counter sat dimly-lit desks. Before I could ring the bell by the dusty potted African violet a blank-faced woman rushed toward me.

Sandy. Square-shaped, middle-aged Sandy. Sandy held a piece of paper in her hand. The paper shook. Her hand shook. I put out my hand to shake hers. "Hi, I'm Cat. I phoned from the Pearl Pond Police-"

"This is it!" Sandy said, "This is all! There's nothing else!" She clamped the paper in her fist. "It's all I found! Just this!"

I reached for the shaking paper. She drew it closer, huffing, "That's it! Just one arrest! No more!"

"May I please see?"

Sandy drew the page closer to her heaving chest.

"Please may I see?"

She white-knuckled the page, then with an angry sigh, gave it over.

It was a graph with many columns and a code I didn't understand.

"What does this mean? 'AR' for 'Arrest'? And 'DWR' for 'Driving While Revoked'?"

"He had one arrest for driving while his license was revoked. That's it. That's all. No more."

"Well...thank you for looking, Sandy."

I stared down at the chipped black and white tiles wondering what else to ask her. When I looked up she was gone. I spied a few other no-faces sitting quiet at desks in the dimness beyond. Then a door down the hall opened and a giant Sheriff in a butterscotch uniform stepped out. He was at least six foot eight. He ducked under the doorway, walked behind me and stepped outside. I spied him through the chicken-wire as he leaned against the building, rested one cowboy boot against the yellow brick and stared into the lowering afternoon.

Why's he just standing there like that? And where had Sandy gone?

I wasn't through with her. She had something, I could feel it.

Something stuck between the pages of her brain.

I opened my mouth. "When Ned was arrested, how long was he held? What exact dates?"

The potted African violet dropped a leaf. No one answered.

I asked a new question. "Where would I find a list of missing kids?"

Another leaf dropped.

Ask again, Cat.

"Where would I find a list of missing kids from around here?"

No answer.

"Where would I find a list of missing kids from this area?"

A voice from the dimness: "Try the library."

Try the library...

As I turned to leave no one said goodbye. Outside Sheriff Giant still squinted into the lowering afternoon. I felt his eyes on my sweaty back as I slid in the Dodge Dart. I slammed the door and didn't look back.

Heading west back towards Pearl Pond, I turned the radio on to shake out the Redtail County Sheriff's Office. As I grooved to the music with my head bobbing and my arms goose-necking the way Rosy Sue used to, I didn't see the little shadows in the back seat bopping and grooving to the music with me or hear them whispering, *try the library, try the library, try the library...*

I leaned on the counter, speaking quietly, "I'm visiting relatives and-"

The librarian at the front desk of the new Pearl Pond Library had a cabernet-colored beehive. She burst loudly, "Oh! Who're your relatives?"

"Well, they're all dead now, but-"

"Well they can't all be dead!"

"No, they're not all dead, but-"

"So, where're you staying? You must be staying somewhere!"

"Well I'm just, here for a summer school report, on some missing kids."

"Oh! The Missing Kids!"

Cabernet twisted her lips and reached down. There was a smooth sliding sound and the click of her fingernails on metal. She brought up several sheets of paper. "If you take these from the desk, I'll need some ID."

I reached in my backpack, opened my wallet and handed over my White Rock Library Card.

She frowned. "Catherine M. McCloud?"

"My mom's from here."

"Well who are your relations? Are you going to tell me? Or do I have to guess?" She drew the papers to her chest and tipped her head.

"The Downs. My mom's Edith."

"Oh, the Downs! Such lovely folks! I knew Rob and Nita. They were your grandparents? Lucky you! I'm sorry about their passing. And Ned too, after that-"

I reached for the papers. "I'm in a hurry, so-"

"Of course! Here you go! Those can't leave the library. Return them here when you're done. And if you need copies, there's the machine. And if that eats your dimes, come see me!" Cabernet gave me a friendly squint.

I found a solitary cubby. The papers were flyers for missing boys from West Brownmound, each with a smiling photo above a detailed description.

MISSING

James "Jimmy" Moon. MISSING SINCE: September 12, 1970. MISSING FROM: Blue Winds State Park. CLASSIFICATION: Non-Family Abduction. D.O.B. June 7, 1959. AGE AT REPORT: 11. SEX: Male. RACE: Caucasian. HAIR COLOR: Black. EYE COLOR: Brown. HEIGHT: 56 inches. WEIGHT: 73 pounds. James "Jimmy" Moon was last seen in his tent in Campsite Number Three of Blue Winds Campground at approximately 12AM. He was wearing blue-checked flannel pajamas, white cotton socks, a navy-blue knit cap and beaded doe-skin moccasins...

MISSING:

Robert "Rob" Munson. MISSING SINCE: August 3, 1971. MISSING FROM: West Brownmound. CLASSIFICATION: Non-Family Abduction. AGE AT REPORT: 12 years old. SEX: Male. RACE: Caucasian. HAIR COLOR: Brown. EYE COLOR: Brown. HEIGHT: 57 inches. WEIGHT: 78 pounds. Robert Downs was last seen leaving his home at approximately 5:30AM headed for the Orangedale Park Bridge to go fishing. His fishing pole was found on the footbridge in Orangevale Park at approximately 9AM. Rob was last seen wearing a white t-shirt, green shorts, blue tennis shoes and a red baseball cap...

MISSING

Timothy "Timmy" Cross. MISSING SINCE: September 17, 1973 from West Brownmound. CLASSIFICATION: Non-Family Abduction. AGE AT REPORT: 12 years old. SEX: Male. RACE: Caucasian. HAIR COLOR: Brown. EYE COLOR: Hazel. HEIGHT: 5 feet. WEIGHT: 85 pounds. Timmy was last seen leaving his home to deliver The Sunday Brownmound Bugle at 4:45a.m. The elderly family dog that accompanied him, a golden retriever named Bessie, returned home at 6am. Timmy's red wagon and his Brownmound Bugle paperbag, with newspapers still in it, were found on the corner of Maple and Seventh...

Corner of Maple and Seventh...
"Miss McCloud!" Cabernet again. She bent over me with her perfumed head. "Here's another Missing. This one's over ten years old but I thought you'd like to know."

Below the boy's description were two pictures, one a grade school photo, the other a grown man. The man looked like the boy, but with a wider jaw, darker brow and thicker neck. He could have been the kid's dad, or older brother, but his face looked odd, the skin dull, like a Halloween mask or House-of-Wax dummy. Under the picture were the words:

AGE PROGRESSION
As he would appear at the age of...

So that was an Age Progression Image...
"Excuse me." Cabernet was back. "Here's another missing. This wasn't originally classified as missing, but I thought you'd like to know." She handed me a newspaper clipping.

East Brownmound Bulletin
September 16, 1969
WHERE'S BILLY BELL?

Billy Bell, age 11, son of Mr. and Mrs. Hank H. Bell, of 504 Bluebird Avenue, East Brownmound, has not returned home since spending August 2 at the Iowa State Fair. Billy approached home on his bike at approximately 10:30PM with his sister Becky, aged 13. Becky Bell reported that Billy turned eastward towards the 119 overpass. His yellow Schwinn "banana" bike is also missing. He was last seen wearing blue overalls, with no shirt or shoes...

One Camping Boy. One Fishing Boy. One Paperboy...
I had too many missing boys. I needed a cigarette. I stopped reading, stretched, and went to the Ladies Room. I smoked a cig in the last stall. After my smoke I made copies of the Missing flyers. As I went to return the originals to Cabernet's desk I stopped dead.
Cabernet was talking to two men. Both had their backs to me. Both wore overalls. Both were family. One was Uncle Ned. The

other was Gramps. *Couldn't be. Both were dead!*

Cabernet spotted me. "Oh look, your relative!"

Who was she talking to? Them or me?

Both men turned my way. One was a beef-faced stranger. The other was Mom's cousin Ben who lived across the road from the yellow house. His mouth fell open.

"Cat! What're you doing here?"

"Ben!"

I stuffed the Missing copies in my backpack.

"Look what I got, Cat!" Ben held up a stack of bright-colored books. "Murder mysteries!"

Cabernet grinned. "Ben loves a good mystery."

"Yes I do. And my favorite librarian here saves the best for me." Ben and Cabernet shared a grin. He crossed to me and whispered, "Cat, why don't you come to the car? Beth's waiting in the parking lot. She'd love to see you."

Caught. Found. Discovered.

I followed Ben out. Heat rose off the asphalt. The door of their shiny blue truck was open. Inside Beth sat fanning herself with an American Farmer magazine.

"Cat! Where'd you come from! How are you? Let me give you a hug!"

Beth felt warm, solid, comforting. I wanted to cry in her arms and blurt out everything, how I worried about Ned and my nightmares and that I'd just discovered five more missing kids not five miles from the yellow house. Instead I smiled.

She looked into my eyes. "What are you doing here, Cat?"

"Well-"

"Are you here overnight?"

"Uh-"

"Well where are you staying? Oh! Stay with us! Who else is down? Cause we'd love to-"

"It's just me. I'm here to look into, um, family history. For a summer school-"

"Oh really?"

"Yup."

"Oh, I love family history."

"Me too."

A SCREAM IN THE DARK

I followed Beth and Ben's truck over the railroad tracks, imagining the fishing boy on the bridge, the paper boy on his route, the camping boy in his tent...

And Ned rising early with the mist over the corn, leaving the house quietly, with a plan...

Sunday morning paperboys are out early, same with fishing boys, up before the sun, no one about. Whoever took those kids, the dissolving mist or the boogie man or Uncle Ned, he'd have watched the boys beforehand and known their routes.

And he'd be- what was the word? *Innocuous.* A quiet man in dim light out for an early walk pondering the line between good and evil.

And where was that line? And how did you know when you crossed over? Was there a ringing in your ear? Or a penny in your throat?

And where would you hide a body in that flat land?

Before I drove down to Iowa, I'd thought *it'd be easy to hide a body in the country.* Just stow it behind a tool shed or in a barn or tuck it between the corn rows. But when I got down there, I saw it wasn't easy. Every cornrow was accounted for. And everyone was watching behind their curtains for strange behavior, and everyone knew everyone, their clothes, cars and habits. No way could you hide a body out there.

So where would you hide a body in Iowa?

In a green splotch on the map, in untilled land.

And where was my Iowa map? And where were my Tareytons?
I needed a cig.
Where did I have them last? At the library. On the paper thingy. In the Ladies' Room. Shit.

After supper at Ben and Beth's where the wallpaper still hung from when Gram was a girl, I followed Ben out to inhale his smoke as the sun set.

The stars came out, the crickets cricked and we stood looking up into the falling darkness. We didn't talk, just stared up. I could have asked Ben 'was there anything funny about Uncle Ned? A funny touch or word? Or a kid who went into the yellow house and never came out?'

But I couldn't ask. Because I was a coward.

Then Trisha and Beth came out wiping their hands. We three walked across the road. There was a FOR SALE sign out front of the yellow house. BURNSIDE REALTY. We entered through the sitting room door. The blood-stained carpet had been ripped up.

Trisha wrinkled her nose. "Yeah, we had to get rid of that."

Beth flicked on a switch. The sitting room was empty. The kitchen was empty except for table and chairs, the dining room and living room empty.

"Looks different."

"Yeah."

"Want to go upstairs?"

I nodded. We ascended past the blank oval where the mirror had hung and the empty niche where the Virgin had sat. All the bedrooms were empty. Except for a rug in Mom's old room.

Beth asked, "Seen enough?"

"One more minute."

We sat on the rug in Mom's room. Trisha pointed to a pale rectangle on the wall. "Right there hung that lily painting.

Remember?"

I nodded.

The white lily with spiky green leaves…

"Well, this is it." Beth scuffed the rug.

"It hasn't sold yet?"

"No," she sighed, "some buyers looked it over, but no sale yet."

"It's looking good."

"Yeah. It's looking good. We painted some of the rooms, and got most of the mold out and made some repairs. And some buyers were interested…"

"But…something about the basement." Trisha made a face.

"It's not a bad smell."

"No." Trisha stretched her legs, "It's just-"

A deep dug basement.

"Trisha, you've got church in the morning."

"Do I have to?"

"No, you don't have to. But don't you girls have some catching up to do? Cat, you can sleep in-"

"Um."

Think quick!

"Uh. This might sound funny and might sound crazy and might sound weird, but for my summer school we're supposed to…spend the whole night…alone. In a house of our family."

Cat you are so full of shit.

"The whole night? Here?"

I nodded.

"Alone?"

"Mm-hm."

"No, Cat! You could sleep with-"

"No, it has to be…alone."

"Well!" Beth scuffed the rug.

"You really want to, Cat? Cause we could-"

"Sorry, Trisha."

Beth harrumphed into the hall. "If that's what you want, Cat, but it does sound crazy."

"Yeah," Trisha giggled. "And don't tell Arnie. Or he'll sneak over and scare you. Arnie's full of tricks."

"No. Don't tell Arnie. And you'll need something to sleep on. And we should open some windows, get some fresh air in here. Trisha, get the box fan."

"You are crazy, Cat!"

Trisha ran down flicking off lights. Beth and I stood at the head of the dark stairway.

"Trisha Anne! Turn those back on!"

As the lights went back on, Beth turned to me, her blue eyes edged in pink. "You sure you want to do this, Cat? Don't you want to come back to our house for a bedtime treat? A nice cold root beer float? Hm? No? Well alright then." She took my face in her hands. "Trisha will be right back with some pillows, you crazy thing."

She pinched my nose. "You take care."

I watched her wide, comforting back descend the stairs.

You take care...

I kicked off the covers and sat up.

What was that?

After Trisha and Beth left me alone in the yellow house I'd decided it was too late and dark to explore.

I'd do my exploring in the morning...

I'd curled on the floor up in Mom's old room with my sleeping bag, unlit joint in my hand, the fan blowing and the food Trisha brought spread before me, ham and cheese sandwich, three homemade chocolate chip cookies and a jar of fresh milk. And all the lights on. Except for the basement. I was too scared to go down there *just yet*.

I was about to touch the lighter to my joint, *crackle-pop*, and inhale, and burn my lungs, *hold it in*, and cough it out, then lean back and let my head pop off in all directions as the mysteries of the universe revealed themselves to me with the chanting of the crickets and the whirring of the fan as I untangled life's conundrums, then wound them back again into my own little ball of understanding-

But I didn't light the joint. Because if I smoked that I'd start imagining Gram there in her dressing room and Gramps waiting in bed and Ned was sitting up reading.

I turned off the fan. The house creaked.

It was just an old house. That creak isn't Ned walking or the camping boy's moccasins or the fishing boy's pole or the age progression wax dummy of Jack creeping up on me-

As the crickets in the yard below screamed *"Ned! Ned! It was Uncle Ned!"* I set down the unlit joint, clutched the lighter and made my way downstairs and out through the sitting room door. I was hoping Ben had left a few puffs on that butt he'd dropped in his driveway. The moon was a fingernail clipping. As my eyes adjusted I made out the bare spot where the barn used to be, the spot where Gramps used to grow snap peas, and the green pump where Trisha showed me her boil, back-when we were little.

Trisha had sat by the pump, her bare foot outstretched and I'd crouched over admiring her big red boil. She'd waved my finger away, saying, *Don't touch, Cat! If you touch that I will die!*

I knew Trisha wouldn't die. Back home we'd touched our boils all the time. But I knew the power of persuasion: an old lady lived in the mirror, fairies lived in flowers, the unpopped kernels in the bottom of the bowl were trapped souls, if you lay still long enough in the middle of the road, you'll see the boy flying over the corn.

Rosy Sue wasn't the only one who made up lies. The others told me not to touch the old TV set with blue tubes in our laundry room. Every time I toddled past that dead set I heard my siblings' voices in my head. *Don't touch that, Cat, or it'll explode, and take you and the whole house with it.* BAM! *We'll all be blown to smithereens. In an instant. If you so much as-*

Smithereens. Boom.

I made my way across the road to Ben's driveway. There were voices coming from the kitchen window. I ducked down. I heard Beth's high voice.

"She's just looking. What harm can it do?

Then Ben's:

"Well, uh, but-"

"Well, what can she find?"

"Well nothing."

"Well that's what I said, 'nothing'."

On my hands and knees in their driveway, I found Ben's smoked Winston. Three puffs left. Back in the yellow house driveway I lit up and looked up. *Big Dipper. Little Dipper. Cassiopeia.* More stars than at home. And the memories... Rosy Sue's arm, cool on mine as we lay in the road... Gram's apple pie in my mouth... Trisha and me trying to clean out the henhouse...Trisha and me bucketing tadpoles up at the pond, and peeling off our suits that night to red stripes as Gram smoothed on the calamine. *What were you girls thinking with your backs to the sun all day!* We weren't thinking. We were oblivious and delirious with the cattails, thrashing tadpoles and glistening water.

I stopped by Gram's garden. *Something odd there, something different.* And beyond in the brambly place, something strange, but I couldn't make it out. The path to the pond was somewhere near. I started down a dark row, remembering the morning of Gram's funeral, when Gramps led Little Mary and me out to the nubbly spring field. He'd bent down, squeezed up some dirt, closed his hand round it and said, "Look at this, girls," then opened his hand. A black tulip sat upright in his palm. "See how that holds together? Now watch this." The black tulip fell open. "See how that falls apart? That's good soil, girls. That holds together then it falls apart. That doesn't happen overnight, or in one year, or one lifetime. How many years do you think it took, to make this good soil?" We squinted up at Gramps. "Well, girls, it took more years than your Gramps has lived. This took thousands of years of creatures, living and dying, to make that good soil."

Thousands of creatures. Living and dying...

I'm hearing them now. Behind the crickets. The bullfrogs...

The pond must be close.

But instead of heading to the pond I went back to the yellow house, crawled into my sleeping bag and covered up every part of me, leaving just one tiny hole to breathe.

And woke to a scream in the dark. A high, clear note as if fifty voices were compressed into one.

Where was that coming from?

There was a dim glow in the hall. *What time was it? Must be just before dawn.* I felt for the light and flicked it on. There were no screamers in Mom's old room. *Just that high clear note.* I shook my head to shake out the screams and as I shook the white lily in the painting turned into a rabbit and the leaves turned into a hoop of fire. The rabbit jumped through the hoop, over and over.

I stopped shaking and the rabbit turned back into a lily and the leaves turned back into leaves but the scream was still there. I kicked off the covers, wiped my eyes and stepped into the hall. The wallpaper cool to the touch, the ringing still there, louder, but not from the hall. I peeked into the sewing room with its slender bed, spools of thread and blue-ribboned scissors.

No screaming there.

I peeked into the bathroom, at the pink countertop, the bottles and jars lined up like soldiers prepped for cleanliness.

No screaming.

Across the hall in Gram and Gramps room, two weightless shadows seemed to hover above the bed, clasping each other in sleep. *But no screams there.*

Out in the hall by the linen cupboard, there were no high-pitched screams. *And none from Ned's room…*

Halfway down the stairs, the virgin in the niche bent her neck and lowered her eyes. She wasn't screaming. I turned from the mirror at the foot of the stairs without looking in and went through the sitting room into the kitchen. The ringing was louder there.

Was it coming from the basement? The deep dug basement? I opened the door and started down past the whisk broom, garden hat and snipping scissors. Six steps down came the smell. I pulled the chain. The bulb flicked on. *Oh! Somebody had been down there.*

Whoever it was had pried up all the linoleum and pushed the

furniture to the sides. Chairs, tables, shelves were in disarray, everything leaning toward the walls. Some chairs fallen against each other. *Someone had been down there digging.*

They'd broken up the foundation, dug into the earth below and left several oblong holes. *And the ringing was very loud.*

In the bottom of one hole was a small brown thing. I couldn't make it out at first. *Something lacy, something dried.* An outline of a kid in a sailor shirt, wool britches and knee socks faded to brown. The friable remains of a boy curled like a seashell. I held my breath so as not to collapse what was left of him.

In another hole was a boy lying on his back. I could just make out his open mouth frozen like one bite in a slice of stale bread. Next to him was the crust of another boy. In another hollow was a girl, just the etch of her, her wee limbs, brown bones, brown skull and once-white dress yellowed as the string of pearls round her turkey neck.

No color was left in these kids. The pink of their cheeks, blue of their eye, rose of their lips, was all faded to brown. And their graves had no stench of decay. Just a whiff of leather like sticking your nose in an antique book. And the scream was very loud here.

But not coming from the mouths of those children. No. There was nothing alive there! Their mouths couldn't scream! But it was them. Yes. They were there all the time. They had screamed long ago and never stopped. *It was them screaming all along. All those years. Just too high to hear.*

I covered my ears.

Still screaming!

I shook my head.

Still screaming!

I curled into a ball beside the girl's dusty hole. *Still screaming!!!*

I sat up in my sleeping bag. The sun hit the wall of the empty room. No painting. No bed. Just me on the floor with my sleeping bag and the leftovers of last night's snacks. I put my hands over my ears. *Still ringing.* I twisted my fingers in my ears. *Still screaming.* I burrowed in my sleeping bag. *Still screaming!* I shook my head to shake out the screams and the sun on the wall where the painting had hung jumped like a white rabbit through fire. I threw off my sleeping bag and walked into the hall. *Louder.* I peeked into the empty bathroom, master bedroom and linen cupboard. *Still screaming.* I peeked in Ned's room. *Still screaming.* Then ran downstairs past the empty niche and the blank spot where the mirror hung. *Louder!* I stumbled through the empty sitting room. *Louder.* Into the kitchen. *Loud, loud! Louder!*

A woman stood at the kitchen sink with her back to me, wearing Gram's old apron, her hair a halo of morning light. She turned round.

THE LITTLE GOLD BOX

"Good Morning, Cat! I didn't mean to startle you. But I didn't want to leave you alone here with all the ghosts!"

Cousin Trisha!

Trisha picked up a screaming teakettle from the stove. The teakettle hissed and went silent. She poured the boiling water into a yellow teapot. "Want some tea, Cat?"

I couldn't open my mouth.

"So, how'd you sleep last night? Anything go bump in the night? Any boogie-monsters? Seriously, I was worried about you, Cat."

She lifted a batter-covered spoon from a mixing bowl and licked. "You like buttermilk pancakes?"

Before I could nod Trisha turned on the gas under the cast iron skillet. "I mean, I wasn't really worried about you, Cat, but I was feeling sorry for you over here. All by your lonesome!"

She dropped a tablespoon of bacon fat into the skillet.

Hiss!

"But you got through it all right, didn't you! And here I am." She ladled the batter onto the skillet.

Spit!

"And it's a beautiful day, and Mom and Dad are at church, and they took Arnie with them, so we have the whole morning to ourselves! What do you think about that?"

I thought I wanted to brush my teeth and wash my face and

get some tea in me before I spoke. I dragged myself to the back bathroom and washed the sleep from my eyes and brushed the copper from my mouth and combed my fingers through my shag, but there was nothing I could do about the purple circles under my eyes or the boulder in my gut or the black mark on my soul. *And how*, I asked my sleepy reflection, *was I going to explore the house for murder-clues with cheerful cousin Trisha shining on?*

"Ding-ding! Come and get it!"

I sat and stared at the rounded lady-syrup bottle as Trisha poured tea. I added milk and honey and sipped.

Ah. Waking up.

"So," Trisha smeared butter on her cakes, "last night, did anything happen?"

I shook my head and waved my fork at the skillet, mixing bowl and egg-carton on the counter.

"Trisha, did you carry all that stuff over for me?"

"YES, that is how much I LOVE MY COUSIN! And I missed you! And wanted to SPANK you for spending the whole night away from me! I don't know what you expected to find here, Cat. I mean," she wiggled in her seat, "what did you expect to find? Skeletons in the closet? Bodies in the garden? Ghosts in the basement? And did you find any? And did they wiggle their bony fingers at you and say BOO?"

As Trisha went on about spirits jumping out of closets and rapping on doors and blubbering from cupboards, I thought about all the things Jill had whispered to me back home, *what it takes for a ghost to speak, what a ghost can move, and how a ghost just keeps on running when they're shot or stabbed. They just keep walking down the hall...*

"So," Trisha reached for her napkin, "I was remembering all the stuff we did here, like that summer we measured the whole house. Remember what we were looking for?"

The Hidden Room!

I'd forgotten about that. That summer we practically lived in the apple orchard. We climbed every tree and made applesauce from all the windfalls. I could still smell those apples rotting in the sun, their brown spots, the softening mush, the greenish-white worms in each, and Gram telling us *not to pick from the trees,* 'don't you girls go picking from the trees! Just pick up the windfalls!' *And that afternoon we spent bending in the pond with tadpoles wriggling in our buckets, oblivious to the sun beating down...*

"Because you had that dream, Cat, remember? You dreamed there was a room in this house, a long skinny room with no windows that smelled of mothballs, where old toys were stored. And you described it so clearly I could smell it, down to the rocking horse and the rubber ball and the little chairs. And remember what your gram said when we asked her if there was a room like that here? She said, 'no girls, there's no room like that in this house, but there *was* a room *just like that* in the old house before it burned down'. Then she said 'how did you know about that room? Did your mother tell you?'"

No one told me. I just dreamed it...

"But we searched anyway, with your gramp's yardstick, to see if there was any space unaccounted for. We tapped every wall for a hollow and measured every closet. And we believed the secret room was where your gram hid her treasures!"

I swallowed. "Yes! We had this list-"

"Yes! Of everything we thought your gram had hidden there. Mink coats, rubies, gold statues of girls pouring gold water down their rumps!"

Trisha pushed her plate away. "Get enough, Cat?"

"Mm." I forked up my last bit.

"But we never did find that secret room."

"No."

But not for lack of trying. We'd measured all morning, every wall, nook and cranny, then went out to play and found a dead mouse in the corn crib, a dried bird in the barn rafters, a child's tea set in the henhouse, a nut-flavored weed in the barnyard, a tarnished ring in Ned's burnpile and tadpoles in the pond but no hidden room.

"And remember your killer boil, Trisha?"

"What boil?"

"You had this huge boil on your foot and you said-"

"I don't remember that!" She began to clear the dishes. "Well anyway, we looked everywhere."

Except Ned's room. That was off limits...

I stared into my empty cup.

"More tea?"

Trisha put the kettle back on, leaned against the counter and sighed. "Something I never told you, Cat. That summer after you went home, I kept looking for that secret room. And I did find something. Well, it was nothing. No big deal. But I felt kind of bad, I mean, what's the word?"

"What?"

"It was nothing. Like I said. But let me show you!"

She grabbed my wrist, tugged me upstairs and stopped by the linen cupboard in the hall outside Ned's room.

"I was always over here helping your gram with one thing and another, and she was always busy with something, so she'd say, 'Trisha why don't you clean out this drawer while I go hang the sheets?'"

Trisha touched a knob on the top drawer. "And one day, while your gram was out hanging clothes, I discovered this."

She pulled the bottom drawer out, knelt and reached into the gap. "You have to get down here to see, Cat."

I knelt and looked into the darkness. As Trisha pushed, the back panel swung inward.

Creak!

"See? And when I felt behind, Cat, I found stuff."

"What stuff?"

Trisha stared at the floor.

"What stuff Trisha?"

"Nothing! Just some rosette soaps, a sachet, a hanky. And I didn't tell your gram. I just took the stuff. And afterwards, I felt so bad." She looked at me. "I'm a very naughty girl."

"Yes you are."

"Yes I am."

"So, Trisha, do you have a cigarette?"

"No! Cat! You're the naughty one!"

We stared at each other.

"Trisha...I wonder."

"What?"

"If...there is anything...you might have missed?"

"I don't know. Shall we see?"

We knelt side-by-side.

"You do it, Trisha. It's your secret hole."

"No you, Cat. You're the one who spent all night with the ghosts."

I got on my belly, reached in, felt blindly, got my hand round something, and pulled it out. A black sock coated in dust.

"Yuck."

"Your turn."

I scooted over and Trisha reached in. She made a face and pulled out a pink hand-towel embroidered with a hot-pink rosebud. She shook the towel. Dust flew.

"Jackpot! I win!"

That high-pitched sound again- the screaming!

SCREEEEEEEEAM!

Trisha laughed. "The teakettle!"

She ran downstairs, and as she clanked in the kitchen, I reached into opening far as I could. I felt something small. Trisha began singing Gram's pie-making song as I got my fingers round the *something*, pulled it out and plucked off a layer of dust.

It was a gold cardboard box. Held shut by a fat blue rubber band. I shook the box gently. Something rattled. I sniffed the lid, tugged the band and imagined what could be in there.

A bloody tooth? A pair of severed lips? A dried-up private part?

Trisha came back upstairs singing, "oh dear what can the matter be!" Before she could see what was in my hand, I thrust the little gold box behind my back, ran to Mom's old room and stuffed the box deep in the toe of my sleeping bag.

THE STARING CONTEST

After breakfast Trisha and I walked Gram's garden in the morning light and she pointed at what used to be.

"That's where her naked lady lilies were. And there her Japanese cherry. And there was the fish pond."

The fishpond was gone, flowerbeds gone. The whole yard just humpy grass.

"Why's it all covered over with sod?"

"I know. Ugly, right? For the buyers. The garden hadn't been tended for years, the beds were overgrown, so we just…covered it up."

"But why the humps?"

Trisha shrugged and kicked at the ground, humpy as my sodded-over grave.

"And I never noticed that before, Trisha."

I pointed to a big silver submarine-shaped thing between the garden and where the brambles used to be.

"The propane tank? You never saw that Cat? That was there the whole time, but your gram thought it was ugly, so she hid it with those old bushes."

The brambly place! The fenced-in tangle where Ned threw his old tires and burned old magazines! Where weeds grew tall as our shoulders, and where I turned into the Evil Queen. That was gone. In its place was just bumpy lawn. You'd never know it had been there. And now the house was up for sale and a family of strangers would move in and sleep in the rooms and run up and down the stairs and sit at the table and eat their breakfasts and think their thoughts and…

"Trisha, I have to go…"

Back on the highway, a hollow grew inside me. My whole trip had been a failure. I'd found nothing. *Except a little gold box.* Because I was a coward. Too afraid to ask. And I needed a cigarette, *a whole, fresh cigarette.* There weren't any in my backpack or the ashtray. And my Tareytons were in the Ladies' Room at the library.

Closed on Sundays. Shit.

And shit!

I was trying to get on the freeway north for home, but the Dodge Dart was heading east. I missed my turn.

Shit-shit! What was the next exit?

PRAIRIEVILLE & REDTAIL RISE 1/2 MILE.

I took that exit and turned right towards Redtail Rise, instead of left into Prairieville. I didn't want to see Sheriff Giant or blank-face Sandy ever again. The road rose past three farms, curved and rose again by a big green sign.

REDTAIL RISE WILDLIFE REFUGE

Maybe there was someone in there with a cigarette.

The blacktop meandered through a meadow and dead-ended in a big, near-empty parking lot. At the far end was a low modern brick building.

REDTAIL LEARNING CENTER.

On the way to the building were path entrances with signs.

SEE THE PRAIRIE RACOON.

SEE THE WHISPERING TORTOISE.

SEE THE FRITTILLARY BUTTERFLY…

The morning was holding its breath, the heat already pressing down. Inside the Learning Center it was cool and quiet. A tall woman with a long gray braid stood at a desk where postcards of baby animals sat beside ceramic statuettes and stuffed toys of the same. She explained to me that Redtail Rise was now tallgrass prairie that had been restored slowly, over the past seven years, one inch at a time, from original seeds carefully garnered, one seed at a time, from old graveyards and railroad beds, and that the land was bought out from farmers slowly, one acre at a time.

"This was all farm land?"

"No." She scratched her tanned nose. "It was partly hunting land, what we call fallowland, where the townfolk would hunt and targetshoot. They lost their hunting rights when we took it for the tallgrass. Some folks weren't too happy about that, but once they see the bison, most of them stop complaining. And hunting can be dangerous."

She looked down at the table of souvenirs. "One boy was killed here on this land, years back, before it was a refuge. That boy loved running. He ran alongside the schoolbus, ran barefoot, he even ran in the winter, but one morning some hunters who not familiar with the area saw a brown blur and one of them raised his rifle and shot that boy dead."

She put her head down and straightened a pile of postcards of baby raccoons peeking out from a hole in a tree. I wasn't really listening to her story. I was wondering if she had a cigarette.

Back in the parking lot of the Refuge, I sifted through my smelly ashtray for a butt but found nothing. I'd already smoked the butts down to nothing. *Argh!* I needed something to fill my lungs in that beautiful place.

There was the joint.

I reached into the steamy backseat, unrolled my sleeping bag, dug for the Saran-wrapped roll and sniffed.

Ah, Santa Lucinda Gold! And that little gold box.

I set the joint on the dash, set the gold box on the seat and drove deeper into the refuge, past the blue, purple and yellow wildflowers, past the darting bees and flirting butterflies, up a long hill. I parked at the top. *No one around.* I got out, stood in the middle of the road and lit up, admiring the vista, the dipping green dotted with flowers.

I held the smoke in, let it burn my lungs, let it out...

Ah, yes. Then I saw. Everything was alive here, trees, breeze, plants, the bugs crawling up my legs, the darting, biting insects sucking my blood, the flying seeds, the spurting birds, the hiding bunnies, all alive. One blended into another, the leaf died, crumbled and turned into soil, the bug died and turned into soil, the cows shit. All a circle, interlocked.

That's why I couldn't ask about Uncle Ned. Not because I was a coward. I wasn't a coward. I drove all that way and stayed in the yellow house. I wasn't a coward. I couldn't ask because I loved Ned. We all did. Ned was family. And you loved family no matter what. Even if they hurt you, even if they pissed you off. Even if they made you crazy.

The hairs on the back of my neck rose.

Someone watching me.

I turned round, to the round black eye of a huge male bison. He was close enough for me to see his coat hanging in clumps and count the flies walking his eye and see my night-water reflection.

Oh. I know what this is. This is a staring contest.

I'd done it back home with rabbits and squirrels, but never with a creature that big. I knew what to do. *Hold still, make myself disappear, put yourself into the body of the other.*

I inhaled and imagined myself in his skin. I felt his hooves on the earth and the air in his nostrils and the clover in his mouth. I was in him, looking back at the girl in the lime-green blouse and cut-offs. That girl wasn't even there. She was just a wisp of breeze. *A nobody...*

And Mr. Buffalo, where was the line between you and me? And who was that man who went after the kid with his fishing pole on a misty morning? Then another kid on his paper route? Then another in a campground? And how fresh was the air that morning with the mist rising, and such sweet silence in that suburb before sunrise, with the lawns mowed and dewy, the dog lagging behind, and the feel of the wagon the boy tugged, the handle in his hands, the squeak-squeak like my popping lawnmower?

And did the man creep up behind? Did he smile and ask for directions? Or pet the dog? And did the dog look up and see the dark in those eyes? Where did those boys go? Were they covered in dirt or destroyed with fire or hidden by smoke? And did the man try to hold himself in till he burst again, and took the next kid from the ball park bowling alley gas station convenience store church picnic? And how did the blood taste at the back of his throat? And was he sorry? And did his family know?

Somebody always knows. Somebody always knows and somebody always hides and somebody always vomits up his liver in the middle of the night. Most killers go to bed with the faces of those they killed staring right at them. *Eye to eye. Forever and ever. Amen.*

Whoever it was he had a family, a mom and dad, sisters and brothers. *Did his parents know? When did they know? What day? What time? What number was the second hand of the kitchen clock on? And where is the line between knowing and not knowing? Is it the same as the line between good and evil? Where is that line? In our brains? Or in our hearts? Or between waking and sleeping? Or the truth and lies? And how do you know when you've crossed over? Does an alarm go off like in the game of Operation? 'Oops! I touched the sides! Oops, I killed the patient!'*

The buffalo said nothing with his blackwater eyes. He just backed up, turned slowly and headed downhill.

Whew.

I got back in the Dodge Dart and headed to the far side of the refuge. Under a spreading maple, I sat down with the gold box in my lap. There was a game Jill and I had played back in White Rock. You cut a hole in the bottom of a small box, put your finger through, wrapped in a ketchup-daubed cotton ball, and held the box out for your friend-

SEVERED FINGER! Ha ha!

I took off the rubber band and lifted the lid. There was nothing in there, no hairy finger or dried body part. Just three pennies, a nickel, a dime, a little silver triangle of folded paper, scented faintly of chewing gum and one half of a torn dollar bill.

Nothing.

And I still needed a cigarette. And was suddenly hungry. And did not see, in the dappling shadows of that maple, a skinny kid in overalls with dirty blonde hair doing backflips. But I did get a powerful urge to head back to Dinah's Diner for a greasy burger.

The bell rang as I walked into Dinah's. The place was empty except for a waitress leaning on the far counter. She was dressed in the same robin's egg blue and white as the diner. I slid into a window booth, put my backpack on the cracked red vinyl, set the little gold box on the yellow formica and pulled out a menu.

The waitress walked over to me. She wore a HI I'M BECKY nametag and had stringy blonde hair and a lone-wolf face. Her right hand was wrapped in gauze. She set down a sweating waterglass.

"Need more time?"

"No, I'm ready."

"What'll it be?"

"Dr. Pepper, fries and a cheeseburger. Rare please."

She put my order in, leaned on the far counter and picked at her bandage as I opened the little gold box.

On the lid's underside was the letter B, hand-written in blue china marker. I lined up the coins, the silver triangle and the half bill.

Not enough for cigarettes.

And no one there to ask. I poked at the dime. If Ned had saved that stuff, I didn't know why. It was probably Little Arnie's or some other cousin's, dropped down the back of that linen cupboard years ago. Dropped and forgotten. I flipped open the matchbook by the napkin-holder: HAPPY DINERS MAKE DINAH HAPPY. Someone had written *Im' off at 7* on the inside and added a happy-face. I set the matchbook aside and looked out at the hot, still day.

Shadows cut across Main Street and over the dog-yellow bricks of the Sheriff's Office. A bumblebee buzzed the glass. I tapped the window. Outside, the bee lit.

What was I doing there, risking my life on the road, snooping in the library and questioning the police? Was I trying to smear my uncle's name? And ruin my family? And what if Uncle Ned was a monster? What did that make my family? Accomplices?

I picked up the small folded triangle of silvered paper and sniffed.

Ah! Juicy Fruit!

I set the triangle down and fingered the nickel as the bee

outside walked the glass. At the far counter, Waitress Becky drew a cig from her apron and lit up.

She's got cigarettes!

I tried to wave her over, but her attention was fixed on the ceiling. I set the nickel down and picked up the half-dollar. It was soft in my fingers, well-rubbed.

What if this half did belong to a missing kid? And what if the other half was out there somewhere? And what if I could find both halves?

I put the bill close to my eyes and studied the wavering edge, the miniscule hills and valleys.

With that torn edge, I thought, *they'd have to take a microscope, do scientific tests, drip chemicals and look with expert eyes to determine whether or not the two halves matched-*

Wait a minute-

From my back pocket I tugged a whole dollar, smoothed it flat and read the words: 'Blah-Blah Our Country Under One Blah. This Note Is Legal Tender For All Blah and Blah.' On the right face-side was a serial number. On the left face-side, the same serial number. *Same and same.* So banks could keep track. So no one could go ripping dollars in half and get twice back.

Stupid me! They wouldn't need science to see if the halves matched! They'd just need the serial numbers. Ha and ha.

Waitress Becky walked up with my order. She set down my burger and frowned at my coin-stacks.

"Anything else?"

"No, thanks. Wait-"

I NEED A CIGARETTE!

But she was back at her perch, picking her bandage and eyeing the ceiling. I lifted the bun off the burger thinking, *Holly was right. Ned was dead. What harm could he do?*

I peeled the pickle slice from the cheese.

And, like Officer Blockhead said, most of those guys never left their houses. For all I knew, Ned never did anything but play in the road and get hit by a car and go into a coma and get brain damage. So what if he had a few pairs of kid's underwear???

I squirted a big bloosh of ketchup on my plate.

I was the one who couldn't be trusted. I was the one who couldn't keep secrets. I was the one who couldn't keep my nose out of other people's business.

I dipped a fry in the ketchup and used the bloodied end to write HELP on the bun's white underbelly as the bee buzzed the glass.

Bzzt.

This whole trip was a huge waste of time. Ever since Rosy Sue whispered, it was Uncle Ned, all the time I've wasted, all the wondering, all the hunching over microfiche, all the nightmares, when I could have been out GETTING KISSED.

I dragged the fry through the ketchup again and wrote HELP on the burger. Waitress Becky appeared and frowned down at my plate.

"Everything all right?"

"Yeah fine."

As she turned away I wrote HELP on the yellow formica. I wasn't that hungry. The bee banged the glass.

Hello bee. I know where the line between good and evil is. It's the line between your eyes where you go cross-eyed from looking at a thing too long, and the line blurs and you're left staring at your own stupid-ass nose. Well I'm done looking at my own nose and done worrying and ready to start living. I was going to drive straight home to tear up the missing posters and throw away that little gold box. And get kissed. *And burn up that half-dollar! Right then and there!*

But first I needed a cigarette. I waved Becky back.

She scratched her bandage. "What?"

"Could you spare a cig?"

She reached into her apron and shook out a Kool.

"Thanks"

"Anything else? Coffee? Pie? More ketchup?"

Very funny.

As she dropped off my bill a shadow crossed the window. I thought the storm was finally breaking. But then the bell rang and a big family walked in.

The Jumbos! From the Welcome Center!

They wriggled into a booth saying, "No lunch, please, we're not that hungry, just two coffees, three Orange Crushes, five pie a la modes, cherry, apple, key lime, cheesecake and chocolate silk with whipped cream."

As Becky poured their coffees I fingered the Kool.

But where was my lighter? And where was my wallet? Not in my backpack. Not in my pocket. Not on the floor. Shit. Did I leave my wallet in the Dodge? Was it on the dash? With the joint?

I looked out at the Dodge. The bee was gone. I tore a match from the HAPPY DINERS MAKE DINAH HAPPY, dragged the tip across the flint, touched the fire to the cig and inhaled.

Ah! Menthol Blue!

I picked up the half-dollar and held a corner to the flame.

Burn, baby, burn!

But before the flame caught the half-dollar, time slowed. Time sowed like the balls in my Fischer-Price Lawnmower. I'm not sure what happened next. Because it al happened at once. Sheriff Giant walked up to the parked Dodge.

Did he see my joint on the dash? And my wallet? And was he about to arrest me for illegal drugs?

And was that the bumblebee on Becky's hand?

Then BAM!

Becky dropped the Jumbos' tray. Their food flew in slow motion. Cherry filling, key lime, chocolate cream, whip cream, ice cream and orange pop danced a frozen tango. Then gravity sucked the whole mess to the floor.

SPLAT.

The food smeared in a psychedelic paisley. One fat drop of orange Crush flew to my matchhead.

Szzt-

Out went the flame. The half-bill was intact. The Jumbos cried out. Becky grasped her hand. Sheriff Giant bent over my windshield-

SHIT! My joint WAS on the dash!

I left the change and half-dollar bill on the table-

For your tip, Waitress Becky!

-grabbed my backpack and ran from Dinah's Diner.

The missing flyers flew from my backpack. Jack, Billy and Jimmy's faces slow-motioned over Main Street like big lazy white leaves. Then I saw the tangerine Opal Cadet speeding right towards me.

SWEET SEVENTEEN

Whew! That was close!

I got across the street just in time. The Opal with the spray-painted black-lace designs whizzed by, Sheriff Giant turned towards the speeding Opal, Waitress Becky ran out waving my bill, and I headed back towards Ben and Beth's, thinking *must have left my wallet up in Mom's old room...*

I hit green lights all the way. As I pulled into Ben and Beth's driveway Little Arnie ran out with a balloon, slipped on the steps and fell. The balloon bounced and he smiled up, yelling, "She's back!" Trisha skipped down the steps calling out, "Cat!" My wallet was in her fist. Beth stepped out of the side door, wiping her hands, "Oh, Cat!" Ben stepped from the shed wiping his hands on a greasy rag and cracked a grin, "Hey! The Cat's back!" "Yeah," I said, reaching for my wallet, "for that." Trisha handed it over. Ben shook out a Winston. "Cigarette, Cat?" Beth scowled. "Well I think she deserves one after what she's been through." Ben lit me up, and as the smoke rose my relatives circled. *Oh no*, I thought, *word is out. They've heard I was asking questions. You can't go sniffing around in a small town and get away with it, and now my relatives are going to kill me and throw my body n the cistern.* Then Beth mouthed *ready?* Trisha giggled "Ready." Arnie yelled "READY!" and from the shed, house and barn people popped, Mom, Holly, everyone, even Jill. People and balloons bounced everywhere, red, yellow, blue, then everyone shouted,

"HAPPY BIRTHDAY CAT!" *One day late. But stupid me!* Turns out Trisha hid my wallet on purpose to lure me back. Arnie leapt off the porch after a balloon, Little Mary circled with a balloon, the nephews chased each other with balloons, the men began loading the truck with coolers, the ladies carried picnic baskets and we all headed towards the yellow house pond. On the way, Trisha tossed me a flowered bikini, and at the pond the ladies flapped out red and white checkered tablecloths, and the men muscled in more tables, and there were tupperwares of potato salad, three-bean salad, chicken-salad and three grills. "Rare for me," I yelled as I stepped from the boathouse tugging down the striped bikini, which fit me perfectly.

Before I could wade into the pond, Tammy pushed me to Mom. All my brothers and sisters were staring at me with stone faces. I was ready for the worst. *You stole Dad's Dodge! You drove illegally! You tried to shame the family!* Instead Mom said the Dodge Dart was mine soon as I got my license. The others whooped, "Watch out world!" *No one was mad at me!* As I waded into the pond, who walked out of the water but a *big, dripping David White!* David White walked up to me, put his hands on my cheeks *and kissed me. On the lips. Me.* I let my head explode with the idea that I'd just BEEN KISSED then splashed in the sparkling pond with the kids pushing balloons under and balloons popping up. Then down the path, *who did I see? Kirk King! My old crush!* Kirk walked into the water and put his arms around me. David lunged toward Kirk, yelling, "She's mine!" "No, mine!" Kirk yelled back. Kirk and David wrestled like two shiny monsters till I pried them apart saying "I'm no one's! But if you behave you may BOTH date me." Then I went underwater in my golden bikini so as not to break out laughing. *WHOO-HOO, SWEET SEVENTEEN!*

We spent hours playing in the pond and feasting on the homemade goodies with watermelon juice running down our chins and Gramps got out the rowboat and Gram set out fresh-baked pies. Even Ned got into the swing of things, spinning kids like airplanes. Then some of the adults were getting cranky in the humidity and the jello salads were melting and black flies gathering over the feast and black clouds gathering in the northwest so I went up to take a nap in Mom's old room.

Rosy Sue sat at Gram's dressing table doing her nails. I sat on the bed and watched her cuticle stick as I chewed on my nagging question. Ever since that Thanksgiving Rosy Sue said it was Uncle Ned, I'd wondered why, by the time she sat down to eat, she said that crap about it being Jack's own fault. *What made her change her mind?* Did she tell someone else after she walked into the house that Thanksgiving? Did she tell Dad? No, she wouldn't tell Dad because she wouldn't want to upset Dad. *Don't upset your Father.* And she wouldn't tell Mom, because what would Mom do? Nothing. *Ignore it and it'll go away.* Did she tell one of the sisters? No, because they wouldn't believe her. Did she tell one of the big brothers? Mark or John? And did they shut her up, because someone shut them up years before? Did they say *never tell or else?* Then did she sit down at the Thanksgiving table and make up that crap?

I finally asked *why did you change your mind Rosy Sue?* And she put down the cuticle stick and put her lips to my ear and whispered on and on, like that night in the road, and her words rose like mist over the corn. I tried to grab her words but they dissolved in the air and I fell asleep.

I dreamed of popcorn popping, each kernel a different face. Then Little Mary woke me with a poking finger. "Auntie Cat! The storm is coming!" Out the window, over the corn magnificent thunderheads rumbled. "Let's open this window, Auntie Cat! Get some fresh air in before the storm hits." "Good idea, Little Mary, but I think this window is stuck." That window had been stuck for decades. We huffed, puffed and grunted, and finally BAM, that window came up. In the ledge were dead flies, June bugs and cicada shells. In came birdsong, cool air and the scent of the oncoming storm.

"Let's open all the windows!" Little Mary and I ran through the house opening windows, then all the doors. Fresh air poured in, and everybody watched and clapped, and Dad gave me his grin like, *I'm so proud of you Cat.* Then an unseen force took over. I saw it with my own eyes and I don't make this shit up. Drawers slid out, cupboards swung open, sheets flew from beds, nails squealed, windows shattered, plaster crumbled, floors buckled, counters snapped, studs twisted and the stairs fell in on themselves. Over all the screeching, Little Mary shouted, "You feel that, Auntie Cat? You feel all those little spirits zipping free?" I did feel them whizzing by, zipping free. "Yes, Little Mary! I feel them!"

Then the whole house fell outward and the glass shelf in the bay window shattered and Gram's conch shell fell into the basement as the sky opened and the storm broke BIG TIME. Little Mary spread her arms and shouted over the roar, "THAT IS HOW YOU TAKE APART A PUZZLE!"

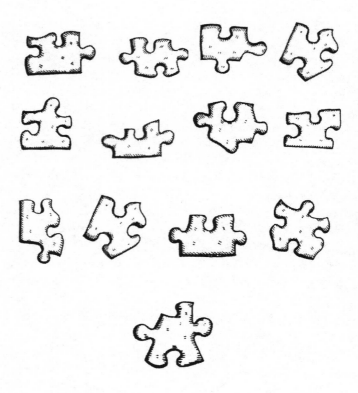

THE GIRL IN THE ROAD

The clouds dumped a tidal wave of rain on the yellow house. Little Mary and my folks jumped in their cars and raced for Savage Road, Gram and Gramps got in the rowboat and paddled to higher ground and the second cousins climbed atop their barn to watch the downpour fill the pond.

The pond filled the creek. The creek overflowed, flattened the corn and tumbled past the grain elevators towards Pearl Pond.

At the railroad tracks, the waters swept into Pearl Pond and climbed the steps of the old library, tore up the plaster gnomes and white fences, licked the bricks of the schoolhouse and covered the petunias by the Safety Station.

Back at the tracks, the waters widened over Savage and gathered into a torrent. The torrent frothed through West Brownmound, tore up shrubs, overturned bicycles and spun kiddie pools, then raged past the Kentucky Frieds, Hamburger Heavens and Shrimp Shacks and washed out the Orangevale Creek Bridge as it sped downtown.

In downtown Brownmound the raging swept past the hospital, the courthouse and the gold-domed State Capital, filled up the lower levels of the parking ramps, whirled round traffic poles, sucked up cars and poured east.

In East Brownmound the whitewater sped round the boxhouses, ripped yards clean of barbeques, trikes and old Harleys, filled window wells, tore clapboard and torrented towards Highway 119.

Down 119, the waters gushed through the main gate of the Fairgrounds and into the Midway, swirling round the Ferris wheel, Tilt-a-Whirl and Death-Drop, splintering Pete's Pronto Pup stand and Froggy's Frosty Lemonade and screaming towards the wildlife refuge.

Instead of pouring right and drowning all the prairie critters, the torrent turned left into Prairieville. There the waters rose up Main and slowed to a river. The river flowed past the Post Office and thinned to a stream. The stream passed the dress shop mannequins and narrowed to a rivulet. The rivulet passed Dave's pink confections and became a trickle. The trickle snaked past Dinah's Diner like a weak garden hose somebody forgot to turn off and stopped at the feet of a strawberry blonde lying in the middle of the road.

The teenager in the cut-offs and lime-green check blouse looked like a rag doll back-handed across a room. Only this time she had more than the wind knocked out of her.

Waitress Becky stopped running and walked to the girl. Sheriff Giant stopped chasing the Opal and walked to the girl. The Jumbos came out of the diner and waddled to the girl as Missing Boy posters fluttered down like lazy white leaves. They all stood over the girl as if standing over a grave.

Ha, that is funny. The summer I was ten years old I dug my own grave down by the lake. I wanted to see what it felt like to be dead. I lay in the hole and watched the blue rectangle above. One white cloud passed over, an ant crawled on my cheek, a purple thunderhead hovered then it started to rain, so I got out of my grave and washed off with a swim in the lake, but I've always been like that, drawn to the dark side. That same summer Jill's brother sold his whole plastic monster collection at their garage sale across the street, yellow fangs, reaching claws, dripping blood. I got two for a quarter as a joke, took them home and put them on top of my dresser. *Very funny ha-ha!* But when I turned off the light they were not funny. In the dark Frankenstein and Wolfman became every moonbeam, blood-hunger and campfire nightmare tangled up just like Dad and Uncle Ned got tangled on that day I yelled STOP.

On that day I yelled STOP, Dad fell to the floor, Ned left in a red-faced rage and the house filled up with silence after Ned left, a gray dread. I picked up the cups and wiped up the coffee and wrapped up the sandwiches but couldn't see into the future. I couldn't see Dad's artery filling up with blood or the cake drying up down in the basement fridge or where Ned went after he left.

But from where I am now I see where Ned went. I see Ned drive mad to the Mini-Mart and grab Halbert Evans. I see Halbert throw his ice cream at Ned. I see Uncle Ned put his sticky hands on the wheel and drive madly towards Rosy Sue's. I see Ned turned away at Rosy Sue's. I see Ned get madder and drunker each time he stops for gas or booze. Each time he stops, he sees a kid in a Halloween costume or smells a kid's sweet smell, and tries to talk to the kid, and each kid makes a face or runs away, and at each stop Ned gets MADDER, till finally he puts on a Wolfman mask, whips out a gun and takes Jack Jackoway.

I see that clearly as Jimmy's bones in the barn-ash and Jack's blood-trace on the ceiling and Billy's remains under the maple out at Redtail Rise. I see that clearly as the boy flying over the corn. That night Rosy Sue lay beside me and the gravel pressed into my back I didn't see the flying boy. But I see him now. Like Rosy Sue said *he only flies over these farms and these fields and these roads because he's looking down for the boy he lost when he was broken into, and when he finds a boy who looks like he did, he looks in their eyes for the hurt, and if he doesn't see the hurt, he makes the hurt, so he can share what he felt when he was broken into.*

I see that clearly as the blank-face stranger I killed in my sleep. That wasn't a dream. I did kill. My blank-face stranger was Jack Jackoway if he'd had a chance to grow into a man. Like the age-progression wax-dummy in the HAVE YOU SEEN ME poster. I killed Jack when I opened my mouth and said STOP. I said STOP to keep Dad from hitting Little Mary. I broke the Rule of Silence and started them fighting, Dad and Ned, like interlocked monsters. I set Ned on the avalanche path.

You'd think that would teach me to keep my mouth shut but no. Sleeping monsters are everywhere waiting for an excuse to yell or hit or kill and sometimes you have to open your mouth and say STOP even if you do wake up the monsters. And because I said STOP Little Mary wasn't backhanded and didn't hit the wall and didn't turn her heart to stone.

That is funny. I used to think that's what I did with my heart. Made it hard and small like a stone. But from where I am now I see what I did with my heart. I made it hard and small *like a seed*. A seed can wait a long time to sprout. A seed can wait thousands of years underground in the layers of an Egyptian mummy for that one drip of water and that one shaft of light.

And when it's safe I will open my heart one infinitesimal crack and let in one sliver of light and one drip of water, then slowly one white stem will rise up, and at the top one tiny bud, like the sunflower in Gramp's coal bin, and that bud will flower like you cannot believe, like Gram flowering out at her funeral, out in all directions, glistening up to the light, lovely and free.

And no one will be able to get their hands on me, because Gram taught me: a forced bud will not flower. Not once, not again, not ever. Once forced, you can't put a bud back the way it was, not with tape or wire or hopes or prayers or yellow ribbons or glue, so there is nothing left to do but let each little bud flower in its own sweet time, in its own sweet way, forever and ever amen.

And if anyone ever messes with a kid or a flower again, I will feel it instantly. I'll feel it in the bones of my ear, and I'll come from wherever I am to wherever you are, *zip*, I'll be with you. And so will Billy and Jimmy and Jack. And you can't run and you can't hide, because if you run to an igloo on the North Pole or a straw hut in Africa or crawl into an Egyptian mummy or hide in the blue-tube future, we will sniff you out.

And Billy will slip between your ribs and Jimmy will crawl into your brain and Rosy Sue will sit by your ear and with each beat of your heart Billy will kick and Jimmy will shine the faces into your optic nerve and Rosy Sue will whisper their names, so even if you close your eyes and cover your ears, you will see the faces and hear the names of those you hurt, *forever amen.*

And I will fly round the globe fast as sunlight, and pull from the earth, from the trees, from your clothes, from your back seat and from the whispery corners of your kitchen the hidden clues, the things you left in your wake, the invisible traces of your skin and hair and the miniature cells of your hopes and fears, and I will whisper the clues into the ears of the living, and into the dreams of their sleep, and whisper courage into their veins so their mouths can open and the questions can be asked and the earth turned over and what is buried brought to light.

And Jack will cradle you close and hold you tenderly and look deep into your soul. Jack will let your tears fall, Jack will spread your tears out like the daily paper and read each drop, so he can understand what hurt you, so you can be turned inside out and the vowels and consonants of you mixed up and turned round, so there is a chance for you to be born brand new, as a flower or a duckling or little kid, because that's what we ghosts do.

ACKNOWLEDGEMENTS

This book had a long, slow birth, so I may have forgotten the names of some of my helpers, but I'm grateful to each one. Thanks to the police officers and librarians, including Officer Randy Lebsock, thanks to the Minnesota State Arts Board Artist Initiative Grant for the research support, and to the readers of the seemingly endless march of early drafts, including Miriam Arneson, Amy Arneson Wangensteen, Adam Arnold, Jennifer Birch, Eve Blackwell, Jennifer Carnes, Rachel Coyne, Geraldine Donnelly, Jay Gabler, Judith Guest, Noel Holston, Robert Metcalf, Alan Muscelevitz, Lee Orcutt, Jon Spayde, Mim Solberg, Kim Staley, Wesley Tank, Rebecca Welty and Michael Wolke. Thanks to Barb and Steve Coleman for the cabin writing-retreats, to brave Patricia Drury Sidman and Ken Varnold for their self-publishing tips, Kim Hines for her gutsy professional advice and Christy Perry for her generous formatting skills. Thanks to Terry Hokenson for leading the way in our writing family with his two novels, *The Winter Road* and *Leif's Journey*, to my longtime friend Nancy Kohlsaat for cheering me on, and Brian Garrity for stomaching the early drafts. Thanks to Kristen Freobel and Tessa Bridal for reading the whole monster out loud to me while sharing their own manuscripts about silence. My story was born by Tessa and Kristen speaking it to life. Thanks to Tessa for her friendship, advice and final, eagle-eyed read. Thanks to my family of origin for inspiring me, loving me and putting up with my brutal fictionalization of a good clan. Thanks to Salvatore Salerno for clearing a space at his kitchen table, feeding me, listening to my rants and believing, when I did not, that this story could be told. Thanks to Chad Augustin for his patient, skillful, long hours at the computer with the cover and all the images! And thanks to the heart of my heart, daughter Alberta Mirais, for her clear vision and her exquisite drawings.

Heidi Arneson, June 1, 2016

ABOUT THE AUTHOR

HEIDI ARNESON is a many-armed troublemaker. She writes, paints, and performs in her attic studio that she finished by hand. She has written many plays, including *DeGrade School*, *PreHansel & PostGretel* and *BloodyMerryJammyParty*, performed her one-person shows in Minneapolis, New York, Chicago and California, received the Bush Artist Fellowship, the Minnesota State Arts Board Initiative Grant and the Loft/Jerome Minnesota Writer's Initiative Grant for her creative work, and has taught storytelling to male inmates, but she is happiest curling up with a mystery or digging in her own backyard. Interlocking Monsters is her first novel.

ABOUT THE ILLUSTRATOR

ALBERTA MIRAIS has worked as a visual artist, musician and performer. Her artworks have hung in collections across the US and overseas. Among her finished works and repertoire are recordings, films, giant books, live bands and surreal burlesque dance theatre. She currently sings and composes in her lounge group *Holiday*.

Heidi Arneson and Alberta Mirais are mother and daughter.

32806662R00172

Made in the USA
Middletown, DE
18 June 2016